Ed Goodall published his first novel *Cicadas* in 2004. He lives in Belfast and is married with four children.

Cold Cross

Ed Goodall

BLUEBERRY

First published in Great Britain in 2007 by
Blueberry Publishing,
4 Parkmount Road,
Belfast BT15 4EQ
www.blueberrypublishing.com

Copyright © Ed Goodall 2007

The right of Ed Goodall to be identified as the author of this work has been asserted by him in accordance with the Copyright, Design and Patents Act 1988.

A catalogue record from this book is available at the British Library.

ISBN 978-0-9548705-2-2

All rights reserved. No part of this publication may be reproduced, transmitted or stored in a retrieval system in any form or by any means, without permission in writing from Blueberry Publishing.

Printed and bound in Great Britain by Shanway Press, Belfast.

'A cold coming we had of it,
Just the worst time of the year
For a journey, and such a long journey:
The ways deep, and the weather sharp,
The very dead of winter.'

Journey of the Magi, Thomas Stearns Eliot

*To the memory of
My mother, Patricia
My father, Augustine
and
My friend, Eric*

Acknowledgements

Fyodor M Dostoevsky:
The Brothers Karamazov

Stephen Cameron:
Death in the North Channel

Thomas Stearns Eliot:
Journey Of The Magi

1

HCMS WINDSOR swayed in the black water as Luke Wilson led the boys up the boarding plank. A Mate helped him find his feet and he turned to his leading acolyte. 'Tell them there's nothing to worry about, Matt. It's quite safe.' He pushed back the thick lock of grey hair which had fallen across his eyes and adjusted his glasses. 'Lead the way, Sir. You're aware that the Captain is expecting us. I was his Chaplain during the Second World War. A hard time we had of it.'

The sailor betrayed no reaction and barked at the group behind to keep in line. Each boy stuck to the one ahead as they were led to the Captain's sanctuary. They could see the yellow lamp glow as their guide rapped the cabin door.

'It's great to see you, Father. It's been a long time.'

'You're looking well, Joe.'

'Sit down and we'll have a drink. Arthur, show the boys around the sub and give them lemonade.'

Matt Quinn whispered to Barney Mulvey. 'Once the boss gets a few rums under his belt, there'll be no shutting him up tonight.'

Casey turned. 'We'll be passing through the men's quarters soon. I advise you to keep quiet. They will be trying to sleep after a long spell of duty on the way here.'

The fetid air hit them as they entered the narrow passageway between the bunk beds. They heard rattles and groans on both sides as they tiptoed towards the dim light above the cabin exit. Matt noticed a thick grey sock protrude from the last bunk as he inhaled the smell of stale Guinness. A curtain twitched open. A man stuck out his head, cursed and pulled back the rough cloth.

Casey explained to them how the submarine was propelled and showed them the finer points of the engine room. 'The current fleet is powered by diesel but, in the future, they will all be nuclear although I'll not be around to see it.'

He brought them to a small refectory where a tray of soft drinks had been prepared for them. Relaxing now, Casey drank tea as he told them his wartime tales. 'The Captain told me about your boss but I'd heard of him before on another command. Not many men of the cloth performed to his standard.' He smiled but did not elaborate. 'Let's get back. The Chief needs to keep a clear head for later.'

'Well, boys,' boomed Wilson, 'you've had the kind of education you don't get in schools.' He thanked the Captain for his hospitality. As the two men shook hands, they grasped each other's wrist. 'It's not a Soldier's Farewell this time, Joe. You must come and see me before you leave Belfast.'

As Casey swung shut the cabin door, Matt saw the Captain glance at empty glasses and move to the drinks cabinet. Ahead of him, Wilson stumbled as the submarine was hit by a strong swell. Casey caught his arm but he waved him away. The December evening was coal-black as the group edged down the plank. The driver of their minibus switched on his lights in welcome and they ran to the back door.

Within ten minutes, the bus circled the City Hall and stopped at the Windsor restaurant. They knew that it had been chosen for its name. Wilson always did them proud on their Christmas outing. The boys hurried down the cellar steps to the feast.

Two middle-aged ladies, dressed in black and white, stood waiting in the room that had been reserved. A long table was covered in snow-white linen and thirteen places had been set. A waiter greeted Wilson and the dining arrangements were confirmed. The priest moved to his position at the head of the table. 'Dear Lord, for what we are about to receive, may we all be truly thankful,' he intoned and commanded the boys to take their places. The bus driver sat to his right, Matt and Barney sat to his left. The waitresses brought lemonade for the boys and the driver. The waiter opened a half bottle of Chianti for Wilson. He sniffed, drank and the waiter filled his glass.

Jingle Bells played softly in the background as thick vegetable soup was devoured with gleaming silver spoons. After a short pause, the main course was delivered. Instead of the expected chicken, thick sirloin steaks were slapped on everyone's plate. Then came mushy peas and a silver salver of fat chips.

'The boss is well oiled,' whispered Barney to Matt. 'It's going to be double hard to keep him quiet when we get back.' They looked at the vacant eyes of the driver as Wilson regaled him with a watery tale, one which he had related many times before.

As their steaks settled, small bowls of pears and custard were placed before them. The waitresses poured tea from huge kettles, Christmas crackers were exchanged and Wilson thanked his team for their dedicated service throughout the year. 'You boys could serve the Pope himself,' he finished. 'And maybe some of you will.' Flushed and tired, he sat down as the boys clapped.

The music was switched off and, taking the hint, the driver helped the priest to his feet. As they ascended the steep steps from the restaurant, snowflakes flickered in the yellow lamplights surrounding the City Hall. The minibus sped through the silent streets. Shop windows glowed with Fairy lights and Christmas decorations.

At ten o'clock, they arrived at the parochial house on the Northern outskirts of the city. Some walked home while the driver delivered the younger ones to their parents. As the senior boys, Matt and Barney knew that Wilson would invite them in for tea and present them with a gift afterwards.

'Warm yourselves up, boys,' he said, 'while I put the kettle on.' Matt and Barney sat by the fire that had been banked high by the housekeeper. Wilson bustled in with a tray of tea and ginger snaps. 'Tuck in while I see to this fire.' He shoved a large poker into the heaped coal and the flames broke loose. The worn settee was pulled closer. He sat back with a cup and saucer perched precariously in his lap. They were asked how they had enjoyed their day. Matt and Barney responded with appropriate enthusiasm. 'How long did you serve in the Navy, Father?' asked Matt although he knew the answer.

'Ten years, from 1939. Joe Higgleston – the man you met this afternoon – and I sailed together on many a journey. I remember the time...'

The boys listened to a familiar story. The fire roared and Wilson left to fetch more tea. Matt winked at Barney. 'It's better to humour him. We'll wait and see what he has for us. When Wilson returned, Matt detected a fresh aroma of rum in the warm air.

The fire cast its yellow glow along the walls of the book-lined room. The priest had lost the thread of his previous tale and was silent for some minutes. Matt redirected his attention in order to extract a new story. 'It must have been dull coming back here after all the excitement.'

Wilson pushed his glasses up over his forehead and rubbed his eyes. 'Joe said the same thing to me this afternoon. Yes, it was hard settling down. I admit that. They gave me a curate's job in a dockside parish...near where you visited today. I was there for four years before being moved to here.' His eyes grew sad and he paused. 'I suppose there's no harm in telling you what happened to me before I left my old parish. After all, it's not a tale from Confessions. Something Joe said to me this afternoon brought it all back.'

Matt and Barney relaxed in their armchairs. Their parents knew they were here and it was only a short walk home. Between a gap in the curtains of the front bay window, they saw snowflakes drift in the wind as Wilson told his strange tale.

One cold and raw February night in 1953, he had been finishing a nightcap when he heard a rap at his front door. The housekeeper had gone home and he was alone. At first, he ignored the noise of the brass knocker. Although not worried about safety, he was sometimes bothered by a beggar who occasionally was given a bed for the night in the adjacent Stella Maris hostel. The man, if drunk, yelled abuse if his request for money was rejected. The knock came again but was not insistent. He decided to open the door.

It was not the beggar but a stranger dressed in a military overcoat. Despite its protection, the young man was shivering. 'I know it's late, but I had to talk to someone. Otherwise, I will go out of my mind.' As he came through the entrance porch, the harsh light shone on the prominent cheekbones in his ghostly face. His black hair was slicked back and parted in the middle.

After exchanging comments on the wild weather, the soldier opened up. He spoke with the twang of an Ulsterman who had spent his recent years in England. 'I deserted from the British Army in January. I was based in the South of England and made my way to London where I found lodgings in the East End. My money ran out and I used the last of it to buy a train ticket from Euston Station to Stranraer.'

'How did you cross the Irish Sea with no money?'

'I had to take a chance. I made myself known to a deckhand who was loading the ferry to Larne. He smuggled me on board and ordered me breakfast in the third-class canteen. At first, I was grateful.'

'And why would you not be?'

'We'll come back to that later. I got into conversation with a man who said his name was Jack Sullivan...a big, plump man in his late thirties. He sussed out my situation. Said he'd been in a similar fix himself once and could help me. After the War, he'd jumped ship in New York and made his way by train to San Francisco. There he caught a cargo boat bound for South Australia, earned a fortune in the goldmines, changed his identity and came home.'

'What about your family here?'

'I'm an only child and my father is dead. My mother has a farm near Doagh but I can't go back there yet. They'll be looking for me but they'll give up eventually.'

'This Jack Sullivan. Did he help you?'

'He gave me an address to go to...about two miles from here. After a bit of trouble, I found the terraced house where a single woman lived by herself. A blonde called Teresa. She asked no questions, fed me and gave me a bed.'

'How long have you been there?'

'About two weeks. I didn't go out and I'd have been content to stay there until Easter.'

'Why have you come to me?'

'Last night, I heard a commotion in the middle of the night but went back to sleep. When I got up this morning, I found Teresa lying dead on the kitchen floor with a big poppy bruise on her forehead.'

'Did you go to a neighbour or anything?'

'How could I? Not in my situation. What would they have thought?'

'What *did* you do?'

'I scarpered with my few belongings. I've been wandering the streets. Earlier today, I sat for a while in your Chapel and saw you going into the Confession Box. Afterwards, I followed you.'

'You've put me in a spot. Go upstairs and lie down in the back room. There's nobody else here. We'll work out a plan after Morning Mass. In the meantime, all I can do is pray for you.'

'Thanks. I'm beat out.'

'Before you go to bed, you had something else to tell me? After you boarded the ferry, you remember. Which one was it? I know them all. I was in the Navy during the War.'

'You'll know this one well. It'll not be sailing anywhere again.'

'You don't mean?'

'Yes. The *Princess Victoria*.'

It was after midnight. The boys waited in vain for a finale. 'There's nothing much more to tell,' said Wilson. 'We talked most of the following day. He agreed he would have to give himself up. He left and I never saw him again.'

'What about the woman?' asked Matt.

'I listened for news of the assault on the radio and later made discreet enquiries. The police knew nothing about it. Shortly afterwards, the Bishop moved me here. Boys, I've talked too much. Your presents are ready. It's time to go home.'

2

THE SNOW had not settled as Matt had expected when he arose on the Saturday morning. His younger sister, Anne, was still asleep and his father, Jim Quinn, had left for work. Before drifting off to sleep, the soldier's tale had floated around in Matt's mind. Why would the man tell lies? The story had all the force of truth. 'Do you know anything about a ship called the *Princess Victoria*?' he asked his mother as she scooped a poached egg from a saucepan.

'Who could forget? I remember the day it sank very well. There were terrible storms the whole weekend. You were only a child at the time.'

'Father Wilson mentioned it last night when he was talking about something else.'

'The *Princess Victoria* left Stranraer early on a Saturday morning and ran into big trouble right away. There were gale-force winds and gigantic waves. Its back doors burst open and the sea poured in. It was supposed to be going to Larne but ended up near Donaghadee on the other side of Belfast Lough.'

'That's were it sank?'

'Yes. Over a hundred and thirty people drowned although a few dozen survived to tell the tale.'

'How did they escape?'

'Most of them were found in a lifeboat by a rescue vessel from Donaghadee. Many had almost frozen to death. Bodies were being washed up everywhere for days. Why did Father Wilson bring it up?'

'After our dinner, he invited Barney and me back for a cup of tea. Then he told us a story about a man who had been on the *Princess Victoria* and survived.'

'Who was he?'

'He said he was a stowaway – a soldier who had deserted. Someone he had met on the boat gave him a safe address in Belfast where a woman called Teresa would look after him. He stayed with her for weeks. Then, one morning, he came down the stairs and found her dead with a giant bruise on her forehead. He did a runner and came to see Father Wilson.'

'This sounds like a tall story.'

'It happened before he came here. He said the man came to see him one night and disappeared the next day.'

'There was a famous murder case in the same year that the *Victoria* sank. A student called Patricia Curran – a judge's daughter – was assaulted as she was coming home one evening from Queen's University.'

'Did they get the person who killed her?' Matt paused to wipe egg yolk from his chin.

Marie Quinn looked at him curiously. 'A young Scottish soldier was arrested and imprisoned. Iain Hay Gordon was his name.'

'Why did they not hang him?'

'They said he was insane. I believe he's in an asylum up near Antrim.'

Matt rubbed his chin, eyes bulging. 'That's a coincidence, isn't it. Two soldiers…coming from Scotland.'

'There was a lot of doubt as to whether Hay Gordon was guilty. Many people thought he'd been framed.'

'Who do they think killed her? Patricia Curran, I mean.'

'One of her family. Maybe her brother who had been friendly with Hay Gordon. Even her mother or father.'

'You said her father was a judge.'

'He was. You never know what happens when someone loses their head. I never heard of this other murder.'

'Father Wilson made enquiries afterwards. Nobody knew anything about it, he said.'

'Finish your breakfast. We'll ask your father when he comes home.'

Later that afternoon, Barney called to watch the football results with Matt. Mrs Quinn had gone shopping. Matt told Barney about the morning's conversation.

'Maybe this man Gordon is innocent and the other soldier murdered both women,' said Barney. 'He wanted help from Father Wilson but he wasn't going to admit he was a killer.'

'No body was ever found. Remember that the visitor gave himself up and Father Wilson went to the police.'

'Maybe he didn't turn himself in,' said Barney. 'Nobody knows for sure.'

'It's twenty to five. Let's catch the results. They're coming through on teleprinter.'

At five o'clock, they heard a key turn in the front door and Jim Quinn came into the room. 'Well, boys. How did United perform this afternoon?' When informed of a scoreless draw, he commiserated, sat down and rubbed his hands in front of the coal fire. 'Your mother should be home soon. I could murder a fry-up after driving since early morning. Tell me all about yesterday's outing while we're waiting.'

Matt skipped through Friday's trip to the submarine and the feast that followed. He related Father Wilson's story to his father.

'Mum told me this morning about a famous murder case that happened about the same year. A girl called Curran down near Whiteabbey.'

'So you know all about Hay Gordon. It was all the talk on the buses. I never heard the end of it. Mind you, I didn't think he was guilty. The whole case stank.'

'Mum said you might know something about the other business.'

'No, I can't say I do. Had Father Wilson been hitting the rum?' He grinned.

'It sounded true to us,' answered Barney. 'We always know when he's having us on.'

'OK. I shouldn't have said that. As for the *Princess Victoria*. Well, there could be plenty of truth in that one. There were stories of mystery stowaways who disappeared. Nobody knew whether they'd lived or died.'

'Did you know anyone on it, Mr Quinn?'

'Not personally. But something's coming back to me. As you know, Barney, I'm from Donegal. Matt's grandmother once worked with a woman in Letterkenny whose daughter drowned in the disaster. When we go up in the New Year, we'll see if we can find anything out.'

Matt and Barney did not see Wilson again until Sunday afternoon. They had already served at an early morning mass officiated by a visiting priest. However, on the third Sunday of each month, a special mid-afternoon service was held for the Servite Order. Their special saint was Saint Peregrine who was the patron for sufferers from cancer.

Afterwards, they helped Father Wilson in the sacristy as he struggled with the ties of his alb. He usually left promptly afterwards but today he hesitated. They waited as he stared from the window across the Lough at a build-up of sleet. Then he turned to them. 'I've some bad news for you,' he began. 'I didn't know for sure until yesterday when the Bishop rang me. I've been here seven years and it's time to move on. I'm being shifted up to a parish in North Antrim. You two boys have served me well and I'll remember you always.'

Matt and Barney were stunned by the news. He had been their only master since they had joined the altar. Initially, they were silent and then found the words to express their regret. Matt asked. 'When will you be going, Father? Who will replace you?'

'Everything hasn't been decided yet but I expect to go early in the New Year. Keep it quiet for the time being.' He paused. 'Just one more thing, boys. The story I told you late on Friday night. Perhaps you've talked about it already to your families but I'd appreciate it if you didn't gossip about it to anyone else. Parishioners might get the wrong idea.'

As they walked home in the gathering gloom, Matt and Barney discussed the startling news. 'I'll miss him,' said Barney. 'He could be sharp with you at an early mass but always mellowed as the day wore on.'

'I can't get that last story out of my mind,' said Matt. 'And it was odd the way he asked us not to spread it about. He should have told us on Friday night.'

'I'd love to become a detective and find out.'

'Maybe you will, Barney.'

The following Friday was Christmas Day. At twelve o'clock, Matt served altar for Wilson one last time. In the sermon, a sustained attack was made on the creeping evil of materialism and its impact on the special Season of Advent. 'Our Lord was born in a stable. He came to save the world. Remind yourselves of the words from 6.25 of St Matthew's Gospel. Therefore, I say unto you. Take no thought for your life, what ye shall eat or what ye shall drink; nor yet for your body, what ye shall put on. Is not the life more than meat, and the body than raiment?' He developed his theme as his flock looked at their feet and twisted their cuffs to catch a glimpse of the time. With Christmas dinners sizzling in nearby ovens, Wilson warned them that the Good Lord might come for them like a thief in the night. 'Maybe in that lonely hour between four and five when the night sweat is upon you. Remember then that there are no pockets in a shroud.' Afterwards, he informed them of his imminent departure from the parish and expressed the hope that they might meet again some day. 'If not in this world, then perhaps in the next.'

As he changed from his Christmas robes, Matt reminded Wilson that the Quinn family were going to Donegal and would not be back until the New Year. 'We haven't seen my grandmother since the funeral in the summer. She's by herself now and isn't too well. I'll see you before you go, Father?'

'Of course you will, Matt. Donegal, you say. God's own acre.' His eyes closed. 'Barney will keep me right while you're away.'

Two days later, the silver Austin carrying the four Quinns left early on its journey for the North-West. Matt sat in the front passenger seat. His mother and sister sat squashed with luggage in the back seats. By the time they had reached Toome, they were asleep. Jim Quinn asked Matt about Wilson's departure. 'No word of a date yet...or the new man?'

'I think he's called Laverty,' replied Matt. 'He's expected sometime later in January so there'll be plenty of time for a send-off.'

'It's all very sudden, isn't it? He was a character. I was thinking about that story he told you. You know, the one about the soldier. If it was true, I can't understand how a body was never found or nobody reported her missing. She must have had relatives or friends somewhere. Surely the neighbours would have noticed her disappearance.'

'Maybe she wasn't really dead,' said Matt. 'The soldier made a mistake and got into a panic.'

'I suppose someone might have knocked her about and she recovered after her lodger left. From what we've heard she kept herself to herself and didn't want anyone to know her business.'

They heard a groan from the back. 'I was having a nightmare and woke up to hear you talking about that dead woman.' Marie Quinn rubbed her eyes. 'She would have had something delivered to the house. Bread, milk...newspapers. It would have piled up.'

'For the same reason,' said Jim Quinn, 'surely someone would have caught on about the lodger. They'd have noticed extra deliveries.'

'Not necessarily,' replied his wife. 'She'd have been cute enough to cover herself. It's making me tired again thinking about it all. We'll never know what happened.'

The Austin struggled over the Glenshane Pass as a blizzard threatened. Sheep sheltered behind stone walls in the shadows of the Sperrin mountains. The car cleared Derry and, at the Border, a customs official warned them about illegal imports. They stopped to eat sandwiches above the River Foyle, then made their way through Letterkenny for the penultimate lap of their journey to the coast. The roads narrowed and were pitted with holes which shook the chassis of the aged Austin. It was late Sunday afternoon before they approached deserted Dungloe. Anne Quinn woke up as the family car reached Mullaghderg.

After a tearful reunion and talk far into the night, they collapsed into bed and awoke to the sound of heavy rain. The days settled into a routine. A late breakfast, a lunch of floury potatoes with bacon and cabbage, an evening supper of boiled eggs into which they dipped their wheaten bread. The meals were punctuated with odd jobs about the farmhouse or walks on the wild strand that it overlooked. In the evenings, Jim Quinn joined old friends for drinks in the pub. The rest of the family sat by the peat fire and exchanged news from both sides of the Border. At night, Matt's sister was dispatched to bed early and Marie Quinn soon followed. His grandmother stayed up late and smoked as she awaited her son's return. The week was nearly over before the subject arose.

'That's a freezing night,' said his father when he came back from the pub on Saturday. 'But fresh. I heard a fella in the pub say that, this time last week, the air round here was so cold and clear that the dead in the cemetery got up to look for their Christmas dinner.'

Matt's memory stirred. 'You said you would ask granny about the *Princess Victoria*,' he reminded his father. Jim Quinn prompted his mother about the tragedy and of the woman she knew. 'Ah, yes,' she responded, inhaling deeply, 'When we heard of the disaster and that a local woman had drowned, we followed everything very closely here. Your father kept all the cuttings from the newspapers. I believe I still have them in the back room. Read them tomorrow.'

Matt studied the old newspapers but could not find what he wanted. The Quinns had to leave on the following day and he asked his grandmother for the box of clippings. Marie Quinn protested but gave in. He clutched it to his knees on the return trip and later stored it under his bed.

On Monday morning, when Jim Quinn had left for work, an excited neighbour called with Marie Quinn to break the news. 'Father Wilson didn't say any masses over the weekend. A stranger came in to do the job. I called with Margaret, his housekeeper, after twelve o'clock mass when the visiting priest had gone. She warned me not to breathe a word to anyone. But as Matt's the senior altar boy, I thought you should know.'

'What's happened?' asked Marie Quinn. 'Some awful news?'

'Late on Friday, the police called to see Father Wilson. Margaret overheard questions about a woman who'd been found dead in the River Lagan. They said she was gagged and bound. On Saturday morning, he left Margaret a note to say that he'd had to move more quickly than expected.'

3

THE SUNLIGHT sparkled on the Upper Bann river as Matt drove in his yellow Spitfire along the road from Kilrea to Coleraine. It was late morning in the early summer of 1976. He had not seen Barney for many years, the selection examination results of 1960 having led to divergent paths. Matt knew that his old friend had joined the police. Their meeting with Boyle and Co., Solicitors, was scheduled for midday.

Afterwards, Charlie Boyle invited them to have lunch with him in The Salmon Leap. 'Father Wilson and myself became friendly about two years after he arrived here. Some time later, for reasons which we'll talk about shortly, he asked me to represent him in an official capacity. You'll have questions about the details of his will. It's an odd one, I grant you.' He gulped his pint of Harp and scanned the menu. 'As it's Friday, I recommend the cod. Detective-Sergeant Mulvey, perhaps you'd like to begin.'

Barney put the menu aside and stroked his chin. 'Matt and I will need to discuss matters between ourselves later this afternoon. However, I understand from your reading of it that Father Wilson has left us £5000 each and a property which, if sold, would command a substantial sum. However, there is an important string attached?'

'It's connected to what I said earlier.' Charlie Boyle paused to extract a bone from his fish. 'I can provide you with some background notes to assist you.'

Matt interrupted. 'In relation to a crime with which he was linked in the 1950's.'

'Allegedly linked, you mean,' said Barney. 'I understand that he was never charged.'

'I must inform you that it's been a close-run thing over the years and it broke him in the end.' Charlie Boyle stabbed at his chips and wiped his mouth. 'We're moving too fast. Let's get back to the will. He followed the progress of you two over the years and always spoke of you with fondness. If I may put matters in a nutshell, he wants you to clear his name. If you can do this to my satisfaction, you inherit the house.'

Matt pushed back his long black hair from his pale face. 'I don't see how I will be able to help. This is Barney's territory.'

'Not so easy for me either. I've heard rumours about the accusations from colleagues but I can't go round tramping on toes to obtain information about a case that's not officially mine.'

Boyle sighed. 'Walk away if you wish, gentlemen. No one's forcing you. I don't think Luke would have done this if he hadn't been mentally tortured in the last few months.'

'What will happen to the house if we don't comply?' asked Matt.

'He has already donated £5000 to the Church. The residue of the estate will go there as well if you don't want to proceed.'

Barney lit a cigarette and inhaled. 'I could use that kind of money.' He looked over at Matt. 'Let's talk this over. Maybe *we could* do something.'

Charlie Boyle undid the lower two buttons of his waistcoat and stood up. 'I have appointments all afternoon. One of you can get back to me when you've thought it over. I hope to hear from you soon.'

When he had gone, Barney ordered two glasses of Bushmills and they moved away from the diners to a quiet lounge overlooking the river. 'I'll be getting as fat as Boyle if I keep this up.' He sipped the whiskey and paused. 'Well, Matt, it's been a long time. How has life been treating you?'

'I've done OK, I suppose. I teach computer students at the College in Jordanstown.'

'Not married yet?'

'Plenty of time for that. What about yourself?'

'I settled down too young. Once I started earning money, I married the first girl that would have me. We're separated. Jean's got the kids. The divorce hearing is coming up. I need all the money I can get.'

'What caused the break-up...if you don't mind my asking?'

'Long hours away from home. Drink. Gambling. The usual.'

'I'm sorry.' Matt paused. 'I respected and admired Luke Wilson. I never believed that he was guilty.'

'You learn to keep an open mind in my business, Matt. I've seen the problems that arise when the horn rules the head.'

'We've never had an opportunity to talk about it since, Barney. I remember that time when I came back from Donegal. We never had a chance to wish him farewell.'

'Something had been eating him up when you were away. He was never at his best in the mornings but he reeked of rum at early mass. New Year, 1960, wasn't it?'

'Yes. My mother told me he'd been questioned about the death of a woman who'd been found gagged and bound in the Lagan.'

'The corpse was badly decomposed. There was gossip that she'd been dumped from a cargo ship. I heard nothing more at the time. The body was never identified. No one was ever charged...as far as I know. Did *you* ever hear anything?'

'No. As you say, the reports dried up. Although I was reminded of it one day when I was coming home from school. You remember I went to St Malachy's?'

Barney grimaced. 'When I was dispatched to Technical School. The world's ill divided. Shall we have another whiskey?'

Matt went to the bar to order the drinks. 'We can talk these off. It was a wet November day. There was a bus strike so I had to walk. That's why it's lodged in my mind and the fact that we'd been studying a book called Typhoon by Joseph Conrad. All about a storm at sea and how the Captain handled the passengers and the crew. Father Wilson's story about the stowaway soldier came into my mind. The rain was pelting down and I found shelter beneath the awning of a corner shop at the top of a wide Avenue. As I waited for the rain to stop, a big row of three-storey terraced houses caught my attention. In the distance, you could see the giant Harland and Wolff cranes. And that's when it came back to me.'

'The blonde who lived in a terraced house near the docks. What was her name?'

'Teresa. I've never forgotten. It occurred to me that the Avenue in front of me led straight to Wilson's old parish. We'd imagined her living in a row of houses just like our own...opening directly onto the street. I couldn't understand how she would have hidden anyone.'

Matt paused and sipped his Bushmills. 'However, if she lived in a house like one of those across from where I was standing, that would make it easier. They had basements and front gardens with hedges dividing them.'

'I couldn't fathom then why she would admit a stranger just because they shared a contact. When I thought about it later, I supposed she might have been a prostitute. Luke wouldn't have mentioned that part of it to us. Not at our age. Did you find out anything more?'

'When the rain stopped, I crossed the road and walked along the Avenue. The houses had white curtains and were well maintained...apart from one that stood out. Its garden had been covered over with black tarmac that was strewn with leaves. I was studying it when a man came up behind me and asked what I was doing.'

'What did you tell him?'

'It was not long after Halloween and I just said that the house had spooked me. There was something eerie about it. He told me that it had been empty when he'd bought the adjacent house ten years before. The couple who owned it had emigrated but had never put it up for sale.'

'You made no more enquiries?'

'It began to drizzle. The man advised me to get a move on. I plodded home. That's it really. Talking to you brought the memory back.'

'You can't remember the name of the Avenue?'

'This was twelve years ago. I'm rarely up that way. Maybe we could have a look around sometime.'

Barney nursed his empty glass. 'We'll have to make a decision. What do you think we should do?'

'You haven't told me everything, Barney. You mentioned something from years later.' Matt heard what Barney had to say and then agreed to ring Boyle on Monday morning.

The drinks wore off on the hour's drive back from The Salmon Leap to Jordanstown. The Ulster College campus was deserted. Matt had no difficulty parking the Spitfire. He walked to the office that he shared with two colleagues, Graham Watt and Derek Scott, and unlocked the door. Matt saw Watt's black briefcase sitting below his desk. He usually left before five o'clock to catch a bus home. It probably meant that he was working at the solitary computer terminal in the maths laboratory. Matt had hoped to work on it for an hour before returning to his apartment.

He opened a book but could not concentrate. A door slammed and Matt heard the slap of footsteps along the narrow corridor between offices and lecture rooms. Watt was carrying a brown folder and looked flushed as he entered the room. He nodded at Matt, sat down at his desk and rammed the folder into the briefcase. After checking that it was secured, he turned.

'I thought you were off today,' he said. 'Something about a will.'

Matt caught his stale breath. 'I hoped to spend some time on the computer,' he replied. 'Something sprang into my mind on the drive back and I decided to run with it while my mind was hot, Graham.'

'I know how it is. With the two of you gone this afternoon, I managed to catch up on my own research. My perturbation paper is coming along nicely.' He looked at his watch. 'Is that the time? I'd better rush. My wife will be expecting me.' He rushed out of the office.

Matt waited for five minutes, opened the door and peeped out. The office cleaner complained bitterly about black scuff marks on the floors and Matt saw that Watt had done it again. Even in high summer, he wore thick black brogues with a heavy polish. The coast was clear and he found the terminal free.

Watt had shattered his mood and he found it difficult to begin. The room smelt clean. At this time of year, the air was often fetid almost to the point of gagging when the laboratory was filled with staff and students. Matt inspected the floor. No scuff marks. The cleaner finished at five on Friday. He wondered where Watt had been working. He gave up, returned to the office and packed his briefcase. As he bent over, he noticed a sealed white envelope lying on the floor near Watt's desk. He put it in his inside pocket and left for the Halls of Residence.

Matt had obtained a post as Assistant Warden, a job that provided him with free accommodation. In return, he had to insure that residential students observed the Hall rules and did not get out-of-hand when they returned from the local pubs or Student Union Bar. In his own block, he shared the duties with Sue Neil, a Yorkshire woman who acted as Domestic Bursar. As he left the central spine of the main building, he saw her ambling across the car park.

'Hi, Matt. Fancy a drink? I'm going over to the Common Room for a quick gin before dinner.'

'I'll pass on that, Sue, if you don't mind. I had a few this afternoon. Maybe we could meet up later.' She smiled and strolled on, her long blond hair streaming down her back.

Matt let himself in to his apartment and switched on his portable television to watch the evening news. Afterwards, he made thick cheese sandwiches with Branston Pickle and opened a bottle of Beaujolais. At ten, there was a rap at the door. 'Sue, come in.'

She glanced at the half-empty bottle and smiled up at him. 'I thought you might like to pop across the way for last orders. Mind you, it was deserted earlier this evening, apart from the usual bores. I have some nice wine in my place. I'll get it, if you like.' Before he could reply, she had turned to leave. He heard her flip-flop down the stairs. A few minutes later, she was back.

Matt poured a glass of Beaujolais and opened her bottle of Rioja. 'It's been a long day, Sue. I told you yesterday about the reading of the will in Coleraine.'

'How did it go? I can just imagine you as a goody-goody altar boy. Black soutane and starched white linen. Brylcreamed hair and crooked smile.' She crossed her bare legs and reached out for a top-up.

'I met an old friend who served with me on the altar in the 1950's. Father Wilson was the curate. As a matter of fact, we heard today that he'd left us quite a bit of money.'

'You can take me out to dinner some night next week. Get us out of this place. What does your friend do?'

Matt hesitated. 'He's in the police. I hardly recognised him at first. Put on quite a bit of weight. Very short hair. Veins starting to sprout on his nose.'

'I've never known a cop before. Will you meet again?'

'Something else came up. A complication with regard to the rest of Wilson's estate. The solicitor thought we might be able to help.'

'And, after all that business, you still called into work on a gorgeous Friday evening.'

'I didn't get anything done. Watt was still there and it wrecked any concentration I had left. I'm still feeling whacked.'

Sue caught the hint and drained her glass. She smiled. 'We can finish the Rioja tomorrow evening.' She smoothed down her denim skirt, got up and left.

Matt poured a second glass of Rioja. He heard her move about downstairs and then all was quiet. The Examination season was in full flow and many students had returned home to prepare, free from temptation on campus. Tonight, *he* had been tempted. Often he heard her return from the Common Room, then the laughing and clinking of glasses. Later, the cries and screams. It had been at least a month since that had happened.

His thoughts turned to the outcome of the meeting with Boyle and Barney Mulvey. The latter needed the money more than himself. However, Matt didn't want to spend the rest of his days teaching students. He intended to create his own business. Computers were the future. Many, including Barney, were sceptical but Matt was convinced. Boyle had shown them a photograph of Wilson's detached house surrounded by an acre of land. It would fetch a substantial sum. Then there were the parting words of Barney to consider.

'I started this job when I was nineteen. Just around the start of the Troubles. Haven't had much luck recently, have I?' He had stared resignedly into his glass. 'Some of my colleagues haven't been easy to work with. A few of them are always ready to snipe.'

Matt interrupted. 'You were going to tell me about the gossip.'

'It was more than that. I'd been in the Force about six years when an Inspector called Sam Boomer called me in to join a meeting. It must have been around September 74. A young guy had been tortured and killed in a Romper Room in South Belfast. I knew the lad from

Technical School and they wanted to know about his background. My head was bursting and I jumped the gun about who was responsible. I shouted something about all the guilty bastards wandering the streets and no one able to touch them.'

'How did Boomer react?'

'He exploded. Sarcastic remarks were made about professional men from both sides who'd been walking free for years because of their connections. He snarled about a certain RC priest who'd been at his dirty work long before the Troubles. He mentioned Father Luke by name…maybe to fire me up. I don't know.'

Matt looked out across the blue Lough at the yellow lights twinkling from across the bay in Bangor and Donaghadee. The sea was calm tonight but he had seen it in the throes of a storm on a gale-force night in winter. The stowaway soldier's contact on the *Princess Victoria* had to provide the key. He searched his mind for the name.

Later, as he prepared for bed, he extracted the white envelope from his jacket pocket. It was not addressed. Why not have a look inside? The water in the kettle was boiling and, before pouring it onto the teabag, he used the steam. A black and white photograph fell out. A hooded woman lay spreadeagled on the floor of a barely furnished room. Her hands were tied behind her head. Above her waist, she wore a military uniform whose buttons were undone. Beneath, she was naked.

4

A KING PRAWN curry from The Dragon King was washed down with Colt 45 lager. Barney rinsed the dregs of the yellow sauce under the warm tap and flipped the plate over to dry. He heard the hiss of the kettle, switched it off and poured the water onto Nescafe granules. In the small living room, he sipped coffee, grimaced and lit up a Benson and Hedges.

A bell for an early evening Sunday service chimed across College Green, its manicured lawn deserted in the summer sunshine. Barney had signed a lease for a year on a third floor bedsit that was two minutes drive from Donegall Pass police station. The afternoon visit had wearied him and he dozed in the solitary armchair.

Jean Mulvey had been in fractious form. 'Just leave the money by the phone,' she had snapped and went upstairs to fetch his young son and daughter. They trooped down the stairs without her, barely acknowledging Barney before following through the open door.

'I thought we'd go to the Zoo again.' The comment produced no reaction as he packed them into the back of his red Ford Escort. When they arrived at Bellevue, he bought crisps and lemonade to cheer them up. Lions dozed in their cages. Only the chimpanzees seemed alive to the possibility of a free world outside.

As they watched a seal bask in the sun, Linda spoke at last. 'When will you be coming back, Daddy?' The question filled him with quiet desperation. His mumbled reply produced no follow-up and she whispered his response into David's ear.

After the visit was stretched to the limit, he drove them home. His daughter rang the front door bell. As it opened, he engaged first gear and accelerated away towards the City Centre. After reading the News of the World, his appetite picked up and he walked the short distance to the new Chinese takeaway.

He woke up at eight with a start, rinsed his face and prepared for the evening's session at the York Hotel, the only place open for a Sunday drink.

The owner, Doug Stewart, served him two bottles of Red Heart Guinness with a scowl. 'I don't know how you do it. It was two before I got rid of you and your mates last night.'

Barney shifted uncomfortably on his stool which looked along the tiny bar. 'Nothing else for it, Doug. Don't worry. I'm going to have an early night. Six o'clock start.'

'The only reason you're going early is because I close sharp at eleven on Sunday nights.'

Barney watched the regulars fill the bar. At nine o'clock, nurses whom he did not recognise found a table with four chairs. One caught the sleeve of the passing waiter and ordered four vodkas. They removed their dark blue capes and bundled them below the table. As they settled down to their drinks, one seemed to catch his stare. He drank his Red Heart and looked away.

His thoughts turned to Matt and Wilson's legacy. The extra money would take the edge off matters for a few months. He could clear the overdraft, the Access card and his gambling debts. The bank manager had been sympathetic but it couldn't last forever. Every month was the same. Jean's mortgage, support for the kids and his own new bills cleaned him out. The drinking and gambling had been subsidised by tick. It was going to be dodgy poking around on the case but he knew there was no choice.

Billy Craig was the colleague Barney trusted. 'You got right up Boomer's nose in there,' he had said. 'It was like touching a live wire.'

'I shouldn't have lost my head. When I heard that the bastards had ripped the lad's belly open after dropping concrete blocks on his face, I snapped. Especially when we've a good idea who was involved.'

'You know we can't prove it. Still, it was strange the way Boomer reacted. I've heard him talk about that priest before.'

'When was this?'

Billy rubbed his chin. 'Before you were stationed here. Let me think. It must have been late last year. A girl had been found dumped at the back of a Social Club near the Lagan. We'd appealed for information and had been sent an anonymous letter. There's a file somewhere.'

'I wouldn't mind having a look at it sometime. Can you remember anything else?'

'Boomer was in the Chair as we sifted through information at a meeting. A Sergeant who has moved on pulled out photocopies of the letter. I remember the Chief staring at it for a long time. He began to count on his fingers.'

'And then?'

'He stopped in the middle of his second hand and started to tap on the table. That fucking priest Wilson again, he said. One of these days the lid's gonna flip up on him.'

'Did they find the girl's murderer?'

'No, but Boomer didn't seem too interested in following up the letter. It *was* anonymous but we could have put out a fresh appeal. That's all I can remember, apart from the fact that he told Kerr to place a copy in Wilson's file...the one I mentioned.'

'You'll dig it out for me? Don't forget.'

Barney ordered two more bottles of Red Heart. The bar was filled with drinkers with many crowding around the bar to order double last orders. At eleven o'clock sharp, the towels were placed over the beer taps by a barman who followed Doug Stewart into a side office. Barney knew that they would emerge after ten minutes to clear the lounge. He was tempted to hang on and persuade Doug to serve him a quick double Powers. No, better not, he decided. As Barney passed the table where the nurses had been, he noticed an ID card.

On Monday morning, Matt rang Charlie Boyle. 'We've decided to see what we can do, Mister Boyle. Is there a time limit?'

'Six months. Let's say Christmas. If you haven't got anywhere by then, you never will. I'm glad you're going ahead. You'll have expenses and they'll be cleared within reason. For example, you may have to go abroad at some stage.'

'Why would we need to do that?'

'You'll find out when you read the letters.' They agreed on Friday afternoon for collection.

Matt rang the police station and was informed that Barney was busy. It could wait. He unlocked his desk and pulled out a bundle of examination scripts. At ten o'clock, his peace was disturbed when the third occupant of the office, Derek Scott, bustled in.

'No sign of Watt yet? Let's open the window before he arrives.' Derek fetched a long pole from a corner of the room and tilted open the glass. 'You know how muggy it gets. How did you get on last Friday?'

'I was left some money...myself and an old friend, Barney Mulvey. You wouldn't know him. He joined the cops a few years ago. There's a chance of quite a bit more money but there's a big string attached.'

'Anything I could help with?'

'I can't give you all the details now. There's something you might be able to throw a bit of light on.'

'Go ahead.'

'You've been teaching maths to the marine architecture crowd in the last year. I'd like to find out all I can about the sinking of the *Princess Victoria* in 1953.'

'I remember that myself. It happened in my early teens. Why, in the name of God, would you want to know about that?'

Before Matt could answer, the door opened and Watt came in. He nodded at them and sat at his desk. Before opening his briefcase, Matt noticed him glancing cautiously around the floor. Then he began to edit a file of papers.

Matt paused and looked at Derek. 'My parents told me about it years ago and it struck me how it had faded from memory although people still talk about the Titanic. Anyway, it's time for a cup of coffee. Graham, would you like to join us?'

Watt twisted round to face Matt and said that he would catch them up. Matt waited while Derek locked his desk. As they left the office, they grinned at the scuff marks on the corridor floor. 'There's something I'd like to show you, Derek,' said Matt. 'I meant to bring it with me this morning but the other business had to be sorted out and I forgot.'

'To do with Watt?'

'Possibly. See what you think tomorrow.' As Matt pushed open a door leading to a flight of stairs, he saw Watt lock their office and scurry away in the opposite direction. At the top of the stairs, a door opened onto the main mall of the Ulster College campus. In the Winter and Spring, it was usually packed with staff and students. This morning, there was only a light sprinkling of administrative staff clutching paper cups of tea. Matt and Derek strolled to the Academic Staff Room.

'With a bit of luck, Paul Kerry will come in,' said Derek. 'He's the man you need to talk to about the *Victoria*.' He ordered coffee and they found a table.

'You were curious as to why I wanted to know? It's a complex story and I don't want it to go any further.'

'You can trust me to keep quiet.'

Matt told him about Wilson, the mystery stowaway and the dead woman. Then, how the priest had fled after a grilling by police. He omitted Barney's more recent information.

'It's doubtful that Kerry will be able to help you with any of that.'

'I know but I have to start somewhere.'

'There he is now. I'll catch his attention.' After routine remarks about the sunny weather, Derek steered the conversation to Matt's interest.

Paul Kerry reflected. 'As a matter of fact, a new book discussed it last year. A guy called MacHaffie wrote it. I read it a few months ago. It brought it all back to me. Had you relatives on the ship?'

'No...not as far as I'm aware. I was at a meeting in Coleraine last week and the subject came up. I heard about the tragedy many years ago and I'm interested in finding out more detail.'

'The ship shouldn't have sailed in those conditions that morning. Vessels don't sail these days when winds exceed force 9. The *Victoria* sailed from Loch Ryan in Scotland into a force 12 gale.'

'Surely the Captain was aware of the risks?'

'Maybe but Captain Ferguson would have been under heavy pressure from his employers, British Railways, to sail. The ship carried the Royal Mail and train timetables fitted in with its arrival.

Of course, it wasn't simply the weather. The Inquiry later reported big problems at the rear of the ship.'

Derek interrupted. 'Weren't there accusations about bad design?'

'Not proven at the time although car vessels crossing Belfast Lough weren't built in the same way afterwards.'

'What was the problem?' asked Matt.

Kerry paused. 'The car deck at the open stern of the ship was about twelve feet above sea level, protected only by five foot doors. A man of average height could stand on the car deck and look directly into the sea. On a previous journey, Ferguson had complained of the deck's cargo being heavily drenched.'

'What do you believe happened that morning?'

'We'll never know for sure, Derek. From what I've read and my own experience, I think that, as the ship left Loch Ryan for the open Irish Sea, the Captain realised the true ferocity of the storm and decided to turn back for Stranraer.'

'What prevented him?' asked Matt.

'The force of the gale was coming from the North West. As the crew tried to turn the ship around, a mountainous wave ripped open the stern doors and the sea flooded onto the car deck. Further attempts at reversal would have exacerbated the danger as even more water would have swept in. The Captain's only option was to make a dash for Larne.'

'He got quite a bit of the way over,' commented Derek.

'Yes...in the circumstances. After the stern doors were breeched, the ship developed an immediate list of 10 degrees to starboard. This rose to fifty degrees as the ship crossed the Irish Sea. A few miles from home, it sank.'

'How many survived?' asked Matt.

'About one hundred and forty were lost. Over forty survived to tell the tale.'

'How many?' Matt burst in.

Kerry looked at him curiously. 'I can't remember the figure exactly. I'll check it if you're so interested.' He glanced at his watch. 'It's time I was getting back. I can't linger here all day like you arithmetic boys.'

When he had gone, Matt asked Derek if he had offended Kerry in some way. 'I thought he left very abruptly.'

'Don't get paranoiac. Paul is a very precise person. I suppose he has to be. He was probably just irritated that he couldn't answer your question. Come on, let's go. We'll have to get those exam scripts out of the way.' They saw a solitary female member of staff read a newspaper in a far corner of the room. As they left, they saw Watt approach from the mall.

'We couldn't wait for you any longer,' said Derek. 'Thought you weren't coming.'

Watt tensed. 'Got carried away again. Suddenly remembered you might be waiting for me. No harm done. I'll catch a quick cup by myself.' He rushed towards the Staff Room.

When they returned to the office, Matt thought of mentioning the photograph again and decided against. Shortly afterwards, Watt came back. Matt and Derek marked scripts while Watt edited a research paper. The phone interrupted their silence. Derek picked it up. 'It's for you, Matt. I think it's the guy you were talking about earlier.'

'Barney, thanks for getting back to me. I know you must be up to your eyes with cases. I talked to Charlie Boyle first thing this morning and told him we've decided to go ahead.' He sensed that Watt was listening. 'I agreed to go up there on Friday. He'll get everything together for us.' Matt switched the phone to his other ear and turned around. 'You can't make it? OK. I'll see if tomorrow suits. I'll ring you back.'

Barney's Ford Escort arrived sharp at eight o'clock on the corner of the Jordanstown road and Matt jumped into the front seat. 'He insisted that both of us must go to sign for the file. I thought you might be on duty earlier in the week. That's why I suggested late Friday.'

'I'm on this weekend so I managed to wangle this morning off. I gather it's easier for you.'

'We're finishing off the examination season. Then I'm fairly flexible until September.'

'Lucky for some. Anyway, now that we've made our minds up, we may as well get started. Nothing new since I last saw you?'

The photograph flashed into Matt's mind. He remembered that he had been going to show it to Derek. 'No...apart from the fact that I talked to a guy yesterday about the *Victoria* disaster. He works in the Marine Engineering Department and was able to fill in quite a few details for me.'

'Anything about our stowaway?'

'I couldn't get into that angle although he's going to check out how many actually survived. Perhaps it'll lead somewhere. Nothing new at your end?'

Barney searched in the right hand pocket of his jacket and extracted the ID. He threw it into Matt's lap. 'Have a look at this. Anything strike you about it?'

Matt studied the photograph of a girl, in her twenties, wearing a dark blue cape. 'Looks like a nurse. I don't recognise her. Should I?'

'We were talking earlier about the stowaway on the *Princess Victoria*. Did you ever remember the name of the man who offered to help him before the ship sank?'

'No, I couldn't recall it.'

'I couldn't remember it either until this ID came my way. The older man's name was Sullivan. What signature do you see at the bottom of the photograph?'

'Ellie Sullivan.'

5

BARNEY MULVEY waited for Matt's reaction. 'I almost turned left at the Glenavna Hotel...about a half-mile up the road. It set me thinking about the Patricia Curran case. It was tried in the same year that the *Victoria* sank.'

Matt looked up from the ID. 'They still talk about it around here. The guy who was convicted, Hay Gordon, was released from a mental institution only a few years later and went home to Scotland.'

'The Currans sold up and their house was converted into a hotel. They must have been rich. I noticed the big driveway surrounded by trees.'

'Judge Curran was rumoured to have had large gambling debts and his wife a hair-trigger temper.'

Barney smiled. 'Just like myself. Then there was the brother who converted and became a missionary priest in South Africa. Very strange crew.'

'You seem well-up on it all.'

'Another case that isn't closed. I've heard Boomer on about it as well. Let's get back to this ID. Any thoughts?'

'Where did you find it?'

'I was having a drink on Sunday night in the York Hotel. As I left, I saw it lying on a table where four nurses had been drinking. I asked the barman about them but he said it must have been their first visit.'

'Why didn't you leave it with him in case she came back for it?'

'Something clicked in my mind when I studied it but it didn't really come to me until later. I left a message with the owner, Doug Stewart, to say that I could be contacted at Donegall Pass police station if the nurse came looking for it. Later, in bed, I had a nightmare that I was drowning. It must have been the conversation we had with Boyle.'

'That's the way things come to you sometimes.'

'Well, I was lying there in the dark, half-awake, when it struck me that the stowaway's friend had been called Sullivan. I believe his first name was Jack.'

'The girl didn't return for her ID?'

'No, I checked with Doug last night. We'll wait and see.'

'Bit of a coincidence, Barney, don't you think?'

'Maybe it wasn't coincidence.'

'What makes you think that?'

'It seems odd. After all these years, we meet again to discuss Wilson's estate. The affair of the dead woman is raised. Only you and I knew of this story about the soldier.'

Matt interrupted. 'That's a major assumption.'

'Sorry. I didn't quite mean what I said. He must have told the story to the police in an attempt to clear his name. Boyle must know as well. What I really meant was that only you and I heard it together when he hadn't been accused of anything.' Barney looked around at Matt.

'We don't know that either. He might have known what was coming and was taking precautions.'

'With two innocent young boys? Maybe. We're going around in circles. Let's get back to the ID.'

'Are you suggesting someone else knew about our meeting with Boyle and is trying to help us? It seems like a long shot.'

Barney paused. 'I don't know what I'm suggesting. I just wanted to kick it around. Can't do it with anyone else.'

Barney had chosen the main dual carriageway to take them to Coleraine. Traffic was light and, at nine-fifteen, he parked the Ford outside Boyle's office on the outskirts of the town. A girl with a rural lisp showed them into a small Conference Room where Boyle sat at an antique oak table.

'Gentlemen, nice to see you again. Have a seat. I haven't much time as I have a court session at ten o'clock.' Boyle flipped open the lid of a large box file and extracted a bunch of documents tightened by a black ribbon. 'I needed you to sign for these in my presence. There is also the matter of gaining access to Father Wilson's home.'

'I wish we'd heard about his death earlier in the year,' said Matt. 'I'd like to have gone to the funeral.'

Boyle adjusted his spectacles and glanced across at him. 'It was sudden in the end. You obviously missed the obituary notice in the *Irish News*. Now...the key to the main front door. I can't let you have it on an unrestricted basis. However, if you'd like to have a look around today, I'm sure I can trust you with it for a few hours but I'd like to have it back.'

'I understand,' said Barney. 'We might bed in there and you couldn't get us out.'

'Now, Mister Mulvey, no need for that.'

Barney smiled. 'I appreciate your position. As a matter of fact, I'm on duty at one o'clock and don't have much time. We could do it another day. It'll be more important to have a look through these documents.'

Matt broke in. 'I wouldn't mind having a peep at the house, Barney, if there's time on the way back. Can you give us the actual address and directions?'

'No problem. Here it is. If you drive back by Kilrea, you will find the house about a mile before Portglenone. You shouldn't have any trouble. Look, I really must go. Any other questions?'

Matt asked about the foreign connection. 'You said we might have to go abroad?'

'At least one of you. You'll find out why when you've had the opportunity to go through these papers. Good morning, gentlemen. Irene will show you out.'

Barney threw the file onto the back seat of the Ford. He reversed, drove back to the roundabout near Boyle's office and found the exit for Kilrea. 'We have time for a quick cup of coffee. Let's try the Salmon Leap again. I'm parched.'

The waitress brought them two huge mugs of coffee as Barney inspected the documents. 'This lot is going to take some work. Maybe it's better if I look through it first.'

'You're the detective. I'd like us to get together as soon as you've finished.'

'Sure. Boyle's arranged everything in chronological order from the date of their first official correspondence.' Barney scanned the contents of the first letter. 'It's dated Fourteenth of February, 1967. Very brief. He requests Boyle for a meeting in an official capacity to discuss an important legal matter. He must have been living in the parish house at the time. A different address from where we're headed.'

Matt grimaced as he sipped the hot coffee. 'Boyle told us last Friday that Luke moved in after he resigned from his religious duties. He didn't get much joy out of it.'

Barney replaced the letter, closed the box and glanced at his watch. 'We have to get a move on if we're going to have a quick look at the place.' He gulped down the remainder of his coffee and stood up. 'You'll have to direct me. I don't know this back route.'

The roads were deserted in the June sunshine. Barney navigated a sharp turn at the Brown Trout Inn and drove to Kilrea. Matt directed him towards Portglenone and studied the address. 'We'll have to ask someone nearer town. The house may be well away from the main road.'

They stopped at a small garage. As Barney filled the Ford with petrol, Matt inquired about the address. 'Another half-mile away,' said the owner. 'You can't miss it. Grey stone covered with clinging ivy. Were you friends of Father Wilson?'

Matt hesitated. 'We knew him many years ago in his old parish. Didn't know he was dead until last month.' Barney joined them and paid for the fuel. The man looked at him suspiciously and then at Matt's long black hair. He said nothing.

They found the house. Barney parked the car beside the white gates. The hedges had not been cut and the grass swayed in the breeze. As Barney hurried up the pathway to the front of the house, something occurred to Matt. 'We never asked Boyle where Luke was buried. That's something else we must find.'

'I'll leave that to you, Matt. This is a great place.' They peered through a bay window at a room filled with bookcases that surrounded an imposing fireplace. 'Very like the old parochial house in Belfast. Ours, I mean.' Barney followed Matt to the other bay window. A large room was deserted apart from a table below which sat a cardboard box.

They walked to the back of the house and saw an adjacent field leading to a stream running beside a barbed wire fence. The fields rose to a distant farmhouse with its red barn gleaming in the morning sunshine.

'Matt, this place has to be worth quite a sum.' Barney looked at Matt and turned away. 'You and I know that Luke couldn't have killed anyone despite what that fucker Boomer said to me.'

'He was in the Navy, Barney. Remember what we heard when we were on the submarine. Anything's possible.'

'Don't talk bollocks, Matt. That was different. We'll clear his name...if it's the last thing we do. As soon as I come off duty, I'm going to get into this file. Then we'll talk again. Let's go.'

Shortly after midday, Matt returned to his apartment. He heated up a tin of tomato soup and thought about the morning's visit. Barney had said little after they had left Wilson's property. Matt's attempts at conversation had been met with a shrug or a grunt. He gave up and dozed off in the front seat of the Ford. Later, as they parted, Barney said that he would contact him at the end of the week. After lunch, as he thought about the nurse's ID, he remembered the photograph which he had found beneath Watt's desk. He found the envelope again and pulled out the contents. It was not a clipping from a magazine but an actual shot of very high quality. Matt wondered if Watt had taken the photograph himself or purchased it through some speciality service. Assuming that it *had* belonged to Watt.

After lunch, as Matt walked down the stairs, he saw Sue Neil come out of her apartment. He hesitated then caught her upward glance. She waved over and smiled.

'Hi, Matt. I hope you haven't finished my Rioja yet. Meant to call over at the weekend but got waylaid. You know how it is.' She opened the external door of the Halls of Residence. 'I see you have your hands full with that briefcase and file. Ready for action again?'

'I'm getting behind with the examination scripts. Had to go up to Coleraine again this morning about the estate business.'

'Don't forget that dinner you promised me. Maybe at the weekend?'

'I'll get back to you about it, Sue. I hope you don't think I'm putting you off but I've got to see my detective friend again to sort a few more matters out.'

'I thought it was all cut and dried.'

'There's an additional complexity. I'll explain it to you sometime.'

'Sounds very cloak and dagger.' Sue paused. 'Look. Over there. Your creepy friend Watt seems to be going home early.'

In the distance, Matt saw Watt hurry along the main driveway in the opposite direction. 'Slow down. With a bit of luck, he won't see us. We're not exactly bosom pals, you know. Did you say creepy? Do you know something about him that I don't?'

Sue smiled. 'I didn't like to say anything before. After all, you share an office. I must admit I do find him creepy. And I'm not the only one.'

'Are you going to tell me or not?'

'Well, I've heard a few stories from a friend in the Secretarial Centre. Some of the girls travel home with him on the same bus. It becomes very crowded at times. Apparently he's fond of pressing rather too close. Of course, maybe it was only their imagination.'

Matt stopped. 'Thanks for telling me. He's certainly a strange one. I'll have to keep an eye on him.' They parted on the main mall and Matt descended the stairs to his office. He unlocked the door and saw that he had the place to himself.

Matt spent the afternoon marking the remainder of his scripts. The only interruption came at four o'clock when Derek rang from home. 'Matt, I wasn't sure if you'd call back after your trip to Coleraine. I ran into Kerry at morning coffee. He said he'd gathered together some data for you. He'll be in his office until six if you want to catch him before he goes. One of my kids has caught a bug so I left at lunchtime. Is Dr Watt there?'

'No, did you want to speak to him?'

'Not particularly. Just wanted to check before saying anything. He was in very bad humour this morning. Distracted and snappy. Another good reason for me to get offside. I'll maybe work from home for the next couple of days. Catch you later in the week.'

At five o'clock, Matt walked to the Department of Marine Engineering and found Kerry's office. He knocked gently and opened the door. 'Dr Kerry. Sorry to intrude. Derek Scott left a message to say that you might have something for me.'

Kerry looked up from a clean desk and beckoned Matt in. 'Ah, yes. You were asking me yesterday about survivors from the *Victoria*. I've done a little research for you. Your inquiry was a very interesting one and a subject of considerable debate. I've talked to my colleagues and consulted relevant material which we possess.'

'It's very good of you to have gone to all this trouble. I can assure you that I had a very good reason for asking.'

'Not at all...but I'm afraid I'm unable to give you an exact answer. Not today, anyway. Let's go over what I have. You're not in a hurry?'

'No, I haven't any commitments.'

'The Final Report from the Inquiry stated that there were 49 crew and a total of 127 passengers on the ship. However, in an emergency message, transmitted shortly before midday...about two hours before she sank, the radio operator, George Broadfoot, stated that there were 60 crew and 123 passengers on board.'

'Wouldn't British Railways have been required to keep a proper record of their passengers?'

'They would today...especially with the Troubles and terrorist attacks to worry about. But, in 1953, there wasn't a legal requirement.'

'Coming back to my original question, how many were estimated to have survived?'

'No women or children survived according to the records we have. Ten male crew members and 34 male passengers were rescued in lifeboats and from rafts. All were clearly identified...apart from one which we'll come to shortly. Let me show you the list compiled by Joshua Gilbert.'

'Joshua Gilbert?'

'Josh is a member of our Department who's been working on a contract with Harland and Wolff. They've been providing training and advice for a major shipyard in Greece. He's out there for two months. It was Josh who collected this material for our library.'

Matt studied the list. 'Who's the mystery man?'

'Let me digress for a moment. Remember that the ship had been docked overnight in Stranraer after arriving from Larne on the previous evening. There were two night stewards, John Wallace and Albert Steele. They were coming to the end of their shift when the Chief Steward told them that he required one of them to stay on board for the return journey to Larne. The request was due to the number of passengers being larger than expected.'

'Why was that...given the terrible weather?'

'There were businessmen and politicians whose airflights from London to Belfast had been cancelled on the previous day. They had travelled by train from Euston to get home for the weekend despite the weather. They included the Deputy Prime Minister for Northern Ireland and the MP for North Down.'

'You were telling me about the stewards?'

Kerry paused. 'They tossed a coin to decide who would travel. Steele won and left the ship. John Wallace sailed and was drowned. His colleague's recollections of that morning are on file. Near the end of his shift, he was approached by an Ulsterman who had neither ticket nor money but said that he must get home. They took pity on him and brought him on board through the doors on the car deck. They got him breakfast and left him to mingle with the crowd in one of the lounges.'

'Are you saying that he survived but was never identified?'

'Josh believed so...according to these notes.'

'Have we any closer description?'

'Albert Steele suspected that he was a deserter from the Army. Beneath the man's overcoat, he caught a glimpse of a uniform.'

'Is there any record of a name even though you say he wasn't clearly identified afterwards?'

'We know that he was on board Lifeboat No. 6 with thirty other people who were brought safely ashore at Donaghadee.'

'What name did he give?'

'He was known as Perry and never traced. If he was a deserter, he would have given a false name when asked.' Kerry looked into Matt's eyes. 'I can see you're very taken with the story. You never explained to me your original interest. Anything to do with this soldier?'

Matt looked at his watch. 'Maybe we could meet again. I suddenly remembered that I *do* have an appointment.'

'That's a pity. I have something else here for you to think about. Josh was convinced that there was at least one other person on board who was not *listed* among the survivors but may have belonged to either group.'

'How did he reach that conclusion?'

'I'm not quite sure. You will need to talk to him personally. He'll be back later in the summer.'

6

BILLY CRAIG shifted uncomfortably on his barstool beside Barney as he emptied the remains of the Red Heart into his glass. Thursday night was quiet in the York Hotel, especially in the summer as there were no seats outside. The remains of the evening sun streaked through the faded blue curtains facing Botanic Avenue. 'You remember that I tried to dig out the file for you but there was no sign of it. I could hardly ask Boomer so that left Sergeant Kerr who'd moved back up to Ballymena. I rang him on the pretence that I was interested in something else and tried to slip it in at the end.'

Barney gulped his Guinness and sighed. 'But he twigged on right away. You had to back off as Boomer and Kerr had always been very friendly with each other.'

'I didn't want him contacting Boomer to ask what it was all about. You never showed any further interest until this week so I didn't bother with it. What's got you excited again?'

'The meeting in Coleraine last Friday. Wilson left me some money. You remember how Boomer blackened him at that session about eighteen months ago. You couldn't have a second crack at finding the file?'

'I don't know, Barney. Maybe Boomer has it hidden away somewhere, especially if Kerr tipped him off.'

'See what you can do. I'd appreciate it. Now, let's have one for the road.'

Billy excused himself by saying that he had hardly seen his wife since Tuesday. Barney ordered a double Powers from Doug Stewart and asked about the nurses.

Doug shrugged. 'It's been quiet since I saw you earlier in the week. Why don't you just leave the ID with me?'

'She probably can't remember where she dropped it. I'll hold on to it but have another look at it in case she comes in.' He sipped his whiskey and Doug moved away to serve a customer. Barney rubbed the side of his forehead and tried to concentrate. He had meant to study Boyle's documents as soon as he came off duty on Tuesday night. A new case had tied him up and yesterday had been the same. Then the morning's post had brought a tough letter from Jean Mulvey reminding him of his financial obligations. He gulped the Powers, hesitated and rose to leave.

In his bedsit, he toasted the heel of a loaf and brewed tea. As the teabag settled, he unlocked his small safe and extracted the box file. He flicked through the letters and documents. If they were stolen, Boyle still retained the originals. Barney decided to have a second set of photocopies made just in case, but not at the station.

The second letter was an immediate response from Boyle to Wilson suggesting a date to meet in late February 1967. Ring his secretary to confirm. Boyle's précis of the subsequent meeting followed. Barney finished the tea, pulled out his pen and made his own notes. He went to bed at one o'clock. The alarm clock whirred five hours later. When he came off duty in late afternoon, he was dog-tired. He longed for a drink but decided instead to visit the Royal Victoria Hospital.

After the exchange with Kerry, Matt had spent the evening alone. There would have been no point in telling him the background to his interest and the white lie did not bother him. After a shower, he made a bacon omelette and poured a second glass of Sue's Rioja. The late sun sparkled on the Lough as Matt thought about the information he had been given.

No one called Sullivan had been on the official list of survivors. However, someone could have found a raft and been washed ashore without being detected. An experienced swimmer might have reached land despite the horrific conditions. Given what was known about Sullivan's past, he might have had good reason not to reveal his survival. Assuming, of course, that he existed at all.

On the following morning, Matt rose early and reached his office before Watt's usual arrival time. He unlocked his drawer, pulled out the examination scripts and made final checks on the total marks awarded. After completing these, he went to the end of the corridor where the Head of Department had his office. Entry to it could only be gained via the room of a Personal Assistant called Deirdre.

Although usually punctual, there was no sign of her. He walked on through and knocked on Walton's door. At first there was no reply but Matt detected the sound of voices and papers being shuffled.

'Enter!' said a voice that Matt did not recognise.

Matt opened the door. The Head sat at his desk. A tall stringy man appeared about to leave. 'Sorry to interrupt, Dr Walton. I knew you would want to get these exam papers to the External Examiner. I'm finished with them.'

Walton looked across at him with bloodshot eyes. 'That's fine,' he said wearily. 'Do you know Bill Armstrong from Admin? Probably not. Bill, this is Matt Quinn from my Department. I'm sure you'll meet again. I don't think there's anything more we can do about this matter now. No doubt you'll be getting back to me.'

Armstrong adjusted a file beneath his arm. 'Perhaps you can shed some light on it.' He paused and stared at Matt. 'The cleaner has been complaining about dirty marks on the floors of this Department. No sooner has she polished the area when they reappear. Bit like the Forth Bridge.'

Matt hesitated. 'I've noticed them myself. Like black polish, I believe.'

Armstrong looked down at Matt's Adidas trainers. 'So you're pleading not guilty. Well, if you think you know who might be responsible, perhaps someone could have a quiet word with the person.' He turned to Walton, thanked him for his time and left.

Walton sighed. 'Deirdre rang me last night to say that she'd caught some kind of bug. Won't be in for a day or two. I'll have a look through these papers today and then send them on to the Extern. He'll be over to see us at the end of next week. In the meantime, you can get on with some research. I haven't seen any publications from you yet.'

'I've been too busy with teaching.'

Walton smiled. 'Don't keep putting it off. These are salad days for a young member of staff like you.' He watched Matt shift uneasily. 'Close the outer door on your way out, would you? Once word goes around that Deirdre's not here, they'll all be in to stock up on pens.'

A strange man, thought Matt. No harm in him but always manages to get a dig in. Matt had little interest in research although he knew he couldn't progress quickly here unless he made an effort like Watt. As he approached his office, he saw black scores on the floor. He walked past, ascended the stairs to the mall and returned to his apartment in the Halls of Residence.

He made coffee and looked across the Lough. As Armstrong had rushed out of Walton's office, Matt had caught the heading on the file...G.J. WATT. Senior Personnel did not meet with a Head of Department to discuss shoe polish. It had to be something else. He needed to talk with Sue. He would invite her for dinner when he had spoken to Barney again. His thoughts turned to Wilson as he finished his coffee. There *was* one matter that could be checked.

He parked the Spitfire across from the main gates of St Malachy's College and secured the hood. At midday in early June, the main road carried only intermittent traffic. In the distance, a bell jangled and he saw a number of boys running down the College Avenue to the gates. Nothing much had changed.

As Matt walked away from the school along the Antrim Road, the dilapidated homes caught his attention. Many terraced houses were boarded-up. In others, where once there had been spotless linen curtains, makeshift sheets hung within faded window frames. The area had suffered in the Troubles. There had been murders along this route after darkness had fallen. Lone drinkers stumbling home from the City Centre had met their fate in nearby Romper Rooms. The shops near Duncairn Gardens had wire mesh protection attached to their windows. At the Northern Bank, a woman lay asleep in a flood of urine beside the entrance. An empty can of Carlsberg Special Brew blew across the road.

Matt stopped. What could he do? He walked on. The Public Park surrounding the old Waterworks area was sprinkled with groups of teenagers drinking from cans. Empties lay dead on the grass and litterbins overflowed with rubbish. When a skinhead shook his crotch at him, he crossed the road and reached a set of shops. In contrast to the general air of malaise, these were clean and wore a mild air of prosperity. He focused on the area where he thought that he had sheltered from the heavy rain all those years ago.

The final shop in the row sat adjacent to a branch of the Ulster Bank. The latter faced a busy intersection where a residential Avenue cut across the main Antrim Road. The area looked subtly different but Matt felt sure that it was near here where he had sheltered from the rain and thought about Teresa. He turned right at the bank and saw a grocery store about ten yards beyond it. Tension gripped his stomach as he looked across at the three-storey terraced houses.

Many had FOR SALE signs planted. As Matt walked across the road, he saw the yellow gantries in the distance. It had to be near here. Two gardens had been covered in tarmac. Through the front window of one he saw an elderly man reading a newspaper. Matt felt that it must be the other one.

He walked back up the Avenue and stopped to tighten the laces on his trainers. As he did so, he studied the house. If this was the right place, it had been reoccupied at some stage for it appeared well maintained. However, there was no sign of activity inside. Matt noted the number and decided to leave it for now. Perhaps Barney could help.

He walked back to the Spitfire and opened the hood. The boys had disappeared and the district was eerily silent. Matt imagined what it must be like at midnight. He glanced at the huge stone wall running alongside the pavement and recalled that it surrounded an ancient cemetery.

He turned the car and drove back along the Antrim Road. The sleeping woman had stirred and was searching for her can of Special Brew. At the intersection, the traffic light signalled red and, as Matt waited for it to change, he scrutinised the silent Avenue. There was something wrong but he could not fathom what it was. As the signal switched to orange, he decided to break his return with a visit to his mother.

Since his father's death two years ago, her health had not been good and she was being treated for angina. 'Your sister's just off the phone,' she said. 'She'll be back from London at the end of July. The school holidays are different over there. Can I get you some lunch? I'll open a tin of salmon.'

'That would be great. I'll make some tea.' He enquired about her latest treatment and then told her about the money but not the additional incentive.

'You might have told me sooner. Last Friday, you say?'

Matt forked a chunk of John West salmon. 'I didn't want to tell you on the phone and this has been my first chance to call in,' he lied. 'Besides, you don't want to get too excited. In any case, it'll be a while yet before we receive anything.'

His mother glanced at him suspiciously. 'We? Who's the we?'

Matt swallowed. 'Sorry. I should have mentioned it right away. You must remember Barney Mulvey? My old friend from the altar boy days. We met up again in Coleraine.'

Mrs Quinn sighed. 'Yes, I remember the Mulveys. They moved away from here years ago. Maybe just as well in the present climate. We heard he joined the police. Is that right?'

'He's a Detective-Sergeant.'

'I suppose he's settled down. Not like yourself.'

Matt smiled. 'He has a wife and two kids but they've separated. He lives by himself at the other side of town.'

Mrs Quinn tutted. 'Hard to believe he would do a thing like that…coming from where he did.'

'Join the police? That's very harsh. Your uncle was in the police.'

'That's not what I meant. I'll bet he was bad to his wife.'

'How do you know that?'

'I know more than you think. Am I right?'

Matt grinned. 'Maybe. You're nearly always right. But Barney's not a bad guy although he has his weaknesses.' He saw that she was ready to change the subject.

'Tell me, Matt, about Father Wilson. Did he ever get over the scandal?'

Matt twisted in his armchair. 'Charlie Boyle…his solicitor…said that it always preyed on his mind although he was never found guilty of anything.'

'It was terrible to accuse a priest of a thing like that. There's some evil boys in this country.'

'Calm down, Mum. There's something I must get while I'm here. Barney and I talked about the time Father Wilson had us shown around a submarine. Then, afterwards, he told us the story about the mystery stowaway on the *Princess Victoria*.'

'I remember. What is it you're looking for? All your old stuff is up in the attic.'

'We were in Donegal that New Year and I brought back a box of old newspaper clippings about the *Victoria*. I wonder if they're still up there. I'll climb up and have a look.'

When Barney arrived at Reception, a surly clerk was preparing to leave. 'I was visiting a relative and thought I'd check if anyone had lost this ID card. I found it the other night in a pub. Might be one of your nurses.'

The man looked at it without interest. 'This is a big organisation. I wouldn't know the names of all the staff. Leave it here and somebody will find out next week.' He turned his back to fetch a jacket.

Barney waited. 'It mightn't be from here at all. I'll keep it in case the girl comes back over the weekend.'

The man scratched his grey stubble. 'Please yourself.' At that moment, a female clerk entered Reception from a side door, smiled at her colleague and wished him a good weekend. 'Not much chance of that where I live. I'll try my best. Maybe you can help this fella.'

She studied the ID. 'Ah, yes. I know this nurse. The last time I saw her she was on Ward 6. Don't think I've seen her this week. I'll ring them if you want to wait. Have a seat.'

Barney thanked her and sat down. The phone was not answered for some minutes and then he heard a faint voice at the other end. The girl doodled on a notepad. His eyes stung with tiredness.

'Yes, I was right,' said the girl. 'Nurse Sullivan was on Ward 6 until last Sunday night. She's off on holidays for a fortnight. I'll give it to her when she returns. Let me have your name and address. She'll want to thank you.'

'Tell her she can buy me a drink the next time she sees me in the York Hotel. I'll leave her my details. Maybe I'll get lucky.' He smiled and turned to leave. He knew what the girl was thinking. Fat chance. 'I wouldn't mind having a break myself. Somewhere in the sun. Is that where she went?'

She looked up. 'The Sister said Greece. Didn't say which part.'

7

THE YELLOW CLIPPINGS added a deeper note to the tragedy. The blurred print was tiny in the aged Donegal newspaper. Matt read the summary of the ship's last voyage on 31st January 1953 and studied the report on the woman whom his grandmother had known. It said that Lily Russell had lived in Kiltoy near Letterkenny. She was aged 27, unmarried and had been returning home from her job in Carlisle to visit her ill mother. When the ship sank, her final minutes had been recorded by a survivor called John Fitzpatrick. She had jumped into the water and got on to a raft beside him. The treacherous seas soon swept them off it. He had managed to climb on again and saw a screaming Lily cling to another raft. This, in turn, was hit by a fifty foot wave and she was washed away to her doom. An exhausted Mr Fitzpatrick had been eventually picked up by the crew of the Donaghadee lifeboat, the *Sir Samuel Kelly*. His arms had been practically frozen to the raft.

Matt put aside the report and looked out from his apartment across the Lough. In the distance, he saw the Copeland Islands near where the *Victoria* had gone down. A ferry came into view and sailed down Belfast Lough as if being tugged by an invisible thread. Matt turned back to the report. The Donegal newspaper had concentrated on the local angle, the background to Lily's death and the recovery of her body. Afterwards, the details of the funeral were recorded. Letters and notes of deepest sympathy filled the pages throughout early February.

Matt had somehow expected more detail. He tidied up the jumbled cuttings and organised them into a proper file. As he did so, a section of the front page from 2nd February 1953 caught his eye. This had focused on the weekend efforts of rescue ships to find survivors and the bodies of the drowned. Much of the work had been done by the lifeboat men from Donaghadee. Additionally, many Royal Navy ships and aircraft had been diverted to the scene of the disaster. The newspaper noted that one of the latter had stood ready near Carrickfin strand in Donegal but had not been called upon.

Matt wondered what to make of this information. The strand was near where his grandparents had once farmed. He remembered that there *had* been a small airstrip along the sea behind huge sand dunes. However, it would not be well known that the Republic of Ireland allowed Royal Navy aircraft to occupy their territory, over thirty years after the establishment of the Free State. It was strange and, as he put it to the back of his mind, he heard a knock on the door.

Sue bounced in and sat down. 'What are you doing with all these newspaper cuttings?' She picked one up, glanced at it and put it back. 'I didn't know you were interested in shipping disasters.'

'Not really. I'm just doing a little research in connection with the estate matter I told you about.' Matt found a folder and packed the cuttings away. 'I can't offer you a glass of wine, I'm afraid. I finished your Rioja last night but I'll make it up to you when we have dinner. What night would suit you?'

Sue grinned. 'Any night does me. When you've finished with your detective friend, perhaps you'll be more relaxed.'

'Let's make it Saturday. Anyway, I suspect that's not what you called for?'

'Correct. I had another chat at lunch with my friend in the Secretarial Centre. Got some more juicy bits for you about Dr Watt. Hot off the press.'

Matt raised his eyebrows. 'That's a coincidence. Something odd on that front happened this morning. Let's hear your news first.'

'One of the girls in the Centre was deputising in Personnel on Monday. A female lecturer arrived in a bit of a state and went in to see the Head...a guy called George Burley. The girl overheard some of the conversation. There'd been an incident in the Common Room involving Watt. She was quite sure of the name. All the girls talk about him.'

Matt thought back to Monday morning. 'As a matter of fact, Watt was supposed to be having coffee with Derek Scott and me. He turned up just as we were leaving. There *was* only one other person...perhaps the woman you mentioned. Any idea of what actually happened?'

'That's it as far as that incident's concerned. You said something odd happened this morning?'

'I happen to know that our Head of Department, Walton, had an early morning meeting with Bill Armstrong from Administration.'

'Armstrong is Burley's new Deputy. He used to work in Estates.'

'That figures. I was dropping off exam scripts. The PA, Deirdre, wasn't there. I went in to see Walton just as Armstrong was leaving. He had a file with Watt's name on it.'

'Ah, Deirdre. That's a second piece of gossip you must hear. She has tea with one of the girls in the Centre. Apparently, there was a recent clash between Watt and Deirdre when they were alone in her office. She didn't want to stir things up and so she didn't report it at the time. I don't know exactly what happened.'

Matt thought of telling Sue about the photograph but held back. 'Watt's building up a reputation for himself.'

Sue smiled. 'Yes, he's beginning to sound like quite a horny bugger. What did you say his wife was like?'

'I didn't. I've never met the woman…nor has anyone else in the Department.'

She looked at her watch. 'I must go. If I find anything else out, I'll keep you posted.'

Matt smiled. 'Thanks. We'll find out sooner or later.' When she had left, he thought of how he could extract himself from the dinner invitation. She would probably tell him everything without any further intimacy being necessary. Then he felt guilty about using her and decided to go ahead with the date.

After leaving the Royal Victoria Hospital, Barney drove home, parked his Escort and walked to the York Hotel. He ordered two bottles of Red Heart, the first of which he almost cleared in one gulp. The bar was quiet. Stewart left him alone with his thoughts.

Luke Wilson had met Boyle at the end of February 1967 and the latter had drafted a minute of their meeting. The priest had produced a blackmail note found in his letterbox. The enclosing envelope had no stamp. The note itself was not in Barney's set of documents. He would have to check with Boyle.

According to the solicitor's minute, the blackmailer had demanded £1000. The money was to be left at a designated drop-off point at nine o'clock on the subsequent Friday night. If the demand was not met, a letter was going to the police. Its contents would link the priest with a savage assault on a local girl in the November of the previous year. The letter also hinted that he...if it was a *he*...knew all about other similar attacks carried out by Wilson.

Barney finished his second Red Heart and ordered two more. Wilson had informed Boyle of the interrogation by Belfast police before his departure for Portglenone. He had stressed his innocence. Boyle had advised him to report the blackmail attempt to the police but had been met with a firm refusal. The set of minutes had finished with an accusation by Wilson that he believed the blackmailer to be Jack Sullivan...a man with whom he had served in the Navy during the Second World War.

The subsequent minute was dated in June of the same year. It seemed from its content that there had been no interim developments. It could be inferred that Boyle had advised Wilson in February not to proceed with delivery of the money. Whilst this may have been the best course of action, there had been a severe impact on the priest's nerves and he was on a course of medication prescribed by his GP, a Dr Hamill. Attached to the minute was a typewritten A4 summary of the historical interaction with Jack Sullivan.

Barney finished his fourth Red Heart and signalled to Doug Stewart for a fifth accompanied by a glass of Powers. He needed to discuss the summary with Matt as it repeated the story of the stowaway. One additional statement had hit him with the force of a hammer. It confirmed the existence of a woman believed to be the daughter of his blackmailer.

The remainder of the file incorporated further minutes of meetings between the solicitor and priest. They occurred at infrequent intervals with no apparent pattern. On several occasions, Boyle had represented Wilson at interviews with the police. There was no mention of blackmail. Barney saw that Boomer's name was recorded twice.

Doug Stewart interrupted his thoughts. 'Same again, Barney? I take it you're off duty tomorrow.'

'Yes but I'm back on Sunday.' Barney hesitated. He thought of the file and changed his mind. 'I'll be in later for last orders. I'm going to have a bite to eat.'

'No news of your nurse?'

Barney ignored the question. 'I'll see you later.' He slipped off his stool and walked out into the evening sunshine towards The Dragon King. He ate a double portion of noodles with fried chicken in black bean sauce washed down with a pint of Harp. Afterwards, he walked home, made a mug of Nescafe and studied Boyle's documents.

On 23rd October 1967, the police had contacted Wilson with regard to their renewed investigation into an assault on a young music teacher called Celia Teeny. She lived with her elderly parents in a farmhouse near the village of Crosskeys, a few miles from Portglenone. Her mother and father had gone to an evening Novena service in their local church. It was their custom on these nights to visit friends afterwards for tea and sandwiches. At nine o'clock, Celia had opened the door to a man of about fifty who, from his dog collar and black Crombie overcoat, she assumed to be a priest. When her parents returned at ten o'clock, they found her on the kitchen floor, drenched with blood flowing from a wound on her forehead. As they had no telephone, her father had gone to a nearby pub to call for an ambulance and the police.

Celia's recovery had been slow. At first, she had been reluctant to open up to the police. Progress on the investigation had been intermittent. Her caller had said that he wished to see her parents on urgent business. He insisted on waiting until they returned and accepted the offer of tea. As she turned away from the boiling kettle, the last thing she remembered was the raised hammer. There was no subsequent evidence of direct sexual interference.

As the interview with Wilson progressed, the police said that they had received a number of letters in the Autumn accusing the priest. However, they didn't have sufficient evidence to progress a charge. A fortnight later, a subsequent interview covered the same ground with the same negative result.

Barney noted that the police had come from Ballymena and that Detective-Sergeant Boomer had conducted the interviews. He knew that he had risen in the ranks at around the beginning of the Troubles in 1969. His ascendancy had eventually brought him to Belfast. His rural accent, like Kerr's, had remained intact. Barney glanced at his watch, closed the box file and returned it to the safe. He hurried down the stairs, walked the short distance to the York Hotel and arrived just as the barman was about to cover the taps with towels.

Matt had waited until late Friday before attempting to contact Barney. The receptionist at the station said that he had left.

'Any idea where I might reach him?'

'I'm afraid not. Even if I did have a new number for him, I can't give it out to anyone. Is it very urgent?'

'I'm an old friend of his. Will he be back tomorrow?'

She hesitated. 'He will be here on Sunday. If you want to give me your name, I will leave a message.'

'It's OK. I'll catch him at home.' Matt put down the phone in the Entrance Area of the Halls of Residence. He hadn't anticipated this problem. Neither Barney nor he had direct home telephone numbers. Some computer genius should invent a mobile phone. He thought of contacting Jean Mulvey but dropped the idea immediately. It was nearly five o'clock. During his visits to his office in the previous two days, no message had come through from Barney. Matt decided to drive over to Barney's new address before having dinner.

A plump, unshaven man wearing only a string vest on top of flannel trousers opened the front door. 'You've pressed the wrong buzzer, son. Who is it you're looking for?'

Matt paused. 'Mister Mulvey. Sorry to bother you. You don't know if he's in?'

'He must be the new fella on the top floor. I haven't heard him up there since early this morning.' He slammed the door shut.

Matt wondered what to do next. Barney had talked about the nearby York Hotel. He had probably gone there for a drink. A minute's drive brought Matt to it. A security man gave him a casual glance and let him pass. The bar was almost empty and there was no sign of Barney. Matt felt uneasy about asking for him and gave up.

He drove back towards the Ulster College campus, stopping off only to buy two bottles of Rioja. On returning, he opened one and drank three glasses with sirloin steak and salad. He studied the newspaper cuttings again, then thought of Barney. He should have phoned him earlier in the office despite Watt's presence. This reminded him of the photograph. He found it on top of his bedroom wardrobe. At that moment, he heard a knock on the door. Before answering, he slipped the photograph under the clippings.

'Just wanted to check that everything's fine for tomorrow evening.' Sue waited in the doorway.

'I'll pick you up at seven thirty. I've booked the Glenavna so I don't have to worry about drinking and driving. Won't you come in for a drink? I've bought more Rioja.'

Sue smiled. 'It will keep for tomorrow night. I'm going to meet a friend. Bye.'

Matt poured another glass and looked out over the darkening Lough. A pale moon cast a yellow glow across the still water. Then he tidied up his file and returned it to the bedroom. On Saturday afternoon, he drove to Barney's again but there was no reply.

That night, as they ate their Prawn Cocktails with a glass of Muscadet, Sue told him that there was little more to report about Watt. They knew that Deirdre had not been back at work. The waiter returned and they both ordered duck with strawberry pavlova to follow. By the time the second bottle of Morgon had been demolished, Matt felt tipsy. He told Sue about his business with Barney and afterwards they stumbled back to the Halls, by which time the red mist of desire had descended on Matt.

He slept late on Sunday. After a lunch of bacon, eggs and potato bread, he felt better. She had left a note to say that he should call down for supper around nine that evening. She would be ready and waiting. In the afternoon, he rang Barney's station but the receptionist informed him that Detective-Sergeant Mulvey was a busy man and was unavailable. At half-eight, he went down to Sue's apartment. A gentle knock produced no response. He returned after nine but there was no reply.

On Monday morning, a commotion downstairs pulled him out of a deep sleep. Shortly afterwards, he was woken again by a pounding on his door. He opened it and saw a uniformed cop with a plain clothes colleague flourishing his pass. They informed him that they were investigating the murder of Sue Neil who had been found strangled in her room...blindfolded and wearing only a nurse's cape.

GOLD

8

THE MELTEMI breeze settled sufficiently for the ferry *Naios* to leave Pireaus fours hours behind the scheduled departure time of 8.00am. It was five o'clock in the afternoon before it reached the island of Syros. The ship dispatched its cars, motorcycles and passengers with maximum efficiency before taking on board their replacements. Within a half-hour, it was on its way to Paros and Naxos.

Ellie had not known what to expect. Her attention was caught by the twin hills that dominated the town of Hermoupolis, their slopes crowded with blue and white houses rising to meet two spectacular buildings at their peaks. She heard a shrouded nun say that these were the Roman Catholic Churches of Saint George and Saint John. She walked in the blinding sunshine to a taverna and pulled off her backpack. A waiter appeared and she ordered a Coke. In the distance, the tentacles of a crane browsed along the bowels of a tanker.

As she paid, she asked the waiter how she could reach the village of Vari. He pointed to a taxi rank and said something which she could not understand. There was no sign of a taxi but, as she waited, an ancient green bus drew up and two old ladies in black got off. A sign at the top whirled from Hermoupolis to Vari via Manna. Ten minutes later she was on her way and, in the early evening, Bart Vamvakaris showed her into a tiny bedroom apartment overlooking a bay. When he left, she lay down and fell asleep.

She awoke an hour later, showered and laid out her belongings on the single bed. After choosing beige linen slacks and a white blouse, she found the miniature bottles of gin from the flight and mixed one with ice cubes. There was just enough room on the small veranda for a cane chair and a white table. Ellie felt the warm glow of the Gordon's as the sun cast its pale rose rays across the horizon. The search for the perfect taverna could wait for another night and she decided to eat downstairs.

Bart spread a white linen tablecloth for her and placed on its centre two cruets of olive oil. Some time later, he asked her into the kitchen to inspect the evening's dishes. 'Iste etimi? We have stuffed tomatoes, spaghetti, macaroni.' He paused to look at her. 'My wife can do beefsteaks if you like.'

'No fish?'

'Small fish or calamari.'

'I'll have the stuffed tomatoes.'

'Would you like some giant oily beans? Or perhaps a Greek salad?'

'The salad, please. And a glass of white wine.' She went back to her table. Two other diners had arrived. Ellie heard their voices bray across the taverna. She sipped Retsina and grimaced.

Afterwards, she had a cup of Greek coffee and Bart offered her a complimentary Metaxa on which she passed. 'Dutch?' he asked. 'Perhaps not, judging by your dark hair. Your accent is strange to me.'

Ellie smiled. 'No, not Dutch. Irish although a lot of my life has been spent in San Francisco.'

'Where do you live now?'

'I work in a hospital in Belfast.'

Bart simulated a gun with his forefinger and put it to the side of his head. 'Ah, yes. Boom Boom. How do you live in such a place?'

'It's not as bad as you think but it can be rough at times. We get a lot of bad cases in my hospital.'

'And how long will you be staying in Greece?'

'For two weeks. This place is so nice I might base myself here for the whole time.'

Bart grinned and rubbed his grey stubble. 'You are very welcome. If you need anything, ask me.'

'Thanks. I'll catch up on my sleep tomorrow and get some sun. After that, there are some places on the island I'd like to see. You could help me there.'

'Of course. Why did you choose Syros and then Vari?'

'The first bit is a long story. I was reading a cookery book by an English writer called Elizabeth David. She loved traditional Greek food when she lived in Vari over thirty years ago.'

'Tomorrow night we will be cooking pork souvlaki. It is my wife's speciality.' He saw her yawn. 'I will see you tomorrow. Kalinichta.'

The cackle of a rooster woke her early in the morning. She went out to the veranda and sat with a glass of cold water. There was no activity

below. She guessed that early breakfast was not an option in Bart's taverna. In a chest of drawers, she had found a guide book and Ellie flicked through it while she waited for signs of life beneath.
On page 20, she read:

The years of prosperity

The establishment of the Greek state coincide with Hermoupolis becoming an international hub for trade and other exchanges between Western Europe, the Mediterranean and the East. The port is improved. A waterfront is built, the first Public Transit Warehouses in Greece (1834) and the new Lazaretto (1839-1842). At the same time remarkable shipbuilding is developed, 60-80 ships are officially built per year of total tonnage more than 130,000 tons. A lot of money was appropriated for that reason and so ship timber was imported directly from Romania and Russia as well as metal from other countries. Private shipbuilding units flourish and are staffed with experts from Chios, Pasara, Hydra and Spetses. In 1835, nearly 2000 people worked in shipbuilding. The abundance of shipbuilding materials, the guaranteed quality work and paying facilities prompted captains, even from ports in Egypt, the Middle East and the Black Sea, to choose shipyards in Syros for the building of their sailing-ships.
The efforts for full-scale organization culminated in the opening of the Chamber of Commerce (one of the first in Greece). In an official report we see the order of foreign products in the port warehouse according to the country of origin: England, Trieste, Marseilles, Livorno, Malta, Russia, Constantinople, Alexandria. The enormous range in trade exchanges is testified by this.
On the other hand, various industries start to flourish with the tanning industry having the lead (since 1828). It is followed by the iron industry and the soap-making industry. Insurance agencies are founded in 1830 and in 1845 the Hermoupolis Branch of the National Bank of Greece is opened.
In the second half of the 19th century, the town reaches the peak of its prosperity. During that 'golden' period, eighty percent of Greek sailing ships are built in Hermoupolis. In a 30-year period the sailing-

ships registered in Syros reached the amazing number of 5000! The shipping business is thriving, particularly after 1856, with the establishment of the first shipping company with headquarters in Hermoupolis ('Hellenic Shipping Company'). The ships of the company link the islands with Asia Minor and the mainland of Greece and overseas. At the same time the company expands its activities opening a shipyard called 'Neorion and Machine – works of Syros'. The first Greek steamship is built in Hermoupolis in 1854, in a private shipyard. The Municipal Shipyard is founded in 1866.

Furthermore, ships coming from other Mediterranean ports or the Black Sea are docked and repaired at a minimum cost or coaled leaving a lot of currency. The local press from that time testifies the role of Syros as a key marketplace for the whole of the Eastern Mediterranean (1858).

Both the distribution of Western industrial products and the collection and dispatch of agricultural products takes place in Hermoupolis. Its port is full of cargo ships of various nationalities. Until 1867, the foreign trade, practically free of taxes and with little competition from other ports, shows steady improvement.

Ellie heard the clink of glasses and tables being moved. She went down to the deserted taverna. Bart appeared from the kitchen with a notepad and explained to her the breakfast menu. She ordered coffee and an omelette. Shortly afterwards, she heard the revving of a motor cycle from behind the taverna and saw Bart disappear up the hill behind it. In silence, she read the guidebook and waited.

About a half an hour later, Bart brought to her table a blue and white plate on which was spread an orange omelette decorated with herbs. 'I had to go to the farm to collect what the chickens had produced this morning,' he explained. 'I believe the Americans call it the method of 'just in time.' Am I right?'

Ellie laughed and agreed. The eggs were delicious and had been cooked with immaculate care. The sliced crusts of bread were almost as fresh. Bart fetched more coffee and asked whether she required anything in her apartment. 'I just need to stock up my fridge with basic necessities. I don't think I will be doing much cooking while I'm here.'

'Won't you be lonely by yourself?'

'I'm used to it. That's what I like.' When he had gone, she studied the guidebook again and the map tucked in at the back. Some names had not been translated properly into English and did not always correlate with the corresponding text. Nevertheless, she soon found enough to plan her strategy for the coming days.

After breakfast, Ellie strolled to the minimarket that Bart had recommended. She bought teabags, orange juice, a half-kilo of feta cheese and a seeded loaf. Gigantic tomatoes were everywhere but Bart had left her enough to last for weeks. Finally, she added a bottle of London Dry Gin and a pack of canned tonic water. She returned to the apartment, changed into a bikini and found a sheltered spot beneath a cypress tree. A Greek family sat beneath a sun umbrella on the far side of the beach. Only the occasional strumming of the cicadas disturbed the silence.

Ellie did not make her first move until two days later. In the late morning, she caught the bus back into Hermoupolis. She spent an hour wandering around the shops and checking banking facilities. She returned to the taxi rank and explained to a driver her desire to visit the Church of Saint George at the top of the left-hand hill. On the steep drive, he confirmed her destination as the old Roman Catholic Diocese of Ano Syros. He dropped her off at a cobbled square called Kamara and pointed to the Church that dominated a warren of whitewashed streets. Ten minutes later, she read the plaque which said that the site had been a holy one since 1200 A.D. The view was breathtaking and provided a panoramic view of the port of Hermoupolis.

Her mouth was caked dry and she found a small taverna where she drank an ice-cold Amstel beer with a Greek salad. She pulled out the guide book. Her destination was approximately three kilometres away. There was no question of walking there in the heat and so, after lunch, she returned to Kamara Square where a shopkeeper ordered her a second taxi. This did not arrive for some time and Ellie did not arrive at Chroussa until late afternoon. She asked the cab driver to wait for her. The view was even more spectacular. Wide terraced slopes of dry stone walls descended to a gully in which sat a farmhouse surrounded by a vineyard. A short walk brought her to the tiny church of Saint Theressa that sat like a whitewashed jewel set in stone. Ellie found what she was looking for at once, noted the time and walked quickly back to the cab. She put on her sunglasses and asked to be driven to Vari. There, she drained the remains of a bottle of ice-cold water, then lay down and fell asleep. In her dreams, a pirate sprinkled black blood from a thoruble onto her white blouse but she did not stir.

On the following day, she remained in Vari. The taverna was attracting more customers in the evenings. Ellie did not mind waiting. As she drank the rough Cretan wine that she had come to enjoy, she recognised the couple looking for a table. Ellie picked up her guide book and nibbled at her sardines smothered in lemon juice. The tap on the shoulder was not a surprise.

It was the woman coming back from Bart's kitchen. 'Didn't we see you here the other evening?'

Ellie smelt the gin-soaked breath. 'I'm booked in here for a few days.' She did not wish to appear rude. 'It's very quiet. Where are you staying?'

'A few miles up the coast. A place called Finikas. Jim and I have come for a week. We try to eat somewhere different every night. Sorry, didn't tell you *my* name. I'm Sophie Trewsdale.'

'I'm Ellie. It's nice to meet you.'

Sophie steadied herself against a chair. 'Your accent is odd.'

Ellie explained. 'It fools a lot of people but I don't mind that.'

'So you're not Irish really. Why don't you join us? I assume you're not expecting anyone.'

'I wouldn't dream of disturbing you. It's very kind of you to offer. I'm just about to eat and you haven't even ordered yet.' Ellie smiled as she saw Bart approach with her souvlaki.

'We must have a chat before we leave. Compare notes on the island.' Sophie walked unsteadily to her table.

Bart planted a portion of small potatoes on Ellie's table. 'And your pork souvlaki with rosemary, thyme and garlic bulbs to cleanse your blood.'

Ellie pulled a kebab from its silver skewer and set aside the violet tinged onion skin in its green pepper envelope. She swallowed her wine and felt the glow. As she did so, she wondered how she could escape the Brits. A minor distraction, she thought, would not hamper her plans.

After finishing the remains of the feta, she waited for a while before going into the kitchen to pay the bill. If she did not do that, it would take an hour before Bart would fetch it, collect drachmas and bring the change. Before leaving, she paused at the Trewsdale's table.

Spaghetti sauce dribbled from Sophie's chin. 'Why don't you sit down? Jim won't mind. He's fed up talking to me.'

Jim Trewsdale extracted a piece of onion from his teeth. 'I haven't got a word in since we sat down, love. It's the other way round if you ask me.'

Ellie grinned. 'You're in the middle of your meal. I'm just going up to my apartment to make coffee. It's not a speciality of Bart's. If you're here another night, we could meet up.'

Sophie rubbed her mouth. 'We're going into town tomorrow evening. Sunday night is the big one in Hermoupolis. If you're doing nothing, we could pick you up on the way there.'

Ellie relented. 'That would be great. What time will you be here?'

'Let's say about eight o'clock. We can have a drink in town and get to know each other.'

On Sunday morning, Ellie walked to the Church of the Virgin Mary. She lit a candle and said a silent prayer. Sunshine streamed through the open windows, showing up the peeling plaster of the blue walls. There was no evidence of services although that had not been her intention. On her return, she made a Greek salad and ate it with a glass of white wine on her veranda. She read for a while, tidied up the apartment and, in the late afternoon, spent an hour lying beneath her cypress tree beside the beach. Her skin had lost its white pallor but she did not want to burn. As she dozed, Ellie thought about her next move which would require more care.

In the early evening, she had a long shower despite the warnings about water being restricted. She mixed a gin and tonic and sat on the veranda until she heard the honking of a taxi.

Sophie was already slurring her words. 'Sorry we're late. We've been trying to cram everything in before we go back on Tuesday.' She flopped back in the rear of the taxi, then jolted forward and tapped her husband on the back of the shoulder. 'We've got a surprise for Ellie, haven't we?'

Ellie tensed. This evening was going to be a bore. She felt it in her bones. As matters turned out, she was wrong.

Jim Trewsdale twisted round to talk to them. 'At lunch today, we met one of your fellow Irishmen. He's living in town. Recommended a good restaurant to us. I'm sure you'll enjoy meeting him. His name is Josh Gilbert.'

9

CHARLIE BOYLE received Matt's call at ten o'clock. He burst into the outer office, snapped at Irene to cancel his appointments and to keep his junior partner updated when he returned from the Coleraine Assizes. She later recorded her surprise that, despite his height and bulk, he moved with such speed. He jumped into his Mercedes, reversed and sped towards Belfast, leaving a cloud of dust in his wake. Shortly before midday, the car squealed up outside the police station.

Matt looked at him with relief. 'Thanks for coming right away. You're the only solicitor I've ever had any dealings with.' He was about to say more but Charlie thrust up his right hand at a perpendicular to his arm. 'This is Detective-Sergeant Patterson. I agreed to make a statement and he informed me of my rights.'

Patterson interrupted. 'Mister Boyle. This is a murder investigation into the death of a lady friend of your client...a Miss Sue Neil. She was found dead this morning by a cleaner from the Ulster College Campus. Quinn has admitted that they had intercourse in his apartment on Saturday night after dinner and drinks in the Glenavna Hotel...just down the road from where we are now.'

Matt sighed. 'I fell asleep. When I woke up in the middle of the night, she had gone. In the morning I found a note inviting me down on Sunday evening around nine. I called twice but there was no response. I haven't seen her since our night out.'

Charlie raised his hand again in warning. 'Let's walk before we run. I want to talk to my client for a while in private, if you've no objections.'

Patterson nodded at his colleague who was taking notes and turned. 'We'll leave you alone for half-an-hour.'

Matt thanked Charlie again and provided him with his recollection of Saturday night. 'It was the only time it ever happened. Sue had been about a bit. It could have been anybody. There's one thing I haven't told them about yet.' Charlie listened to his story of the photograph.

'Where is it? And you've hinted the woman was promiscuous.' Charlie stared closely at Matt. 'I'd advise you to say nothing more just yet. You're in a state of shock.'

Matt put his head in his hands, then looked up. 'The photograph is in my bedroom. I swear I had nothing to do with this.'

'Never said you did. But you must be careful. It's bloody strange this happening to you just as it did to Luke Wilson. I ask you with your friend to clear his name and suddenly *you're* up to your neck in similar trouble.'

'I haven't had time to think of it like that. Maybe there is a connection but how could there be?' Matt put his head down again as Patterson came back into the room.

'We're going to let you go. I want you to come back tomorrow morning and make a formal statement. Don't get any fancy ideas in the meantime.'

As they walked out into the early afternoon sunshine, Charlie suggested lunch. 'You have to keep your blood sugar up no matter what life throws at you. You must have a decent pub around here.'

'Most of them don't serve food.'

'What about this Glenavna place?'

Matt looked at him to see if he was serious. 'We could try the Stag's Head although I don't much feel like Irish Stew.'

'Sounds good to me. I'll get a few more details from you while we're eating.'

They went to the upstairs lounge whose back windows overlooked the Lough. Two lone drinkers stared into their pints of Smithwicks. Matt ordered Harp lagers and the dish of the day. The scrag ends of mutton were fatty and he finished his lager before attempting the thick stew. 'You'll have another, Mister Boyle?'

'Let me get them. We're not as mean as our reputations.'

Matt repeated what he had said about Saturday night. 'When we got back to my apartment, it all happened quickly. She was all over me. There was no resistance. You don't want to hear the details.'

'I'm not that old.' Charlie paused to digest a piece of lamb. 'However, if it's not relevant, you don't have to tell me...much as I'd like to hear all about it.'

'It was as I said before. When I woke up, she was gone. What do you think Patterson will do next?'

'They'll have to check her background. What about relatives?'

'I don't know. She was from Yorkshire. Never mentioned them and I didn't feel like prying.'

'We'll leave it to Patterson and Personnel at the College. They'll also need to check out her movements on Sunday.'

'If there were any.'

'If it wasn't you, she certainly saw somebody.'

'You know it wasn't me.'

'Calm down. I have to place myself in Patterson's shoes. It'll take time to get all the forensic evidence and then they'll want to see how you match up.' Charlie wiped his mouth. 'That stew wasn't bad. Can I have the rest of yours?'

'Go ahead.'

'You haven't mentioned your friend Barney. I thought you two would have been hard at work on your legacy.'

'Barney's been studying the file. We were supposed to get together at the weekend to discuss it. I couldn't reach him.' Matt explained the difficulty.

'He should be able to help us with this business. We'll have to get in touch with him. Ring him at the station.' Matt found a phone. Barney was out. Matt left a message to come and see him at the campus immediately.

Matt went back to Charlie. 'If you have time, we'll go back to my place. I have to show you the photograph.' Charlie drove to the car park beside the Halls of Residence. The bottom floor was roped off with white tape. Many of the students were oblivious to the operation. They were used to bomb hoaxes...often perpetrated by one of themselves.

Charlie remarked on the silence of the upper rooms and the beautiful view. 'You haven't seen my file, you said. So I assume you don't know the story of the stowaway and Jack Sullivan.'

Matt looked at him carefully before replying. 'Yes. Luke Wilson told Barney and me. We thought we were the only ones who would have known anything about it. What more does the file say?'

'We'll come back to it. Let's have a look at this photograph you've been talking about.'

'I'll get it for you now.' Matt came back within a few minutes. 'I can't find it. It's disappeared.'

The weekend had been a mixed one for Barney. After an untroubled sleep, he had crept out of bed late on Saturday morning, ate the remains from a box of Shredded Wheat and followed those with a mug of tea. After an hour, his headache subsided. He walked to the newsagents opposite the York Hotel, bought a Daily Express and crossed the road.

There was only one other drinker, an elderly regular whose face was strewn with purple veins. He nodded at Barney and, with trembling right hand, raised a large Powers to his lips. He remarked again to the barman that he would be hung before he gave in. Nobody was ever quite certain what he meant by this remark but there was a consensus that he spoke the truth. Barney ordered a bottle of Red Heart and scanned the sports pages of his newspaper. With the football season over, there was little to interest him on the back page and so he turned to the racing selections. The imminent cash from Charlie Boyle would cover any risk and Barney concentrated on his choices for an accumulator bet.

After a fourth bottle of stout, he left for the bookmakers. Afterwards, he resisted temptation and went back to work on the files. He made a ham sandwich and flicked through the documents. Matt, he knew, would be keen to know more about the contents but what of real significance could he tell him? The information about the blackmailer was new. Also, the alleged assault on the Teeny girl. Barney searched his brain for someone who could help him with that one. Maybe he could get to see Celia Teeny. She might be married with children and so contact might be difficult if not impossible. Also, Boomer being involved complicated everything.

The interviews in the late winter of 1967 had been gruelling. Wilson had had no alibi for the night of the assault nor could he remember what he had been doing at that time. Reasonable enough, as Charlie

Boyle had pointed out to the police, for the attack had happened nearly a year before. Barney wondered why the blackmailer had not begun his work earlier. He appeared to be getting his satisfaction from playing on Wilson's nerves rather than having him locked up. It was as if he had enough to get the police interested but no more. The whole exercise might be a smokescreen to deflect attention from himself...the true assailant.

Barney turned to the testimony regarding Sullivan and combined it with the summary that had been produced for Charlie Boyle in June 1967. The story was that they had served together in the Navy throughout the Second World War, doing their service on submarines. It was a tough and dangerous life. When off-duty, hard drinking often led to vicious brawls, especially when women were involved in foreign ports.

Wilson told the police that Jack Sullivan had a reason to frame him. For obvious reasons, he couldn't expand upon the background. At one interview, Boomer had pressed him on the likely whereabouts of the ex-sailor. The response was that Sullivan had deserted from the Navy in the 1940's and he hadn't seen him since. The police were sceptical and raised the matter of the previous accusations before his arrival in Portglenone. Wilson turned this line of questioning around by repeating the story of the stowaway. He believed that Sullivan had returned to Ireland, murdered the woman called Teresa in Belfast and then literally tried to kill two birds with one stone. He probably lived abroad but had connections here. There was nothing more that he could tell them. After the final interview, investigations fizzled out.

Subsequent documentation began in early 1969. Barney looked at his watch. He turned on the television in time to see the racing results. The cold remains of his mug of tea were knocked over as Barney jumped up from his chair. Two horses had come in. Everything now depended on the evening greyhound meeting in Hackney. He could catch the outcome on the radio later.

The good news had broken his concentration. Before going back to the documents, he sat back to think. There was something not quite right but he couldn't put his finger on it. He turned over the sheet of paper with the name on it. No reason given. Just the name. It had to be the same girl. He would have to wait until she came back from Greece. A week's delay would hardly matter. It was time to get prepared for the evening.

He shaved and ran a bath. As he lay back, he felt guilty about not contacting Matt. Maybe he could track him down at the Halls of Residence. There would be a general number for it in the telephone directory. He remembered that he didn't have a phone. If he was going to be here for any length of time, he would have to get one installed. In any case, Boomer would insist.

After dressing he fried two eggs with four rashers of thick bacon and then added to the frying pan two slices each of potato bread and soda bread. While these were being digested, he spent an hour on the next set of documents from early 1969. No surprises came until the end. Here was something hard that could be checked next week. He turned on the radio. Both dogs had come in. He yelled with excitement. There would be a nice pot of money to be collected after the weekend. It was time to hit the York and forget about tomorrow until it arrived.

On Monday, as Barney returned from Eastwood's Bookmakers, Matt searched again for the missing photograph among his file of newspaper clippings. 'I slipped it under these before I opened the door on Friday night. I'm sure about it.'

Charlie shrugged. 'You must be mistaken.' He looked at his watch. 'I'll have to get back soon and we have to go over your statement for tomorrow morning.'

'I never looked at the file again until now. There was nobody here over the weekend...apart from Sue. Let me think back. I vaguely remember her rummaging about in the wardrobe before she left. Maybe she lifted it.'

Charlie snapped his fingers. 'You might have a point there. This could be very relevant. If you're right, perhaps she thought it was the kind of caper that turned you on. You said she invited you back on Sunday night. She had a big surprise waiting for you.'

'If the photograph is in her apartment and Patterson's men find it, they will take a cold view.'

'Your fingerprints will be all over it.'

'So would those of Watt.'

'You don't know for sure that it belonged to him. This could be tricky tomorrow if the police have found it.'

'They'll think I persuaded her to act out a fantasy game that went too far.'

Charlie rubbed the side of his nose. 'If that happened to be the truth, you could plead manslaughter and get out after a year.'

'Come on, Mister Boyle. I had nothing to do with it.'

'I know. I know. We'll just have to wait and see what develops. If they have it, I would advise you to tell the truth.'

'It's as I told you. I found it beneath Watt's desk on the Friday afternoon after I came back from seeing you about the will. Watt had been there all day.'

'Anyone else?'

'Derek Scott is the other guy in our office. He had left earlier. I can't believe it belonged to him. In fact, I meant to discuss it with him last week but never got around to it.'

'Don't rule anything out. You never know what kind of secrets people have. I've seen some things in my time.'

'This has really put the wind up me. You'd better help me with this statement.'

Matt and Charlie went over the background to Saturday's events. 'I was never in her apartment. They won't find any prints.'

'Good point although they could say *you* were all dressed up yourself. Like one of those rubber men. You know what I mean.'

'You've got me worried again. I hadn't thought of that.'

'I have to be Devil's Advocate. We have to prepare ourselves for every attack. Is that someone at your door?'

Matt opened it. 'Barney! Thank God you got my phone message.'

'I just missed your call. I'd nipped out on a bit of business. I ran into one of our boys down below and so I know all about your fix. A nice mess we have here.' Barney grinned. 'I didn't know you were into porno photographs. You could have borrowed mine.'

10

DUSK WAS DESCENDING as Ellie and the Trewsdales scrambled from the taxi in Hermoupolis. The streets were crowded with Sunday evening strollers deliberating on where to eat. The trio, led by Jim, walked from the seafront until they reached Miaoulis Square where Josh Gilbert had recommended a taverna that specialised in fresh fish.

Ellie saw a man with a well-trimmed white beard wave at them. She felt relief. There could be no question of matchmaking with this guy. Back home, he probably wore an anorak and loved trainspotting.

'Great that you could make it,' he said in a squeaky voice. 'It'll be nice to speak English. I've been here since mid-May. My Greek colleagues attempt to entertain me but the language is a struggle.'

Sophie Trewsdale introduced Ellie. 'She's the nurse from your part of the world that we told you about earlier.'

'I gather you're here on holiday. You've picked the right place.'

'I'm staying out at Vari. I understand you live in town.'

'I'm working on a contract for Harland and Wolff.'

'Surely there's not much we can teach the Greeks about shipbuilding?'

'You'd be surprised. We have expertise in computer aided design which they're keen to learn about.'

Sophie butted in. 'Jim, let's get a carafe of white wine. I can see we're all going to get on well this evening.'

Josh Gilbert ignored the menu. 'I suggest everyone has the red mullet. I saw it being carried into the taverna earlier today.' Despite his size, Ellie saw that he liked to dominate. She remembered that he was some kind of College lecturer and she probed for details.

'I'm based at the Ulster College campus that overlooks Belfast Lough. The Marine Architecture Department has close links with many of the great shipyards.'

'My father served for many years in the British Navy although I know nothing about ships.'

Sophie interrupted. 'But you've been around the world, haven't you? Didn't you say that you had lived in America.'

'My early childhood years were spent in Belfast. I lived alone with my mother as my father was always absent. One day, I remember my mother saying to me that we were going to live in San Francisco.'

Josh Gilbert extracted a fish bone from his teeth. 'And your father?'

'My mother told me that my father wasn't coming back. I hardly knew him so I wasn't heartbroken.'

Sophie finished her wine and asked Jim to order more. 'That's sad. Did you ever see him again?'

Ellie paused before replying. 'No.'

Sophie pressed but was halted by her husband. 'Josh, you've gone quiet. We're going home on Tuesday. What should we see tomorrow before we go?'

'There's plenty to see, Jim, but you can't pack it in to a day. Have you been up to Ano Syros? The old churches are worth a visit.'

Ellie agreed. 'I went up there on Friday. You guys should go there.'

Sophie giggled. 'I want to polish off my tan. I'm not a great one for religion.'

Josh Gilbert stroked his beard. 'Well, in that case, you should make your way around from Finikas to Dellagratsia and Agathopes. There's not a lot there, apart from a small naval station which nobody will tell me anything about. However, there's a long beach which is usually deserted.'

Ellie knocked over her glass of wine. The waiter hurried over to sweep up the broken glass. Ellie apologised. 'The fish was delicious. Thank you. Josh, what were you saying about a deserted beach? I'd like to try somewhere different to swim.'

'We could all go there tomorrow and have lunch. Jim, why don't we send a taxi for Ellie in the morning?'

'Thanks for the offer, Sophie, but I wouldn't dream of disturbing your last day. I'll make my way there some other time this week.'

'I'm afraid I can't join you either. I'm working. Let me explain how to get there. Now, shall we have more wine?'

They spent the remainder of the evening in a pleasant stupor. Occasionally, Ellie caught Gilbert looking at her and wondered had he noticed. No, impossible, she thought. Still, she'd better be careful, especially now that she might find what she'd been after.

On the following morning, Ellie felt jaded and spent most of the day reading, sunbathing and swimming. At dinner, she told Bart that she was going to spend two days on the other side of the island but would be back on Thursday before travelling back to Athens on Friday afternoon.

On Tuesday morning, a cab dropped her off at the Hotel Possidonia where she had no problem obtaining a room overlooking the Bay of Finikas. She waited until the evening before walking the half-mile around the coast to Agathopes beach...the one that had been recommended. She found a taverna and ordered a gin and tonic. About fifty yards away, the small naval compound sat fortified by high white walls. At eight o'clock, as the sun dipped, it cast an ethereal lemon glow across the sea. A few seconds later, a tingle crept up her spine as she heard a bugle play the Last Post.

She ordered dolmades and souvlaki with a half-carafe of wine. Afterwards, she sat in silence. Two lights came on in the naval station but there was no sign of activity. When settling her bill, she asked the waiter about the building. He shrugged but gave no response as he turned to serve a party of Greeks.

It was dark as Ellie approached the station. Its front gates were bolted. She deciphered the sign which strictly forbade photographs and displayed a picture of an Alsatian dog. As she walked back past the taverna towards the Hotel Possidonia, she saw the waiter watching her. Before she went to bed, she drank a Metaxa brandy in the hotel bar and checked her guidebook. The naval base was not mentioned. It did not matter. She had seen and heard enough.

On Wednesday morning, after a breakfast of fresh croissants and coffee, she ordered a cab to take her to Hermoupolis. Instead of going around the coastal route, the driver drove along the alternative road across the island. After cashing a traveller's cheque in the Agricultural Bank of Greece, Ellie walked to the Neorion shipyard where Josh Gilbert had been given an office.

He beckoned her in. 'You're exactly on time. I'm not used to such punctuality. I'll fetch coffee and we can have our chat although I'm afraid I have to see a technician at twelve.'

Ellie sat down in a leather armchair and waited until he returned with two Greek coffees in dainty white porcelain cups. 'Thank you for taking the time to see me. You must be very busy.'

'Oh, it comes and goes. I ran a training course in computers yesterday. There was considerable enthusiasm to use them but the network kept breaking down so it was all a bit of a fiasco. I'm trying to get something set up for tomorrow so I hope this techie fellow will turn up. Please, go ahead. Ask me anything you like.'

Ellie finished her coffee. 'You were asking about my background on Sunday night. Let me explain some more. When I was in my teens, my mother married a guy from Seattle. She'd met him on vacation there and, after the marriage, they set up home in his place. We owned our apartment in Pacific Heights and I stayed on in Frisco to train as a nurse. Mom's father had left her quite a bit of money when he died. She always had a good business head and invested wisely in Real Estate.'

'What part of Ireland was your grandfather from?'

'I didn't explain that part of it to you on Sunday. My mother is American. She was born in San Francisco.'

'How did she meet your father?'

'My mother served in the US Navy during the Second World War.'

Josh sighed. 'Where did she *meet* your father?'

'That's part of why I'm here. After the Germans were driven out of Greece, a NATO base was established in Syros.'

Josh interrupted. 'My older colleagues still talk of the famine here in 1941 when Syros was under German occupation.'

'Both American and British forces used the base after the war. My father's submarine was stationed there for a time in the 1940's and that's how he came to meet Mom. When she became pregnant with me, she had to resign her post. My father arranged special leave, sorted out all the necessary documentation and that's how we came to live in Belfast where I was born.'

'But the marriage didn't work out?'

'I've told you that. The constant separations caused difficulties but there were other problems.'

Josh raised his hand. 'You really don't have to tell me.'

'No, I don't mind. When he was home in Belfast, he was sweet enough initially. Then he went drinking. And that, according to my mother, is when Mr Jekyll turned into Edward Hyde.'

Josh groaned. 'The Irish affliction. If only they would drink like they do in Greece. No harm in a few glasses of wine with a meal. I can't stand the binge drinking culture back home. My students are the same. Free at last, money in their pockets and straight to the pub.'

'This was pretty bad, according to my mother. She made arrangements to return home. He contacted her in San Francisco but the marriage was finished. Many years later, my mother told me that she understood that he had left military service and was pursuing a business career in Australia.'

'Why did you come back to Ireland?'

'After qualifying as a nurse, I wanted to travel and see some of the world. I went to the East Coast and worked for a time in New York where I met Irish medical staff. They were always talking about home. I guess New York was fine for a time, but there's a downside. If you're working in a hospital in the summer with the air-conditioning broken, it's not fun. The winters are freezing and I was used to the West Coast. The crime rate was also a problem. I was mugged once in Central Park.'

'Surely Ireland with its political problems...all the killings and bombings...would have frightened you off.'

'The girls I worked with claimed it was exaggerated and didn't affect the South. I'd made up my mind. I travelled to Dublin, completed the necessary registration courses and lived there for a year.'

'And the final step home?'

'Initially, I went on short trips. It wasn't as bad as I had imagined. I found a post in the Royal Victoria Hospital last year.'

'Let's get back to why you came to see me. How can I help you?'

'You've already helped me. My mother told me that the naval base was near Dellagratsia but my map doesn't have it.'

'The newer guides call it Possidonia. Only the older residents use the term for the region.'

'When you used the name on Sunday, I clicked right away. I had to go and see the place where I was conceived.' Ellie laughed. 'Don't worry. My mother told me everything. I'd appreciate it if you could tell me what it is used for now.'

'Nobody really knows. I've enquired about it myself. Everyone clams up as soon as you ask. I suspect the Americans continue to use it as a NATO base. I'll see if I can find out anything more. Did you really come all this way just to see the place?'

'You're very shrewd. I've always wanted to visit Greece. My Mom always had fine memories of her time here. What finally pushed me was something that happened earlier in the year.'

Josh looked at his watch. 'There's no need to tell me it all.'

'I know you're short for time. I'd appreciate any help you can give me later. In February, I met a man who claimed he knew my father.'

'You didn't think he did?'

'I'm not sure but then, shortly afterwards, a letter came...'

The phone trilled. Josh paused, then lifted it. He glanced at his watch again. 'I'm afraid I'll have to go. Duty calls. Come and see me again before you leave. Here's my number.'

'I'm catching the four o'clock ferry to Piraeus on Friday. Perhaps we could meet at three.'

'Fine. I suggest the Hotel Hermes which is just beside the pier.'

'Thank you. I can find my own way out.' Ellie walked along the seafront. Perhaps she had told this stranger too much. No, it could do no harm. She sensed that she would need his help. A cab passed and she flagged it down. 'Ano Syros, please.'

Near the summit of the winding road, she asked the driver to turn right towards Chroussa and stop where she had been on the previous Friday. As Ellie photographed the grave at the side of the little church of Saint Theressa, she heard a door slam shut and a voice behind her. She turned to see an old man wearing flannel trousers, a faded blue shirt and a cap.

He smiled and spoke again. 'Kalimera.'

'Kalimera sas. Milate anglika?'

The old man pulled off his cap and mopped his brow. 'A little.'

Ellie wondered whether he had caught her focusing the camera on the grave. 'There is a beautiful view from here. I hope you don't mind my taking photographs in the church grounds.'

'Of course not. Would you like to see inside the church?'

'I'd love to.'

He extracted a big key from his trousers and walked to the door of the church. After unlocking it, he gesticulated to Ellie and instructed her to follow him inside. A statue of the saint sat beside a small altar. Six rows of shiny brown pews filled the interior whose walls had been freshly painted.

'Catholica?'

Ellie smiled. 'Ne.' She took some photographs, then sat on the front pew and prayed. 'Thank you very much. I must go now.' She explained about the taxi.

'Let him wait. Come.' He locked the church door and led her to the rear. A dirt track wound up the bare mountainside. After a brief walk, they came to a gap in the hillside. 'Here is the tomb of Ferekidis. A famous philosopher from before the time of Socrates. We have not changed much since.'

He brought her down to the church again. The old man smiled and raised his hand, inviting Ellie to embrace the view. 'God is everywhere. Herete.' Then he walked down the slope towards the farmhouse beside the vineyard. Ellie returned to the cab.

She asked to be dropped off at Kamara Square. The taverna was empty. Ellie ordered beer with a salad. She looked down at the sea shimmering in the blistering sunshine and thought back to the day when she had met Wilson.

11

'YOU'RE THE COLOUR of the sprout on a potato that's been left too long in a dark cupboard,' said Barney to Matt, 'and no bloody wonder.'

'So they've got the photograph,' exclaimed Matt as he turned to Charlie Boyle. 'Can you wait while I tell Barney the full story?'

Charlie sat down. 'Make it brief. I have to get back.'

Afterwards, Barney snapped his notebook shut and looked across the Lough. 'It's going to be tricky, Charlie. According to Matt, he's never been in Sue Neil's apartment...a stroke of luck there at least...but he'll have to admit to having had possession of the dirty photograph. His prints will be all over it.'

Matt ran his hand through his hair. 'I told you, Barney. There will be other prints on it as well.'

'They might be hard to identify. They won't start dusting everyone in a place this size.'

'Watt's will be on it.'

'You don't know that. I'll lean on Patterson to check.' Barney grinned. 'I'll also put a good word in for you but don't count on him paying any attention.' He looked over at Charlie. 'Not much more you can do until tomorrow. You better go.'

Charlie rose. 'Any joy with the Wilson business?'

'Maybe. I'd like to go over a few matters with Matt although he's not going to be in the mood for it today.'

'Charlie thought there might be some connection.'

'I didn't quite say that. I'll see you tomorrow.'

Matt made coffee for Barney and himself. 'Have you managed to find anything? I called over to your place twice at the weekend but you were out.'

'Sorry about not contacting you. It was one thing after another over the weekend. Yes, I've had a look at some of Charlie's documents. First things first. Remember I showed you the ID of a nurse called Ellie Sullivan...the one I found in the York Hotel on the Sunday before yesterday.'

'Yes, the day we went up to Coleraine again.'

'One of the documents reveals that Luke Wilson knew Sullivan had a daughter.'

'Any more details about her?'

'I haven't studied all the documents yet. It's not what's important to us at the moment. If it was the same woman in the York Hotel that night, I guessed she must be working in the Mater or Royal Hospital. I took a chance on the latter and hit the jackpot on Friday night.'

Matt's eyes shot up. 'You mean you've talked to her? Sullivan's daughter?'

'I found out that she works there but she's gone on holiday. Greece, they said. She's expected back in a week's time. I'll get her then.'

Matt sat back. 'Well, that's progress. If the two affairs are somehow connected, you never know what we might find out.'

'Don't raise your hopes.'

'Anything else that might help?'

'Hard to be certain. When he was under a police investigation, he always fell back on the stowaway story and Sullivan. I'd like to go over it with you again when we have more time.'

'How many investigations were there?'

Barney glanced at his watch. 'There was one in 1967 which you should know about. Maybe there is a connection. I don't know.' He told Matt the story of the assault on Celia Teeny and Wilson's defence. 'Before I go, there's something else that has come up which surprised me. I'll leave you to think about it if you're able.' Barney smiled. 'Don't worry, Matt. We'll get you out of this. I know enough about human nature and you to be positive that you're innocent.'

After a sleepless night, Matt rose early, showered and made tea. He walked to the police station and arrived at nine o'clock. Fifteen minutes later, Charlie burst into the waiting room. 'I'm not used to these early starts. It's no life for a man of my age.' He pulled a file from his briefcase and made notes with a silver Parker pen.

A cop beckoned them into a side office with pale green walls. Patterson and a Sergeant sat at a bare table, stained with coffee rings. Matt made his statement, interrupted occasionally by Patterson and splutterings by Charlie. When the questions came, he was ready. 'I found the photograph in a white envelope. It was lying on the floor of my office.'

'When did you find it?'

'The Friday before last. I'd been up to see Mister Boyle about a will.'

Patterson looked over at Charlie. 'Do we need to know anything about it?'

'I can't see the relevance.'

Matt continued. 'It was beneath the desk of my colleague, Graham Watt. I suspected that it belonged to him.'

'But you can't prove it?'

'Sue Neil told me that there had been incidents with Watt and secretarial staff. You'll have to ask Personnel about those. I don't know the full details. I'd advise you to check with a guy called Bill Armstrong.'

'We'll do it today.' Patterson sat back in his chair. 'Continue with your story.'

'When Sue left my apartment on Saturday night, I heard her rummaging in the wardrobe where she'd hung up her jacket. I think she found the photograph and believed it belonged to me.'

'And decided to treat you on the Sunday night.' Patterson made notes in his file.

'Possibly. Someone must have got there before me. I told you there'd been plenty of other men besides me.'

'So you say. We're checking all that out. Go on.'

Matt told them about Sunday. The room went quiet. Patterson rose and signalled to the Sergeant to follow him. Matt frowned at Charlie who advised him to keep cool and hold his nerve.

Patterson returned. 'We'll get this typed up. Call back tomorrow and sign it.'

Charlie groaned. 'I'll have to send my young partner down. I'm in court tomorrow. I take it there's no more we can do today.'

'The constable will see you out.'

Matt gave Charlie the contact number at the Halls of Residence. 'Could you read anything into their attitude?'

Charlie looked up from the front seat of his Mercedes. 'I thought they were a bit more relaxed. Maybe Barney's done you a good turn. However, don't take anything for granted. They'll want to keep you on a hook. Just keep calm. We'll talk later in the week.' Charlie turned on the ignition and accelerated away.

Matt returned to the Campus and found his office occupied by Derek Scott. He could see from his anxious look that he had heard everything. 'No sign of Watt? Good. I'll fill you in on what's been happening. We're going to need strong coffee. Let's go to the Common Room.'

When they returned, Watt was bent over his desk. He turned and nodded curtly. There was no sign that he was aware of anything. Matt pretended to study a research paper for an hour and then gave up. 'I'm going back to my apartment to make lunch. Don't know if I'll be back. I'm not feeling great. Some fresh air might do me good. A pity to waste such a beautiful day in this place.'

On his return, he found Patterson and his Sergeant waiting for him in the corridor outside his room. Matt's stomach turned. 'I thought you didn't want me back until tomorrow.'

'After you left, we had your friend Watt in for an interview. There's a few more questions we'd like to ask you.'

'What did he say?'

'We can't tell you it all. It's confidential. However, one of you is telling porkies and I must say that he was very convincing.'

The diversion to see Matt had delayed Barney's progress on other cases. After returning late on Monday evening, he made cheese on toast and went to bed early. All the files would have to wait. Despite being exhausted, he struggled to sleep. Before he finally succumbed, he remembered.

His chance came on the following day. Station staff got the news from the Duty Sergeant that Boomer had been called to a murder case near the Border. It might tie him up for days. Barney winked at Billy. 'This could be our opportunity.'

Billy looked worried. 'You don't mean?'

Barney grinned. 'Yes, the Wilson file I was asking you about last week. I assume that you didn't find it?'

'No.'

'That's because it may not be in the station but I think I know where it might be.'

'How did you find out?'

'I'm not certain but we're going to have a look while Boomer's not here.'

'We?'

'Yes, just in case. The subject of my old friend Wilson has never come up again and I'm guessing that Boomer has found out that he's dead.'

'How would he know that?'

'Remember Kerr's up in Ballymena. He might have heard about it or read of the death in the local rag. If he did, he'd contact Boomer with the news.'

'How does all this speculation help you, Barney?'

'Boomer's very scrupulous about keeping his desk clear and I suspect he's the same with old files. If an investigation was dead and buried...literally in this case...he'd get the documents shifted to the archive store out the back.'

'Isn't this all a long shot?'

'Possibly but it came to me last night that he *did* have a clearout about a month ago. Get me the keys of the store. If anyone asks us what we're doing, we just have to say that we're checking something in connection with our current cases. Nobody will query it. Come on, let's go.'

Matt held his nerve. 'Come in, Mister Patterson. There's no need to call my solicitor. I've nothing to hide.' Patterson and the Sergeant followed him into the apartment.

'You can amend your statement in the morning if you want. We need to move this investigation fast so we'd like to know if you've been hiding anything from us.'

'What makes you think so?'

'I rang your friend, Detective-Sergeant Mulvey, when he got back to Donegall Pass station. He pushed us to check Watt out. We tracked him down at his home and he agreed to come in this morning.'

'What did he tell you?'

'He denied all knowledge of the photograph. We warned him that we would be checking it for prints so he'd better be telling the truth.'

'How did he react?'

'We'll ask the questions, if you don't mind, Mister Quinn. He was very confident that we wouldn't find his prints on any photograph. Didn't even ask for a solicitor and he said he was quite prepared to have himself fingerprinted to prove what he was saying.'

Matt felt the tremor in his voice. 'Did you tell him that it was me who gave you the story?'

'No, we didn't. We gave him the general background. He convinced us that we wouldn't find his prints on the photograph.'

'There has to be some other explanation. I swear to you that I found the photograph on the floor beneath his desk.'

'You may have to swear to it on oath the way matters are going. There's one more thing I'd like to ask you before tomorrow.'

'I'm telling the truth. Ask me what you like.'

'You say the photograph was in a white envelope. All we found in Miss Neil's apartment was the photograph. It was in a chest of drawers beneath a set of underwear.'

Matt thought back. 'I'd forgotten about it.' He jumped up from his chair. 'I think it's on top of my wardrobe.' A few moments later, he returned with the envelope. 'I'm sure this is the one that contained the photograph.' He reminded them of what had happened. 'Maybe I shouldn't have touched it.'

'It won't matter. We know *your* prints are on it.' Patterson pulled gloves from his pocket and put them on before touching the envelope. 'I guess we're going to have quite a bit of fingerprinting to perform tomorrow. You won't have any objection and your colleague Watt has said the same. See you in the morning. Sergeant, let's go.'

Matt's mouth had gone dry. His hand shook as he filled the kettle with water. He made coffee and searched the bathroom cupboard for a packet of Anadin Extra. He needed to talk to Barney.

Billy Craig followed Barney across the yard at the rear of the station. The concrete store was padlocked and the key was stiff in the lock. They entered and locked the door. Rows of green filing cabinets stood encrusted with dust. However, they were neatly labelled and one at the back of the store began with T and ran to Z.

A small silver key unlocked the cabinet. Barney found W and flicked through the folders. 'Billy, I'm in luck. I've got the bugger.'

Billy stood behind him as he skipped through the file. 'Anything hitting you, Barney?'

'I'd love to get a copy of this stuff.'

'You know that will be tricky. There's always someone up your arse having a nosy as to what you're copying.'

'I know, I know.' Barney paused. 'Let me see what I can make of this. Boomer had a full précis of the original investigation in the early 1960's.' Billy heard the excitement in Barney's voice. 'What's this? The actual enquiry began before Christmas 1959. The body had been found in the Lagan but the original report had been buried in the build-up to Christmas. Probably a one-liner somewhere. Forensic estimated that the corpse had been underwater for about seven years. It had been weighed down but had finally broken loose before surfacing.'

'Then what happened?'

'They began checking on stories of missing women from about winter 52. No relatives had reported anyone disappearing. Then, by chance, someone in a North Belfast station found Wilson's report. He was tracked down for a repeat.'

'Why would they suspect him?'

'They didn't. They were just checking. But, at interview, he appeared edgy and the detective smelt a rat. You know how it is, Billy.'

'And then?'

'They began asking questions in the area where she might have lived...if the stowaway story was true. The trouble was that the preliminary enquiry alone turned up about twenty women called Teresa and reports of twenty more. You see the problem, Billy?'

'A dead end?'

Barney read on. 'Not quite. Their suspicions were aroused by a terraced house that, according to neighbours, had lain empty for years. They gained entry and identified a blood stain on the living room carpet...possibly seven years old. Wilson was interviewed. His story was stuttering...until...'

'Until what...?'

Barney jumped at the sound of a bang on the door. 'Billy, would you go and see who it is?' He flicked through the final pages of the initial investigation. His mind raced. Surely not. This couldn't be, he thought. Then he heard Billy pull open the creaking door and Boomer's voice.

'Well, well. I heard you two were rooting about in here. What are you buggers up to?'

12

ELLIE remembered the freezing February afternoon when Wilson had arrived to give the Last Rites to a spinster from Portglenone. Many of the beds in the geriatric ward were partitioned by screens from behind which erupted groans and coughing. The smell of lint and urine lingered everywhere. As she tidied a bed, Ellie saw at the Reception office a thick-set man with grey hair and black glasses. A Sister came out to speak to him and pointed in the direction of his parishioner. She watched him approach with a brown valise and, as he came to the end of the ward, asked if she could help.

He unbuttoned his Abercrombie overcoat and loosened his red scarf to reveal the dog collar beneath a sweater. 'I'm looking for Miss Stuart. I've been told that she is seriously ill with pneumonia.'

Ellie brought him behind the screen where the woman lay asleep. 'We don't have much hope for her. She's very old and frail.'

'In that case, I better do what's necessary. I doubt if she has many sins on her soul but it will do no harm and will keep her neighbours happy.'

Ellie waited. 'If you need anything, just ask.'

'I will.' His tone was abrupt.

She replaced the partition and, returning to the office, heard the Latin intonations. Later, as she wrote up reports, Ellie heard the knock on the door, looked up and saw the priest peer through the glass window.

'I've given her Extreme Unction. As she may die soon, I will give you my contact number although there's nothing much more that I could do except bury her.'

Ellie pulled a page from a spring–leaf notebook. 'Your name, Father?'

'Wilson and here is my phone number.' As he wrote it down, he paused to clear his throat. 'I hope I haven't caught anything. My own health is not the best. I used to serve in the Navy, you know, and once had a bad dose of pneumonia myself.' He wiped saliva from his mouth with a linen handkerchief. 'Perhaps you will let me have your name.'

'Ask for Nurse Sullivan if you're ringing to enquire.'

She recalled his startled look. 'If you're not feeling too well, why don't you have a seat. Perhaps you would like tea? I'll get an auxiliary to make some.' She had not expected him to take her up on the offer but he sat down.

'Thank you, Nurse. Do I detect an American brogue or perhaps Canadian?'

Ellie explained her background as they waited for tea. 'You mentioned the Navy. Although I never knew my father, I know that he served in it during the Second World War.' She saw the faraway look in Wilson's eyes.

'It may be a coincidence but the submarine on which I served as Chaplain had a man called Sullivan aboard. In fact, he and I knew each other well for many years. Do you know what happened to your father?' He took off his glasses and rubbed each lens with the end of his scarf. 'May I ask his first name?'

'His name was John. My mother and I don't even know if he's still alive.'

Wilson replaced his spectacles and looked down at his gleaming Church brogues. 'My colleague's name was Jack Sullivan.' He glanced up at Ellie. 'I recall that he used to talk of a daughter but it's all a very long time ago.'

Her subsequent questions elicited snappy responses. He finished his tea, said that it had been pleasant to talk to her and left. A shower of hail had sprung up and rattled the external windows. As Ellie checked the temperature in the radiator outside the ward she saw him standing at the end of the corridor that led to the exit. He studied a scrap of paper which was replaced in an inner pocket but he did not move...almost as if he did not know whether to return to her or leave.

Ellie drained the bottle of Amstel, paid and walked to Kamara Square. She rang for a cab to bring her to the Hotel Possidonia. After a shower, she changed into jeans and a tee shirt. She searched for the letter at the bottom of her bag. She had studied it many times but only once since her arrival in Greece. It would be important to make a final check before she returned to Vari in the morning. It had arrived in early April, bearing a postmark from Letterkenny in Donegal. The writer, with only a bare preamble, stated that he had become aware of her existence and her current address. It became rapidly clear that the person knew much more, especially of her Irish origins. He said that he had been a close friend of her father, Jack Sullivan. They had shared many an adventure together on the high seas of life but such tales would have to wait.

Her father was dead. He had always loved her mother and herself but realised the divorce had been caused by him. After further details had been provided, the tone lifted and the writer revealed that her father had substantial assets. He had left instructions with the executor of his will that his estate was to pass on to his daughter should communication with her ever be re-established. When further checks had been made, a second letter would provide the number of a safety deposit box.

Ellie went to the bar and ordered a large gin. She watched the early evening windsurfers circle the Bay of Finikas, then made her last visit to the Naval Station. Apart from a late sunbather the area was deserted. She walked on for a hundred yards and turned around. As she did so, she saw the black periscope rise from the water.

On Thursday morning, after breakfast, she repacked, paid her bill and rang for a cab to take her back to Vari. Bart Vamvakaris was glad to see her return. 'A single girl like you should take care. It is safe here but everywhere is not so pleasant. Your room is prepared.'

In the afternoon, she settled herself on the beach under a pine tree. She turned over to study her ragged tourist guide. Above her, the cicadas strummed in anticipation of their fate. After reading, she thought back again.

The second letter had given her what had been promised and more confirmation of her inheritance. However, a condition was imposed. She was requested to visit Syros and follow the instructions contained in the letter. It advised caution and, in particular, not to arouse any suspicion from the authorities. Whilst she should not be at any risk, it would be better if she was circumspect in all that she did. The Greeks were an excitable people and were excellent bureaucrats when it suited them. It exhorted her not to get too involved. On her return, she would be contacted and matters should move to a satisfactory conclusion for everyone. The key of the box and its address was enclosed.

In the early evening, she had a long hot shower. Her beige slacks and white blouse had been laundered by Bart's wife. There was enough gin left in her bottle for a tall glass with ice and tonic. She sat on the veranda for an hour until the sun had dipped beneath the horizon. The missing piece of the puzzle would have to wait until tomorrow. She went down to eat.

Bart arrived to take her order. He had had his weekly shave and was dressed in black. 'My wife and I will be sorry to see you go. Perhaps you will return next year.'

'You can be sure of that.'

'Perhaps you will have company next time.'

Ellie smiled. 'That will be in the lap of the Gods.'

'Sometimes you must make your own fate and not wait for them. They are very busy men. Now, what can I get you?'

She chose small fish and smothered them with lemon. Bart suggested a white wine from the island of Santorini. He brought her a small carafe. As Ellie dabbled at her Greek salad while she waited for her pork souvlaki, she wondered about the Trewsdales. They had exchanged contact numbers but she felt sure that they would never meet again. She thought that it would be nice to share a vacation here with a partner that you loved. There had never been anyone like that for her. Occasional dates had fizzled out...usually at her instigation. She had found most American men superficial. As for Irishmen of her own age, well...

Bart brought her kebabs skewered in a silver elliptical dish. Tiny potatoes rested in a bed of olive oil beside the pork. 'Somi and Nero?' He placed four slices of fresh crusty bread in a bowl on the table and went to fetch a bottle of still water.

Afterwards, she walked in the moonlight to the Church of the Virgin Mary. The front door was unlocked and she went to sit in the front pew. To her left, four long tapered candles flickered beneath the statue of Our Lady dressed in Greek blue and white. On her right, on the far wall, a moonbeam illuminated the suffering face of the crucified Jesus. Although Ellie could not believe, she prayed.

In the morning, she packed before breakfast. Without being asked, Bart brought her omelette with fresh bread and coffee. She spent a last hour on the beach and then made her final preparations. After Greek salad with a cold Heineken, she said goodbye to Bart and his wife. He ordered her a cab to bring her to Hermoupolis where she arrived at three o'clock.

Josh Gilbert sat at a table underneath a yellow canopy in front of the Hotel Hermes. He was reading as she approached. He looked up and then placed the open book on the check tablecloth. 'Can I get you something?'

'A Coke would be fine.' Ellie sat down. 'What's this your reading?'

'The Colossus of Maroussi, by Henry Miller...an old compatriot of yours.'

'Nexus, Sexus, Plexus, the Tropic of Cancer and the Tropic of Capricorn. I've heard of all his famous books...even read the last two. I haven't come across this one. May I see it for a moment?'

'Of course.'

Ellie read the opening page:

'Marvellous things happen to one in Greece – marvellous good things which can happen to one nowhere else on Earth. Somehow, almost as if He were nodding, Greece remains under the protection of the Creator. Men may go about their puny, ineffectual bedevilment, even in Greece, but God's magic is still at work and, not matter what the race of man may do or try to do, Greece is still a sacred precinct – and my belief is it will remain so until the end of time.'

'This sounds good. I must get it when I go back.'

'It's out of print. This is an old copy of mine. I read it very year. You may borrow it if you wish.'

'No, I'll find it somehow. If you lend it to me, you may never get it back.'

'I'm sure we'll meet again. I'll be back in Belfast in early August. The heat here becomes almost unbearable and there will be far more tourists around...although it's not nearly as thronged as many of the neighbouring islands such as Mykonos.'

'You come here every year?'

'I've been to Greece many times. This is my first visit to Syros. I was delighted to have the opportunity to be actually paid to work and live here for a few months. Now, we haven't much time. You were going to tell me why you came here?'

Ellie drained her glass of Coke. 'I've told you of my family background. I went to see the base again on Wednesday. It's a pretty mysterious operation...whatever they do there.' She paused. 'A priest came to visit one of my patients in late winter. To cut a long story short, it turned out that he may have served with my father during the Second World War.' She saw her companion stifle a yawn. 'Am I boring you?'

'Of course not. I'm sorry. Go on. I had a tiresome time with my Greek friends this morning.'

'Shortly afterwards, I received a letter from the South of Ireland informing me that my father was dead and had willed me part of his estate.'

'And you believe that the two events were linked?'

'I just don't know but I felt they had to be. The writer knew about my parents' time here in Syros. By the way, I'm grateful to you for leading me to the place where they met and...'

'Think nothing of it. You haven't told me the name of this priest or the person who wrote to you afterwards. Perhaps you didn't know the latter's name? Or maybe I'm being intrusive.'

'Not at all. The priest's name was Luke Wilson.' Ellie caught his startled reaction.

'Are you quite sure...especially of the first name?'

'Why? Did you know him? The North of Ireland is a small place.'

'I knew a cleric of that name.' Josh Gilbert rubbed hard at the side of his forehead.

'You seem excited?'

'I will need to think this out. I'll write to you if you give me your address. It's a pity we haven't more time. If only I'd known or realised earlier. Look, your ferry is coming in. You'd better get in the queue if you want to find a decent seat.'

'I'll look forward to hearing from you. I'll give you all my contact details.'

'One thing more, Ellie. Perhaps you would tell me the name of the person who prompted you to come here and also your father's first name?'

'Jack. As for the writer, it may be false. I could show you the letter if we had time. The name at the bottom was A PERRY.' She jumped as Gilbert's chair crashed to the ground.

13

BOOMER looked suspiciously at Barney who noticed the double cut beneath the Inspector's chin that the razor blade had nicked. 'I hope you two aren't skiving. I was told that you were working on a case and needed a file. There's no paperwork here.'

Barney gathered himself. 'We'd just finished. It was only a hunch I had about that business from last week. The suspect's name rang a bell but I was wrong. There's nothing here on him.'

'Forget it. There's something I want you two to check on right away.'

Barney relaxed. 'We heard you were called to a murder near the Border.'

'The scene is well covered down there. The victim is a suspected terrorist from Belfast. Come on, let's go. There's a car waiting to take you to the City Centre.'

After their briefing, Billy got into the front passenger seat and Barney climbed into the back. Both remained silent until they arrived at their destination. Barney told the driver to wait.

'You don't think Boomer caught on? I couldn't hold him back, Barney. You saw the mood he was in.'

'It's OK, Billy. I got the file back just in time. Let's get this over with and then we'll grab lunch.'

After grilling the informer and discovering what they needed, they found a café. They ordered the All Day Breakfast Special with extra fried eggs and sausages.

Billy waited until Barney had finished. 'Did you find out anything significant?'

'Don't know what to make of it. I'll need to see the file again.'

'Keep me out of it next time. Boomer is vindictive. I don't want my promotion fouled up. It's all very well for you.'

'I know, Billy. If I'd gone in by myself, he might have caught me red-handed.'

'At least you know the file's there. Wait until he's on a day's leave.'

'You can never be sure of him. You're told he's off duty then he suddenly appears. He's a workaholic.'

'Did you get enough to keep you going?'

'You don't know the full background, Billy. And it might be better if you didn't.'

'I'll help you if I can.'

'I'm grateful.' Barney closed his eyes and sighed. He told Billy part of what he'd read.

Matt rang the Station but was told that Detective-Sergeant Mulvey was out on a case. He left a message to ring the Halls Of Residence as soon as possible. Thoughts of Saturday evening returned. Sue had been voracious and had all the experience. Despite the red mist, he had found it difficult to live up to the challenge. The hot evening, the heavy sweat and the smell of stale musk came back. He hadn't been able to perform.

His mind in turmoil, he decided to walk down to the Lough. A path led along the sea. The salt air revived him as he made his way as far as Macedon Point. The field that stretched to a rocky wall beside the shore was sprinkled with mothers and toddlers. The tide was coming in and he turned back before the sea could cut off the path. In the middle of the Lough, a trawler made its way to Belfast harbour. Matt thought of Wilson and Sullivan.

As he returned towards the campus, he saw the Head of Department walking in the opposite direction, heavy briefcase in hand. 'Dr Walton, how are you?'

Walton stopped. In the bright afternoon sunshine, his face looked more haggard than usual. The skin was pale and blotchy. 'Matt, I thought you might have come to see me about this tragedy. Armstrong in Personnel has been telling me all about it.'

'Sue Neil lived beneath me in the Halls. We were friends and had been out together on Saturday evening.' Matt wondered how much Walton had been told.

'It must have come as a dreadful shock to you. If there's anything I can do to help, make an appointment.'

'Thank you, Dr Walton. I will.'

'Your examination scripts are back from the External Examiner. Perhaps, if you get a chance, you'll pop in to the office tomorrow and do the necessary. I must go. My GP has told me to take more exercise so I'm walking back and forth from home.'

Matt watched him disappear towards the Jordanstown Road where he knew he lived alone since the death of his wife. He imagined him returning, duty done and pouring a huge whiskey before an evening meal of boiled eggs and toast soldiers.

When Matt reached the door of his apartment, he found a yellow slip of paper sellotaped across the lock. 'Mister Mulvey returned your call. He will be arriving to see you at six o'clock.' As he let himself in, Matt looked at his watch. Another hour to go. He lay down on the settee and closed his eyes. A bloody Teresa splashed about in his dreams. As they drowned for the third time, Barney's knock woke him up.

'Let's go for a pint, Matt. I'm parched. It's been a long day and we have a lot to talk about.'

'We'll go to the Common Room. It'll be quiet at this time of year...especially on Tuesday evening.'

When Barney had cleared half of his glass, Matt told him about the meeting with Patterson. 'I'm panicking, Barney. How should I handle this in the morning?'

'I spoke to Patterson yesterday. Told him it couldn't have been you. I did my best to talk you up.'

'Do you think he believed you?'

'Who knows? Cops are cops. He's just doing his job. I know you didn't do it. The truth will come out. You weren't even in the woman's apartment. Any good ideas on who might have been?'

'Everybody knew Sue but I find it hard to believe any of her partners could have done it.'

'This guy Watt sounds like a bit of a creep. You say he's pretty cocky about the prints.'

'So Patterson says.'

Barney grinned. 'He might have been trying to wind you up. I'll talk to him again if I can reach him this evening.'

He ordered more pints. 'This will have to do me. There's a few other matters we need to talk about. Come on, Matt. Cheer up. Think of all this money we might be coming in to.'

Matt sipped his Harp. 'You hinted that you'd found something out?'

'Maybe. I can't shake from my mind this business about the daughter. How did Luke Wilson know about her? That she was Sullivan's girl, I mean.'

'You'll have to wait until you see her next week.'

'I want to compare notes with you about the whole story. What can you remember exactly?'

When Matt had finished, Barney swished the dregs of lager around in his glass. 'That's how I recall it as well. In the documents which Charlie Boyle gave us, there's a lot of stuff that sets the scene for his initial meetings with Wilson. You can read it yourself when I've finished. At one point, Charlie gets the story on paper.'

'What's the problem?'

'In Charlie's document, the dead woman is referred to as Teresa throughout.'

'Same as we remembered.'

'With one difference.'

'Yes?'

'He told us she was a blonde.'

'Probably a mistake.'

'I can't help feeling it's significant.'

'What about Sullivan's reason for framing him?'

'There is a suggestion that Wilson knew that Sullivan was guilty of something pretty bad. Maybe he had murdered someone in a drunken row and made a clean breast of it in Confession.'

'He doesn't sound like the type.'

Barney pursed his lips. 'We don't know enough about him. I've seen a lot of cases where guys only get violent when tanked up.'

'Jekyll and Hyde.'

'When the drink has worn off, they're meek and mild as lambs. Some of them can hardly remember the half of what they've done the night before.'

'If Sullivan fell into that category, it doesn't square with the type of character who goes in for blackmail.'

'That's true, Matt. Also if he's told something in Confession, he'd be sure it would never come out.' Barney's eyes dulled. 'It doesn't hold up. Look, time's moving on. Let's get back to your problem.'

'Charlie's not appearing in the morning. His partner is coming down to keep me on track.'

'Make sure you check the statement and that you can stand over everything. You say this guy Watt is going to get fingerprinted as well.'

'According to Patterson.'

'You haven't spoken to Watt.'

'No.'

Barney rubbed his forehead. 'Don't lose your nerve. If Watt had nothing to do with it, you've no other ideas?'

'No.'

'You didn't see anything suspicious in the Glenavna Hotel?'

'There was a Saturday night crowd in the bar. If we were being watched, I wouldn't have noticed.'

Barney changed tack. 'You remember the morning I picked up you to go to Coleraine to see Charlie?'

'Yes, the day we went to get the documents.'

'We talked about Judge Curran's daughter being murdered in the grounds of the Hotel in 1952. It used to be their family home.'

'You said the murder had never been solved.'

'Hay Gordon, the guy who was convicted, was released and now lives in Scotland. The smart money says he never did it.'

Matt caught on. 'If it wasn't one of the family, then maybe there's a psychopath living in the area...but these guys don't wait for so long before repeating themselves.'

'Not usually, Matt. There's any number of possibilities. If he didn't scarper immediately, he may have lain low for a time then moved out of the area for a few years. For some reason, he returns and somehow develops an attraction for Sue Neil.'

'He could have come back and found a job on Campus. A security guard or something like that. They'd be watching everything, especially at the weekend.'

Barney smiled. 'Don't raise your hopes too much. I agree it's possible. I'll get a hold of Patterson tonight and put it to him. It'll create a smokescreen if nothing else.'

'This scenario takes us away from any possible connection with Wilson's case.'

'Not necessarily.'

'What do you mean?'

'Think again about the stowaway...a soldier deserting from the army. Maybe he murdered both women. On the second occasion, he covers himself by telling the Sullivan story to Luke Wilson. Then he disappears.'

Matt's head spun. 'We know that Sullivan existed and we have to assume that Wilson told us the truth about that winter night.'

'It was seven years later and another sixteen years have passed. We may have missed a key detail...something that might lead us to the truth. Is there anything else you can remember?'

Matt snapped his fingers. 'I've been sleeping in. With this murder business hanging over me, I'd forgotten.'

'Something Wilson told us?'

'No.' Matt rubbed his temple. 'Last Tuesday, I had a conversation with a guy called Paul Kerry from the Department of Marine Engineering. I asked him about the *Victoria*. Their Department is involved in ship design and they train students for jobs on the cross-channel ferries. Kerry told me that there had been reports of stowaways but only one who may have survived.'

Barney sensed Matt's excitement. 'Did he give you any detail?'

'It's coming back to me. One of the stewards on the boat from the previous night's trip reported a young guy getting on without any money or a ticket. The steward and his mate...the latter sailed on the boat and drowned after she sank...suspected that the man was a soldier. They glimpsed what they thought was an army uniform beneath his overcoat.'

'Could Kerry put a name to this guy?'

'A false name, he thought. Perry was the name he gave when he was rescued by the Donaghadee lifeboat.'

Barney rubbed his chin. 'It could well be the same guy. Does Kerry have any indication of what happened to him?'

'Kerry is not the real expert. He told me he'd got all his information from another man in the Department. A guy called Josh Gilbert.'

'You didn't get a chance to speak to him?'

'No, he's abroad on a contract with Harland And Wolff. They provide advice to foreign shipyards all over the world.'

'Where is he exactly and when will he return?'

'He's coming back later in the summer. August, I believe. He's advising a shipyard in Greece.'

Barney's eyebrows shot up. 'Greece? Greece again? We're now waiting for two people to come back from Greece before we can move on our legacy.'

'I hadn't thought of that. The girl's out there on a vacation. He's working there. It's just a coincidence.'

'I don't subscribe to so many coincidences. I'm a gambling man. No, Matt, that's not why I'm getting excited. There's something I haven't told you yet. I had meant to mention it to you and Charlie yesterday but there wasn't time.'

'Come on, Barney. What is it?'

'You remember I told you about the assault on a woman called Celia Teeny. After that investigation fizzled out in late 1967, Charlie's file doesn't have much in it until 1969. In Easter of that year, the police contacted Charlie again. He tried to reach Wilson but failed. He had gone for a break to a Greek diocese on an island called Syros.'

14

THE FERRY *Naios* departed from Syros on the Friday afternoon of 18th June. Ellie found a vacant seat on the top deck overlooking the stern of the ship. A canopy protected the passengers from the fierce heat. In the distance, above the twin hills stretching behind the town, the two churches dominated the skyline. She photographed them and asked a German girl beside her to take a snap of her with Hermoupolis in the background.

On returning to the seat, she pulled a sun hat over her eyes and placed her feet on the rucksack. Gilbert's reaction had surprised her. He had refused to explain and she had had to catch this last ferry to Piraeus. Her flight left from Athens airport at midday Saturday and there was no other way of making a connection on time. For some reason, the three names had meant something to Gilbert. How could he possibly know her father? Wilson, that was plausible, she recognised. However, when she had given him the name of her correspondent, he had fallen off his chair. She had searched, without success, to identify anyone by the name in the telephone directory. Ellie thought back to her second meeting with Wilson.

Miss Stuart from Portglenone had gone into a coma. He arrived again to see her. Afterwards he had stopped at the ward office. 'Is there anywhere we could have a quiet word?' He put the back of his hand against his mouth to stifle heavy coughing. 'I've caught one of these viruses,' he explained.

Ellie saw his marble pallor and the broken veins showing up on his cheeks. 'You shouldn't have come out today, Father. I doubt if there was anything more you could have done.'

'I had another visit to make near here. Something I couldn't get out of. I thought I'd kill two birds with one stone.'

Ellie smiled. 'Is there anything more that I can help you with?'

He waited until his cough had abated. 'When I was here before, we talked about your father. My memory's not what it was but our conversation came back to me the other day. I wondered whether we were talking about the same person. Have you a few minutes?'

'If it turns out you knew my father, I'd love to hear anything you know about him.' She paused. 'Warts and all.'

'Those were different times. Your father...if it was the same person...was a complex man. If he liked you, there was nothing he wouldn't do for you. If he didn't like you or you crossed him, there was nothing he wouldn't do *to* you.'

'I don't expect to hear about a plaster saint. My mother told me of his violent temper, especially if he'd been drinking. That's what led to the divorce.'

A second bout of coughing followed. 'I wouldn't want to run him down in front of his daughter. But yes, you're right. With drink taken, he could be...'

'Do you want to talk about it?'

'For obvious reasons, I can't tell you more. Let's check whether we are discussing the same man.' He told her what he knew and she reciprocated. 'What you say makes sense. We must meet again.'

He never returned but she had thought nothing of it until the letter arrived in April. Ellie became convinced that, having established the relationship, he had told others. One of those may have been trying to contact her. All there would have been to go on was the original address in San Francisco...from where she had moved in the mid-sixties after her grandfather had died.

She stretched her legs and looked across the flat blue sea. Yards away from the wash of the boat, there was barely a ripple. The German girl was reading Doctor Faustus by Thomas Mann. The pages turned slowly. Ellie remembered the Faustian pact. She had done what she had been asked to do. There had been no sale of her soul to the devil but it might not apply to her father.

At nine o'clock, the ferry approached Pireaus. The sky was darkening and she saw the lights in the suburbs that intermingled with those of Athens itself. The passengers streamed off behind the revving mopeds and transport lorries.

She hailed a cab and, thirty minutes later, she got out near the centre of the city in the Plaka beneath the Acropolis. The driver recommended a hotel of the same name. She checked in and was shown to a spotless room with immaculate white bed linen. After a quick shower, she dressed and went out to look for a taverna. Spoilt for choice, she chose one as near as possible to the Acropolis itself. After a dinner of spaghetti with tomato sauce, she finished her glass of red wine and walked until she reached the Parthenon. From a nearby amphitheatre came the sound of a Maria Callas recording. Tosca, she thought. It reminded her of back home. In North Beach, the café of the same name played Italian arias in the background. Tears came to her eyes and, for the first time, Ellie felt lonely and afraid.

Two days earlier, Matt had woken at four in the morning. He sweated as he tossed and turned. His eyes were closed but his brain raced. At six o'clock, he gave up. He rose to make tea and watched the sun rise at the far end of the Lough. There was no noise from the apartments on the floor beneath. After Sue had been removed for post-mortem examination, an eerie quiet had reigned. At nine o'clock, he met Charlie's partner, a guy called George Wallace who was not much older than Matt. He repeated Barney's warning to check everything. If he changed it later, it wouldn't look too good. They met Patterson with a Sergeant in attendance. Matt examined the statement and made minor changes.

Patterson scrutinised what had been initialled. 'Sign it for me, please. The Sergeant will then take you next door and we'll do the fingerprinting. After that, you can go but don't plan any holidays.'

Matt looked at Wallace and raised his eyes. The solicitor shook his head and raised his hand. 'There's nothing you can do. They've treated you fairly. I've seen far worse.'

At mid-morning, they parted and Matt walked back to his apartment. He guessed that Watt would be at the station and he decided to make a visit to his office. Derek Scott was there and he gave him a summary.

'If the photograph wasn't yours and Watt is confident that he knows nothing about it, how did it get here?'

'Don't worry, Derek. I know it didn't belong to you.'

'I suppose in theory it could have done. No doubt, they'll be interviewing me as well. It's a good thing my hands are clean. That's not much consolation to you, Matt. Let's go for coffee before Watt comes back.'

As they left the office, the phone rang. 'Barney? You've just caught me.' Matt updated him. 'Nothing new?'

'I can't do much for you at the moment but I'm having checks made on the Greek business. I hope to have a result later this afternoon. Ring about four o'clock.' They ascended the stairs to the main mall. As Matt followed Derek to the right, he saw Watt approach from the opposite direction, drop his eyes and turn back.

In the Common Room they sat in silence with two cups of fierce Italian coffee. In a corner of the room, a female academic sipped as she read from a paperback. They did not notice Kerry approach until he asked if he could join them.

Derek looked up, hesitated and smiled. 'Of course, Paul. Matt was telling me you'd been a great help to him last week.'

Kerry sat down beside Derek. 'Ah, yes. The *Victoria*.' He looked across at Matt.

'Thanks for your information. You've probably heard that I've been tied up with something else.'

'I guess you don't want to talk about it.'

'No, that's fine. It's no secret that I was one of the last to see her.'

'I don't suppose there's anything I can do?'

Matt smiled. 'Thanks. I don't think so.' He grabbed the opportunity to change the subject. 'Any news of your colleague in Greece? Josh Gilbert, wasn't it?'

Derek interrupted. 'That's someone I hardly know. He's not here much.'

'I was telling Matt last week that he was the one he should talk to about the *Victoria* tragedy. As a matter of fact, he rang the Department Secretary yesterday. Told her all his Greek woes, but had apparently been cheered up by dinner with a nurse on Sunday evening. She teased him about it but said he was getting on a bit for that sort of thing. In any case, she was out of his class.'

Derek caught Matt's reaction. 'Are you OK?'

'I was talking to a police friend of mine last night. They're trying to locate a local nurse who's gone to Greece on holiday. Your friend didn't mention a name by any chance?'

Kerry closed his eyes. 'Our Secretary might know. I'll check. I'm not quite sure if she was from here. There was something odd about her background. I think she was Irish-American. Her father had been a Navy man and that's how they clicked.' He glanced at his watch. 'I must go. Ring me later if you're still interested.'

Derek waited until he had gone. 'What was that all about?' Matt told him some of it and they returned to the office. A cleaner was on her knees scrubbing the corridor. Watt was not there but a sour smell pervaded the room. At one o'clock, Derek said that he was going home to sort out a family problem. Matt remembered his examination scripts and went to the Department office to collect them. There was no sign of Deirdre and he knocked on Dr Walton's door. The Head pulled out his keys and retrieved the scripts without a word. Matt thanked him and returned to his apartment.

He turned on the radio to hear the end of the midday news. A Radio Ulster announcer finished by reminding listeners that today was the anniversary of Bloomsday and the occasion was being celebrated in Dublin.

Matt went to fetch his copy of *Ulysses* and he read again the stunning opening pages. He thought of Wilson emerging from his sacristy to say early morning mass. If hungover, he would fling the black biretta aside for the altar boys to catch. At Holy Communion they retaliated by watering the wine. Then Matt froze.

Barney sat in his office with a cup of Maxwell House. He knew that Boomer was on the prowl about something but did not care. In the morning another tough letter had arrived from Jean Mulvey's solicitor and had got Barney off to a bad start. The bets of the previous afternoon had dissipated the gains of the weekend. If it was not for Charlie Boyle's imminent cheque, he would be in it right up to his neck.

The phone call came at three o'clock. Barney put his feet on the desk and pulled at the lower part of his left ear as he cradled the phone to his right. It had been a long shot with the travel agency that he had seen in Portglenone when he had driven through with Matt last week.

The caller rambled on but Barney got what he wanted. He put down the phone and took a long pull of coffee. If only Boomer hadn't arrived back on Monday, he could have put the whole business into perspective. The file in the store would have to be dug out again. Then he could work out what to do with Matt.

His friend rang sharp at four. 'We'll not dwell on how I confirmed the 1969 information. It doesn't matter. He booked his passage to London on British Airways for the Wednesday before Easter. On Good Friday, he travelled on to Athens.'

'How long did he stay?'

'We can't be certain. He told the travel agent that he only wanted to book one-way and he would make his return arrangements from the other end.'

'That's a bit odd, isn't it?'

'I suppose so, but not unusual according to the agent.'

'Where do we go from here, Barney?'

'Good question, Matt. What about your own enquiry?'

Matt told him about the morning's meeting with Patterson. 'I'll have to wait and see. Did you have any joy with him last night?'

'I gave him the Curran angle. It put him in bad twist but will keep him tied up for a day or two.'

'He wasn't so cocky this morning. Let's hope that it goes somewhere and he leaves me alone.'

'Don't bank on it, Matt.'

'Let's go back to the other matter. Something I found out this morning.' He heard Barney splutter at the other end of the line.

'I can't wait until Monday.' Barney took his feet off the desk and got up. 'I'll let her settle in. Then, I'll pounce around lunchtime. There's nothing much we can do until then. Ring me if anything develops.'

'I will.'

On Thursday and Friday, Matt polished off his examining duties and prepared a detailed report for the Examination Board meeting at the end of the following week. The External Examiner had been kind to the students and had tended to mark them up rather than down. On this front at least, he could relax. Normally, he would have been looking forward to the long summer break, but he found it hard to shake the feeling of fear.

On Saturday afternoon, he decided to go home and spend the weekend with his mother. She was delighted to see him but grew worried when she heard that he had known the dead girl. Matt told her no more than she needed to know. She asked him to get extra shopping in and she produced a detailed list for the local butcher. He went to bed early and slept properly for the first time in a week.

After Mass on Sunday she prepared a roast with potatoes and carrots. She joined him in a glass of Beaujolais. When he saw her doze off in mid-afternoon, he decided to go for a drive. He removed the hood from the Spitfire and drove along the Antrim Road until he found the Avenue again. He parked the car and walked along until he was certain. He remembered the moment for the rest of his life. Four o'clock on a sunny Sunday afternoon in June.

He gathered his nerve as he came back along the Avenue. The black tarmac was swept clean. The front windows shone in the sunlight. He pulled at the brass knocker and pushed the bell. A few minutes later, as he was about to walk away, Ellie Sullivan opened the door.

FRANKINCENSE

15

THE YORK HOTEL bar had two early evening customers on Sunday. In one corner, Barney sat nursing a bottle of Red Heart. In the other, the elderly regular remarked to Doug Stewart that he would be hung before he gave in and had received a silent nod in response. Barney pondered the telephone conversation from Saturday afternoon.

'Luke Wilson was a good client of ours. He always booked his annual holiday with us.'

'Let's go over it again. Where did he go?'

'North of Spain. Barcelona, usually. That's why it stuck in my mind that he didn't go there in 1969 and went to Greece instead. I've rechecked for you as you asked. I never throw anything out.'

'You don't know for how long?'

'He didn't always book a return flight. One year, he drove over in a hired car and caught a flight back from Madrid. All I can tell you is that he was back in late April.'

'What about his duties?'

'He'd arranged cover. It wasn't a problem. The Belfast guy was only too glad to get up here for a couple of weeks at Easter and enjoy himself.'

'Did he ever go to Greece again?'

'I don't think he did. He went abroad once a year and I can only remember him going to Spain.'

'And this year?'

'As you know, his health was bad and going downhill fast. Belfast was about as far as he got.'

'Thanks for your help, Mister Young.'

'It's no problem. Call in with me if you're up this way.'

Barney ordered a second bottle of Red Heart. He looked across at the table where the nurses had sat only a fortnight ago. As the woman's return loomed, he was having doubts about how he should approach her. What was he supposed to do? Inform her that he was a police officer and begin an enquiry into her background just because she had lost an ID? He would have to be smarter than that.

'You're in a quiet mood tonight, Barney. I'm glad to see you're taking it easy.'

Barney looked up at Doug Stewart. 'Nothing else for it. The end of the month can't come soon enough for me. There's a hard week ahead of me.'

'Anything I can do?'

'Thanks. Not really.' Doug turned to serve his other customer. Barney felt in his inside pocket to see how much cash he had left. Enough for another four bottles. Billy should be good for a loan in the morning.

After the next round, his mood lifted. Charlie Boyle had said that one of them might have to travel abroad. On Thursday, Matt had confirmed the nurse's name. What had Wilson been doing in Syros in 1969? He turned his mind to Boomer's file. Maybe he had misinterpreted its contents. On New Year's Day 1960, the police had returned to interview Wilson about the woman who had been found in the Lagan. He had repeated his story. They seized on the differences and his responses became frayed. Why had the colour of Teresa's hair changed? They had smelt fear. A cop had come into the room and asked to speak to the detective outside. When he returned, it was confirmed that the name of the owner of Teresa's house had been traced by the Land Registry Office. The holiday arrangements had slowed down the enquiry. They apologised and left. Wilson, who had made his preparations, disappeared to Portglenone.

Barney wondered had he panicked at the name of Sullivan. He had got off the hook but his enemy was still out there somewhere. It could explain his reaction to the questions. Barney would have accepted this theory had it not been for a subsequent note on the case that had been deposited in Boomer's file in February 1960. A witness had come forward to state that a man of the priest's description had been observed going into Sullivan's house over the Christmas period. Although the person could not be certain, the file remained with a key question mark over it.

Barney turned his mind to Sullivan's daughter. The more he thought about it, the more suspicious he became. She was bound to have missed her ID by now if she had dropped it accidentally. Why not wait and see if she came back here to thank him?

Doug Stewart called last orders. 'Have this one on me, Barney.' He nudged the Powers optic twice. 'You're not yourself. This might help.' He turned towards the back room.

'Doug, you're a gentleman.' He sniffed the golden liquid, sank it and rose.

Barney woke with the Monday morning blues. He made tea as he rubbed the electric razor over his face. He left before the post had arrived. Billy was waiting for him. 'Boomer has had to go to a funeral this morning. His uncle died on Friday night. He's not expected back until mid-afternoon.'

Barney's mood soared. 'This may be my only chance. Drop everything. Let's go. I have to see the file. You stand watch. If by any chance he returns, we'll have to use the same excuse as last time. Should everything go pear-shaped I'll take the rap.'

Barney found the file and read from where he had broken off. In the Autumn of 1967, police in Ballymena had received a letter from an informant. The letter accused Wilson of attempting to murder Celia Teeny in the previous November. It stated that a previous parish had been a dockside one in Belfast and they should check on any previous form. The police had been sceptical but had followed up. To their surprise, they discovered his connection with a similar crime. And so the interviews began.

There was overlap with Boyle's documents. However, what the solicitor didn't have was the fuel for Boomer's suspicions. He believed the informant to be female. There was something about the style of writing, even the fact that it was so beautifully typed. It had credibility and they believed they knew where it came from.

Barney looked at his watch. There was plenty of time. He glanced over at Billy to check. He read on. Boomer had gone to see Celia Teeny at her parent's farmhouse. They were nervous and wanted the matter dropped. Their daughter had been through a terrifying ordeal but had recovered from her trauma. She had obtained a post as a music teacher in a good school in Belfast and had settled into her new life. They refused to cooperate.

Boomer had become even more suspicious. The letter carried a Belfast postmark. The parents had informed him that their daughter was employed in a Dominican College. There were only two of those and Boomer had no trouble identifying the correct one. He had phoned her to arrange a meeting. At first, she had refused. Boomer had used the tactic that the assailant could be a threat to other women. He understood her reluctance but everything would be treated with the utmost confidence. And so she had agreed to meet him at Fortwilliam police station. Barney found it hard to control his excitement and broke off to piss in the small toilet at the rear of the store. As he pressed his left hand on the sash window he watched the spray of urine bounce off the cracked Shanks bowl. He zipped up and returned.

The station was within walking distance of the school. The session had begun at five o'clock in the afternoon of 14th October 1967. Boomer had noted the woman's composure and self-assurance. Celia Teeny was in her late twenties with porcelain skin and wore expensive gold-rimmed glasses. Sergeant Townsend minuted the conversation. Barney imagined Boomer beginning in his polite rural accent.

'Thank you for coming. I realise what an ordeal all this has been for you.'

'I had wanted to forget about it. I love my new job and I've made many friends. There is a very active musical society.'

'Yes, I've heard of it.'

Townsend broke in. 'It's run by a Mister William Cairns.'

Barney imagined Boomer's cool reaction to an interruption. A look would be enough to stop Townsend in his tracks.

Boomer continued. 'Quite. I'll not keep you too long, Miss Teeny. As I said on the phone, we've received a letter that names your priestly assailant.'

'The man was dressed as a priest. You must have records of everything I've said before.'

'This is new information. Do you know a Father Luke Wilson?'

'No.'

'Are you certain?'

'Does the letter identify him?'

'It doesn't beat about the bush.'

'Are you going to question this man?'

'We can't proceed on the basis of what may be a malicious letter.'

'But the allegation may be correct. Other women may be in danger. You've told me so. That's why I'm here.'

'Not only other women. You could be in danger yourself.'

'Very reassuring.'

'We don't want to frighten you but it's important that we catch your attacker and get him locked up.'

'I realise that.'

'Are you positive you've told us all that you know?'

'Give me more time to think.'

'Are you worried about your parents?'

'Of course but there are others to consider. There's someone I need to talk with.'

'A solicitor?'

'No, no. I have a boyfriend. That's not the right term. He's a few years older than myself. I haven't told him anything about the attack.' After some additional questions, she agreed to meet Boomer a week later.

Barney glanced across at Billy who put a hand to his mouth and tilted his palm to indicate it was time for a break. 'I'll be finished soon, Billy.' He returned to the file. Celia Teeny had rung Boomer a few days afterwards. She admitted sending the letter but wanted to postpone their meeting. The phone call was enough for Boomer to arrange his first interview with Wilson.

At the subsequent meeting with Celia Teeny, Boomer had noted a drop in her composure. After some opening remarks, he began. 'Tell me, Miss Teeny, why you believe that your assailant was Wilson.'

'I can't be completely certain but I felt sure enough when I saw him again.'

'Where?'

'I was leaving the College with a friend in early September. Wilson was talking to one of the nuns at the main gates. I felt faint. We went back inside to fetch a glass of water. On her return, the nun expressed concern. When I recovered I took a chance. On the pretence of making polite conversation, I said that I couldn't help noticing the priest to whom she'd been talking. Wasn't he from a rural parish? She explained who he was and that he had previously served in two Belfast parishes...one in the docks and one on the outskirts of North Belfast. The nun led us to believe that he was quite a character and hinted at a scandal many years before. That was enough for me.'

Boomer had pressed as much as possible. 'If we arrested him, how far would you go to help us nail him?'

'You seem pretty sure he's the man who attacked me. Do you have something else on him?'

'We'd prefer to act on your identification.'

'I'd hoped you'd find other evidence to give you grounds for an arrest.'

'We might have, but it's not enough. I need you to be certain. You could have made a mistake, or someone might have been trying to frame him.'

'Impersonate him, you mean?'

'Yes.'

'I hadn't thought of that possibility.'

'Perhaps you'd like to tell us again about the night of the attack. I know it's hard but you were concussed afterwards. Sometimes an important detail flashes into a person's mind much later.'

'I smelt drink from him...a powerful smell of dark rum. It has its own unique aroma. At first, he looked into the fire and sat in silence. I pressed him about his business.'

'How did he respond?'

'He barked that it was a private matter. My parents were later than expected. I offered tea again and he accepted. It's coming back to me.'

'Take your time.'

'I filled the kettle with water and lit the gas. He appeared to calm down and mumbled about a notice that my parents had placed in a newspaper about a person he had known. He wanted to talk to them about him.'

'An obituary notice?'

'That's what I thought. It would have made sense. My father read the paper every day and spent a long time on the deaths. If a friend died, he always placed a notice of regret and, a year later, a memoriam paragraph.'

'What happened next?'

'I heard the hiss of the kettle. The steam was rising and I ran to switch off the gas. When I turned, he was right behind me and then it all went black.'

'Try to remember everything. I realise how traumatic this must be. Would you like some tea?'

'Thanks, my mouth is caked dry. I've been teaching all day and this is a strain. The smell of the rum on his breath comes back to me in my nightmares.'

Boomer stopped. 'Townsend, go out and fix tea.' On his return, he was informed of what had been said in his absence. As Barney read the crucial evidence recorded without a third party to witness its veracity, two giant woodlice crept across the table where he sat. His skin crawled and, as he swept them away with a pen, Billy tapped his watch. A country song leapt into his mind. There was a time to hold them and a time to fold them. Barney ripped a page from the file and replaced the rest.

16

THE OLYMPIC AIRWAYS flight had departed from Athens on schedule at midday Saturday and arrived at Heathrow after two o'clock local time. Ellie had booked on a five o'clock BA flight to Belfast. Security measures delayed take-off for over two hours. The time was spent queuing in a crowded corridor with irate passengers on the verge of blowing a fuse in the stench and heat. It was almost eleven o'clock before she arrived home.

She went straight to bed after a cursory look at her mail and did not wake until late morning. She walked to the corner shop and bought milk, bread, potatoes and eggs. The assistant congratulated her on the tan. After Assam tea with toast, Ellie unpacked her bags and rechecked her post. There had been nothing personal as expected, simply two utility bills and a bank statement.

In the afternoon, she washed dirty clothes and hung them out to dry in the sunny back garden. She thought of visiting her friend in the area but, on a Sunday afternoon, all the relatives would be there. Ellie knew that the visit would lead to a lengthy interrogation and she did not feel up to it. When the doorbell rang at four o'clock, she had been at the rear of the house emptying the washing machine. Returning to the front, she heard the insistence of the doorbell and the bang of the brass knocker. Perhaps a neighbour had taken delivery of a parcel and had become aware of her return. Ellie was surprised to see a fit-looking guy of her own age standing on the doorstep. She noted the trainers and long shiny black hair. Who was he and what could he want? The answers were slow to come.

Matt apologised. 'I'm sorry for disturbing you.'
'How can I help you?'
'This may sound strange but don't be alarmed. My name is Matt Quinn. I used to go to a school near here. This house attracted my attention many years ago. It was always deserted and I've often wondered about its history. I was in the neighbourhood and curiosity got the better of me when I noticed it was occupied.'

'I've been here since April. I would ask you in but I don't know you.'

Matt showed her his Ulster College Pass. 'Perhaps I could call again sometime although I'd understand if you told me not to bother you.'

Ellie studied the pass. 'No, please come in. As it happens, I also am very interested in the history of this house. Let me hear your story first and we'll see how things develop.'

Matt thanked her for her time. 'I'm not sure where to begin. When I was a young lad, I heard a story about a woman who had been found dead in mysterious circumstances in this area. The crime has never been solved.'

'When did this happen?'

'In the late winter of 1953.'

'You think it was this place.'

'An intuition.' He hesitated. 'Some weeks ago, I came into business contact again with a friend from the past. We were talking about old times and the story came up.'

'He knew about it as well?'

'Yes. As a matter of fact, we both heard the story at the same time.'

'When would this have been?'

'Oh, years later. I should tell you that the person who told us the story died and left us some money. That's how we came to meet up...in a lawyer's office.'

'I was about to make tea. Would you like some?'

'If it's not too much trouble.'

She returned with tea and biscuits. 'I've only been here for two months. It needed substantial redecoration. Most of my spare time has been spent on it.'

'I can see you've been busy. Did you buy it from an old couple?'

Ellie smiled. 'We'll come back to that shortly, if you don't mind. I sense you've more to give me.'

'Sorry, slap me down if I get too inquisitive.' Matt sipped his tea. 'We needn't go into all the background. Our benefactor was a priest who received a visitor one freezing Saturday night. The man said that he had deserted from the British Army and had been a stowaway on the *Princess Victoria*.'

'Some kind of ship, you mean?'

'You've never heard of it?'

'No, I'm afraid not.'

Matt related the history of the tragedy. 'The soldier explained that he had been one of the survivors. Before the ship sank, an older man befriended him and offered to help when he got ashore. He gave him an address where a woman would look after him.'

'It all sounds very intriguing.'

'The woman gave him lodging and looked after him. One Saturday morning, he found her dead. There was a large poppy bruise on her forehead.'

'What happened then?'

'He fled.'

'Why did he go to your friend...this benefactor of yours?'

'I told you he was a priest.'

'May I ask his name?'

'Wilson.'

Ellie knocked over her cup and saucer. She felt a faintly feeling overwhelming her. He caught her before she fell. When she recovered, he poured fresh tea.

'I had a long day yesterday and haven't fully recovered.' She remembered thinking that she could have been in big trouble. 'I haven't told you anything about myself. Please, sit down. I'm fine.'

'I'll call back another time.'

'No, it's OK. Finish your story.'

Matt sat back and continued. 'Wilson gave him a bed for the night. On Sunday, he advised him to go back and make a clean breast of the matter to the Army. As he was innocent, he should have nothing to fear. The soldier appeared to agree. He never saw him again.'

'What about the dead woman?'

'Wilson made discreet enquires and informed the police.'

'Did they find her?'

'Nobody knew anything about it. Or if they did, they never came forward.'

'You believe a murder was committed in this house. I knew there was a string attached when I moved in here. What else have you got?'

'About seven years later, the body of a woman was found gagged and bound in the River Lagan. A police investigation revealed a connection with a house in this neighbourhood. A house that had been vacant for many years. There was an old blood stain but, as I said before, the crime was never solved.'

'I haven't told you my name.' She saw his mouth fall open. 'You seem surprised. May I ask why?'

'Sorry, something else came into my mind.'

'You knew that I was American?'

'I thought so although there is a strain of Irish in your voice.'

'I'll take your remark as a compliment. I was born here but my mother returned home to the US when I was very young. My parents are divorced for longer than I can remember.' She told her story much as it had been related to Josh Gilbert and the Trewsdales. The Wilson part was omitted. There was something weird behind all this and Ellie did not feel confident about giving too much away to Matt Quinn despite her growing attraction.

'You were going to tell me who you bought this place from?'

'I didn't buy it. You've got my background. When I was back here for a while, someone discovered my existence...an old friend of my father's. We haven't met. The person seems reluctant to do so. A letter informed me that my father had died many years ago and left me my birthplace.'

When Matt returned home, his mother was preparing Sunday high tea of cold ham, lettuce, sliced tomatoes and hard-boiled eggs. 'I woke up at five and you had disappeared. Where did you go?'

'I knew you wouldn't surface for a while. Got the hood down and went for a drive. Nowhere special.'

'I'm going to visit an old friend who's not too well. When are you going back?'

'Not until tomorrow. I slept really well last night.'

She gave him a piercing look. 'There's something bothering you. I can always tell. You can't hide anything from me, son.'

'You read too much into things. There's nothing worrying me,' he lied. 'The Halls can get very noisy at nights and make it difficult to sleep.'

'It's nothing to do with this dead girl, is it? Did you know her better than you're admitting?'

'No, I didn't know her well. The police have been questioning everyone. You know what it's like.'

'I'm glad I don't. I'll be back in an hour or two. Don't wash up.' When she had gone, Matt washed the dishes and left them to drain. He read the remainder of the *Sunday Times* but found it hard to concentrate. Barney would be in the York Hotel. He could phone in the morning to tell him to postpone his visit to the hospital. The girl's image floated before his eyes. Dark hair, blue eyes, tanned skin, classy accent. If only there weren't the complications.

He thought back to his afternoon visit. Barney would have played it cooler. Ellie Sullivan had recognised the Wilson name. She knew far more than she had admitted to him. When she had given him her name, *he* had been rattled.

He dried off the dishes and replaced them. A depression came over him. They had agreed to meet again. He had suggested a drink some evening. After explaining that she was just back from a vacation in Greece, she had given him her contact number at the Royal Victoria Hospital where her schedule would be confirmed. Matt imagined the phone call. 'I'm sorry that I can't go for our drink. A girlfriend has been found strangled, dressed only in a nurse's cape. The police have arrested me on suspicion of her murder.'

He switched on the television. There was nothing of interest on either BBC or UTV. At the back of a cupboard, he found a bottle of Bushmills. It was three-quarters full. He poured two inches into a glass and filled the remainder with cold water. The whiskey gave him a buzz and instilled a more positive view.

Ellie knew her name had shook him. She had not recovered from the final meeting with Gilbert. She would have to wait for his letter. She liked Matt Quinn but he was hiding something. It would have been great to meet again without the hidden agenda, but it couldn't remain secret for long. Her thoughts turned to her schedule for the week and she prepared the starched uniform.

At eight o'clock she cooked a tortilla with fresh eggs and new potatoes. She drank the remains of a bottle of Spanish wine that had been opened a fortnight before. It was viler than Californian jug wine but it would help her to sleep.

It was after dinner before she thought about the identity card. When she had gone to the safety deposit box, it contained a letter, one thousand pounds in cash and the deeds of the house with keys attached. Perry, if that was his correct name, explained her right to the property. Ellie had been living in the special accommodation provided for nurses by the hospital. It had been a great relief to hand in a week's notice and move to her own home that had remained untouched for over twenty years.

On this Sunday evening, she walked around the house again. The story from this afternoon had skimmed the cream off her delight in restoring the mouldy property. The damp, the decrepit wallpaper, a greasy gas cooker had not filled her with despair. Rather, she had been motivated by the challenge. It was an advantage that it had not been gutted and filled with sixties garbage.

She needed a good night's sleep. The letter from Perry entered her mind again. It made the request to go to Syros and perform a simple act. He also advised that, in the event of trouble, she must make contact with Detective-Sergeant Barney Mulvey. The explanation ran to the back of the page. Ellie twisted on the squeaky mattress. She found in the bedside locker the King James bible and read again the story of doubting Thomas.

17

THE MESSAGE was passed to Barney as soon as he arrived in the barracks. 'Don't make your visit today. Ring me when you're free. M QUINN.' Barney assumed that Matt had been thinking on the same tramlines as himself. Let the girl settle in. Find out some more about her before pouncing. He made a mental note to phone Matt later in the afternoon. Billy paid for their sandwiches in the canteen and Barney excused himself. Back at his desk he studied the page ripped from Boomer's file. It sat like a firecracker in front of him.

The phone book contained only one Teeny in the area around Portglenone. A harsh voice answered. A few questions made it clear to Barney that this was not the same family. It was ten years ago when the assault had happened. The parents had been old and were possibly dead. Celia Teeny had met an older man called Joseph Toner who had a wine business. It sounded like a solid relationship. He had to assume that they had married and settled in Belfast. She had obtained a teaching post in a Dominican College. Once a teacher got settled in a secure post, Barney knew that they seldom moved unless they didn't have to work. He had enough to go on.

There was only one address in the local drinks industry with the name of Toner. He phoned on the pretext of needing a crate of booze for a party. The directory was incorrect. Toner had moved to a new site near the docks.

'Yes,' answered the receptionist, 'we can arrange it for you although we specialise in fine wine.'

'Perhaps I could drop in sometime. Who should I ask for?'

'It's a big order by the sound of it. Speak to the boss.'

'What was the name again?'

'Joe Toner. He will be back from lunch soon if you want to talk to him.'

Barney put down the phone. The directory included three Toners with the J initial. It had to be one of the two Belfast addresses. Barney looked at his watch. Two o'clock. A harridan replied at the first ring. It sounded as if she'd been expecting an obscene call. The second attempt elicited no response after ten trills. Toner could have gone home for lunch and was on his way back. His wife could be in College.

The phone at the school was not answered for some time. Barney knew from experience that this was not unusual and he waited patiently. A nun came to the phone. 'I've been trying to arrange private music lessons for my daughter. She plays the violin. I heard you had a Mrs Toner who provides lessons after school.'

'I believe she does but you can't contact her now. She'll be teaching. Ring at four o'clock.'

'Who should I ask for?'

'Mrs Celia Toner.'

In the early evening of the following day, Barney drove the Escort away from her home. The sycamores in the Avenue where she lived were in full foliage. He turned the corner at the end and parked beside a cherry tree and recalled the conversation.

'Come in, officer. I hope this won't take too long. My wife's had a tiring day.'

Barney put away his identification pass. 'I fully appreciate it, Mister Toner, but new evidence has come our way and we might be able to close the case with a little more work.' He was shown into a large living room. Expensive prints hung on the freshly painted walls.

Celia Toner offered tea which he declined. 'I would offer you something stronger at this time but I realise that you are on duty.'

Barney felt her cool appraisal of his flushed cheeks. 'It must have given you quite a jolt for me to contact you after all this time.'

'It was a shock. I hope you don't mind my husband sitting in. He is aware of the background.'

Barney looked across at Joe Toner, a man at least ten years older than his wife. He looked as if he had enjoyed the full fruits of his business. 'Of course not. I can assure you that I'm only trying to clear the case up.'

Celia Toner crossed her elegantly clad legs. 'After all this time, you've identified my attacker?'

'It's not so simple. I'd like to go over some details with you, especially the conversation in the few minutes before the actual assault. Take your time. I realise how difficult it must be after all these years.'

'I'll never forget it. It took its toll on my parents.'

'You mentioned on the phone that they had died some years ago.'

'About two years afterwards. They died within months of each other.'

'You have no other family...apart from your husband?'

'My older sister, Liz. She emigrated to America after the Second World War. I had a letter recently from her son. She's very ill. It brings us back to your question.'

Barney shifted uncomfortably in the leather armchair. 'I'll explain as much as I can to you later. I was going over the evidence again in connection with a related case. Something that you said towards the end of your statement caught my attention.'

Celia Toner recalled what had happened. 'I remember asking him about the obituary notice. Wilson said I'd got it wrong... my father had placed an advertisement in the *Irish News* seeking information about the whereabouts of someone.'

'We don't know that it was Wilson.'

'I realise you must be careful, Sergeant Mulvey. Let me proceed.'

'I'm sorry. Go on.'

'I told him *he'd* got it wrong. The person who had placed the advertisement was myself. I'd had no responses but intended to keep searching.'

Barney glanced down at his notebook. 'This was before he hit you with a...?'

'Claw hammer.' She fingered her scar.

'Let's go back to the advertisement. Fill me in on the background.'

Celia Toner closed her eyes and tilted back her head. 'I'd spent the previous summer in America. My first base there was with my sister whom I mentioned earlier. She lived in New York with her husband, John McWilliams. They'd married before emigrating. I stayed with them for a fortnight before taking the Greyhound bus from coast to coast. I had arranged to fly home from Los Angeles.'

'That must have been a great year to make the trip.'

'Yes, it was. There was a heightened mood despite the Vietnam war. Everyone seemed to be rebelling against the system, especially in New York and San Francisco. The Mid West was rather different. We'll not go into the whole trip.'

Barney flipped over a page of his notebook. 'Take your time.'

'The two relevant events happened in New York and San Francisco. Now, where shall I begin?'

'I'd like to know everything. It might be important.'

'Liz and John had one child named Augustine. Everyone called him Gus. He was in his early teens at the time of my visit. If it wasn't for his mother's illness, he might have been visiting us this summer. Sorry, I'm digressing.'

'It's OK. If you think it's relevant...'

'Gus was a bright lad and, for his scientific subjects, they'd moved him in with older pupils. He had become friendly with a girl in her mid-teens. She was called Lucia. I can't remember her surname.'

Barney broke off from his note taking. 'I assume it doesn't matter.'

'It might.'

'Go on.'

'She didn't know her real name.'

'You mean that she had been brought up by foster parents.'

'She had only recently found out the truth.'

Barney looked up. 'Is it relevant?'

Celia Toner answered coolly. 'I believe so. The person whom she assumed to be her father had died many years before. Her mother had died earlier in the year of my visit and she only discovered the truth afterwards.'

'Who was looking after her?'

'The sister of her foster mother. There was conflict between them when the truth emerged.'

'I'm not surprised.' Barney waited.

'Lucia was a mature young woman. Very feisty. She had used some of her inheritance to hire private investigators to track down her real parents.'

Barney scratched his head. 'Those characters can be pretty shady.'

'Over here, maybe. In America, many of them are very professional. In any case, the search had not been productive. One of the agencies thought that they might have a lead as far away as California.'

'It would be expensive to follow up?'

'Yes. Lucia knew that I was going to San Francisco later in the summer. She asked me to check with the local agency branch.'

'Did it lead anywhere?'

'It may be the reason why you are sitting in front of me.'

'Would you like to break for a few minutes?' Barney looked across at Joe Toner who was nursing a glass of whiskey. Her husband nodded.

Celia Toner disagreed. 'No, I'd like to finish off. There's not much more.'

Barney shrugged. 'OK, keep going.'

'I spent some weeks crossing the States. I loved San Francisco. By the time I got there, I'd almost forgotten about Lucia and her problems until, one day, I passed an office of the Pinkerton Agency and remembered her plight. I did my duty as a friend and followed up on her plea.'

'You found her parents?'

'No. The investigator had a lead on Lucia's mother from the documentation he'd been given although he wasn't wholly convinced.'

'What about her father?'

'The agent's theory was that the relationship had been a fleeting one. If he was correct, Lucia's mother had become pregnant by an Irish businessman. The investigator believed that Lucia's father had returned home to Ireland.'

'Can you recall the name?'

'Of course. We'll come to it in a moment. At first, I thought of giving what I knew to Lucia. Then I had the smart idea of doing some detective work myself.'

'Not in America?'

'When I returned home in the late summer, I placed an advertisement in the newspaper seeking information on the whereabouts of the father. It included a brief outline of what the agency investigator had given me.'

Barney held his breath. 'And the name was?'
'Jack Sullivan.'

Barney longed for a drink but fought the craving. He wondered if he could get an advance from Charlie Boyle. Leaning back in the Escort he closed his eyes. The few grand would be welcome but the prospect of obtaining a substantial sum from the property sale was diminishing.

Boomer had been convinced that Wilson was guilty of both crimes, murder and a serious assault. As late as the Autumn of 1974, he had ventilated his rage, hinting at a cover-up. On the positive side, he had never been able to establish reasonable grounds for an arrest. However, it was going to be hard to prove a negative especially with the paperwork veering on the wrong side.

Barney opened his eyes and stared out of the windscreen at the big houses with their lush gardens in a tree-lined Avenue. His financial circumstances depressed him. He envied the Teenys with their elegant home, fine drink and no children to maintain. Two incomes and a quiet life. He knew he had to break the case in his own favour. It was the only way forward for him despite the risks. Rules would have to be broken. His concentration returned.

Wilson had been linked to the house where Teresa had been murdered. Only one witness had come forward. Boomer had probably realised that the pressure on such a person by a good barrister would discredit the evidence. Also, the Sullivan story had credibility. He owned the house where the murder had been carried out. The record demonstrated a man with a violent temper who had deserted from the Army. At the same time, he appeared to be a smart businessman and not just a thug who became violent in his cups. Sullivan would be intelligent enough to obtain a false passport and make intermittent visits to the United Kingdom. Barney snapped his fingers.

Sullivan could have obtained an Irish passport in Dublin. It wouldn't be difficult to land off a ship at Cork or somewhere and travel freely throughout the country. It would be more difficult in current times with the British Army manning the border. Barney thought of his last holiday. Despite the Troubles, there hadn't been much difficulty driving across from Donegal on an approved road, never mind an unapproved one.

Barney focused harder. What had be been thinking of? Worrying about Sullivan's difficulties in coming over the border was not relevant. The last reports of him had been in 1967, two years before the Troubles got going.

What else was unexplained? There was the girl who had been found dead at the rear of a Social Club in the previous Autumn. Boomer hadn't followed up on that one. Perhaps he had the real culprit identified. You never knew what was in Boomer's crafty mind. There was nothing to go on there.

Barney tossed it over in his mind. Sullivan owned the house. Boomer couldn't get away from that one. The assault on Celia Teeny had been as a result of her placing the advertisement in the *Irish News*. It had brought Sullivan out of the woodwork, just like a louse on a warm, wet night. He must have been in Ireland and read the newspaper. Someone is hunting for him. He gets paranoiac and decides to kill two birds with one stone...his usual strategy. However, a few slugs of rum are needed to fortify himself and he also has a compulsion to know more. Yes, Barney thought, it might all add up. He could put a case together and get a result...if it wasn't for what he had heard an hour before.

Celia Toner had been certain. Barney inhaled deeply. How could he explain it? The thought of losing all the money from the property sale oppressed him. She had to be wrong. There had to be a different explanation. Barney recalled the end of their conversation.

He would have given anything for a big slug of Toner's whiskey as Celia continued. 'I was ill for a long time afterwards and I never attached any particular relevance to what I've just told you.'

'You didn't connect it with the subsequent assault?'

'I assumed a maniac had been stalking me and the advertisement had been an excuse to gain entry.'

'The evidence demonstrated no sexual attack.'

Celia Toner looked across at her husband. 'You never know what such characters get up to when a woman is out cold. I've read about their antics. Also, they are clever enough not to leave samples.'

Joe Toner drained his whiskey. 'Please, Mister Mulvey, can't we move on? This is a massive strain for my wife.'

'I realise that, Mister Toner. I'll try to be as quick as possible. I've read through all the subsequent documents. In the following winter, you identified your assailant as Luke Wilson.'

Celia Toner uncrossed her legs. 'I can't remember the police officer's name. He seemed very keen to follow up but it all went nowhere.'

Barney saw his opportunity. 'Wilson served in the Navy where he made a serious enemy by the name of Jack Sullivan.'

'I wasn't given this piece of information but I can see why the investigation was dropped. I remember that there *was* a suggestion of impersonation.'

Barney pressed on. 'Our men would have given considerable weight to Wilson's story when you gave them the information about the advertisement. It tied in with everything he'd said...not only about your case but the trouble he'd been in before.'

'I heard all about it.'

'Don't you think it fits in?'

She looked away. 'I can see the logic of what you're saying. You said earlier that you had other new evidence.'

'I can't reveal it but it's all pointing in the right direction. I've heard nothing to make me believe that Wilson attacked you. Sullivan impersonated him.'

'Don't be so sure of yourself, Sergeant Mulvey.'

Barney stiffened. 'I just want to clear this case up.'

'I don't think it will be completed to my satisfaction.'

'Why not? We'll do our best.'

She recrossed her legs. 'When the police investigation fizzled out, I was extremely disturbed for a long time.'

Her husband interrupted. 'I persuaded my wife to forget about the whole matter and I'm glad to say that she did.'

'I suppose that I pretended, but you never forget.' She hesitated, then sighed. 'I've told nobody, not even my husband. I saw him again, you know.' Barney felt his stomach tighten. 'Wilson?' He looked across at Joe Toner replenishing his whiskey glass.

'Yes. I knew where he lived. It was dangerous for me but I had to find out the truth. One day, I parked my car outside his home. He was working in the garden. I picked up every ounce of courage I had, got out of the car and walked across to his front gate.'

Her husband swallowed his Bushmills. 'How did he react?'

'Our eyes met. He stood transfixed like a rabbit in a car's headlights. He knew that I knew.'

Barney's heart sank. 'Why didn't you tell the police team at the time? There was the DI who interviewed you. You said he seemed keen to nail Wilson.'

She looked at Barney. 'I'm not talking about ten years ago, Mister Mulvey. I saw him four months ago. He was guilty as sin.'

18

MATT'S HEADACHE subsided as he finished off bacon, eggs and soda bread. His mother hovered with additional helpings which he refused. 'You're not so talkative this morning,' she commented wryly. 'I noticed the bottle of whiskey has taken quite a beating. That's not like you.'

Matt worried that he had given too much away on Sunday night. 'I'll replace it as soon as I can.'

'Don't bother. I only have an occasional hot whiskey in the winter nights. You were in very good form, I must say.'

The fog in Matt's head cleared as he sensed that he was safe. 'It's always great to talk about old times. I never knew about your dispute with Mrs Mulvey.'

'She and I never got on. Too friendly with the men, even by today's standards. Don't let it turn you against your friend.'

'It's nothing to do with him. Anyway, it was a long time ago.'

'You might have told the full story about the will.'

'I'm sorry, but it's only a long shot. Barney and I may never be able to prove anything and I didn't want to worry you.'

'You'd be better concentrating on that girl you told me about last night. It's time you started to think about settling down.'

'I've only met her once. Don't read into it.'

'That's not the way you were talking last night. Tell me again how you came to meet her.'

Matt sighed with relief. 'We'll see how matters develop. I'll fill you in next week.'

'You're sure there's nothing eating at you?'

'Only my breakfast.' Matt looked at his watch. 'I'll have to be getting back.' He went upstairs to pack his bag. He kissed her on the forehead before leaving and said that he would call soon.

'Don't leave it too long.' She waved goodbye.

The depression of the previous evening returned in full force as he drove towards the Ulster College. A note pasted on his apartment door requested him to phone the number that he recognised only too well.

Before doing so, he tried Barney's number. DS Mulvey was working on a case. Did he want to leave a message? Matt phoned the other number.

'Patterson here. Ah yes. We were trying to contact you over the weekend. Thanks for getting back to me.'

Matt felt the sweat on his forehead. 'I was visiting my mother. She's a widow.'

'So we established. We'd like you to come in this afternoon. Say about four o'clock. There's a few matters we'd like to clarify. Bring your brief if you want.' He slammed down the phone.

Matt rang Boyle's office. Charlie and his partner were both in court. The receptionist, Irene, didn't know when they would be free. He felt anxious about going alone but didn't want the additional tension from cancelling the interview. The remains of the whiskey nibbled at his groin and he didn't have much trouble clearing it. He sat above the rising smell and groaned.

When it seemed that an eternity had passed, he looked at his watch. The minute hand had hardly twitched and he thought at first that it had stopped. Eventually, his brain moved into gear as he prepared himself for the coming ordeal. He considered all the angles. Ellie's image came into his mind.

At three-thirty, he locked up and walked to see Patterson. Arriving early, he was asked to sit on a plastic chair in front of the receptionist's viewing panel. A bald middle-aged man was the only other occupant of the dreary waiting area. The beech table between them was bereft even of old magazines. The guy asked him what he was in for. Matt mumbled that he had been a witness to a crime. He pressed no further and bent to tighten the laces on his shiny Doc Marten boots.

The receptionist pushed aside her glass aperture. 'Mister Quinn to Room 3.' The skinhead lifted his right thumb and winked as Matt got up.

Patterson pulled open the file in front of him. 'I see you haven't brought your solicitor. That should speed matters up.' Matt made no response and Patterson continued. 'Your prints were on the photograph and the envelope, but no surprises there.'

'Did you identify any other prints?'

'Yes but I can't tell you who they belonged to.'

'Do you mean you don't know or you won't tell me?'

'Let's leave it at that, shall we? The fact that the envelope has other fingerprints doesn't clear you. Don't rely on it. Now, we're not here to give you a hard time. My only purpose is to get at the truth. You weren't in her apartment on the night she died. I'll give you that.'

Matt interrupted. 'I was never in her apartment at any time in my life. It was her who came to pester me.'

'Pester? A bit strong, given what the two of you got up to on the night before she died.'

'I've explained it in my statement.'

'Think what a jury might make of it.'

'If you're going to continue to harass me, I'd better ring Boyle.'

Patterson's lips twitched. 'Cool down. I'm not accusing you. I'm only doing my job. See it from my point of view. I want to check over two matters and then you'll be free to go. OK?'

'Fine.'

'Let's go back to the Friday when you found this photograph.' Patterson looked down at Matt's statement. 'Fourth of June, late afternoon.'

'Correct.'

'When you returned to your office, was the door locked?'

Matt closed his eyes. 'Yes, it was. I'm positive.'

'When Watt returned later, did he try to unlock the door before realising it was open? I'm assuming you didn't lock it again.'

'No, I wouldn't have done that although some staff did if they were concentrating on a tight deadline and were being interrupted by casual callers. As to your question, I can't remember. Is it important?'

'It might be. Let's leave it. We've established that Watt locked the door earlier and, on his return, was surprised to see you.'

'Yes, I'd told him and Derek Scott that I was going to Coleraine for the reading of a will. When he saw me, he appeared flustered. I remember that he was quite flushed.'

'As if he'd been up to something and had expected the office to be empty.'

'Yes, that's it, although he said he'd been working on the computer terminal.'

'You didn't believe him?'

'I had no reason to think that he was lying. Why should I?'

Patterson kept pressing. 'We've heard all about Watt's shoe problem and the black scuff marks that he left as a trail behind him.'

Matt remembered. 'When I went to the computer room, there were no traces and yet the cleaner leaves sharp at five on Friday.'

'What did you think later when you opened the envelope?'

'Guess. He has this photograph in his possession and he's been off somewhere to have a good look at it.'

'This explanation doesn't hold up if his prints aren't on it.'

'Were his prints on it?'

'No.'

'And the envelope. Are you going to tell me whose prints you've found?'

'Our tests aren't complete. We've only identified yours.'

Matt sighed. 'Where is all this going? You knew that already.'

'Be patient, Mister Quinn. I have a good reason for asking these questions. Let's proceed. Just before you left the office, you saw the white envelope lying on the floor. What made you pick it up and take it away with you?'

'I wish I hadn't. My intentions were good. No matter who it belonged to, the cleaner could have come in early on Monday and disposed of it as rubbish. Anything found lying on the floor was at her mercy and yet it might have been important to someone.'

Patterson produced an icy grin. 'An understatement, you'd agree. Later on, curiosity rules. You persuade yourself that it could have been for you.'

'It crossed my mind. We usually pick up our own mail from the Departmental Office. Deirdre sometimes gives me post for the other two. If she's in a good mood, she'll deliver it herself.'

Patterson looked up at the ceiling. 'So, to come back to my question, you've explained why you put it in your pocket and opened it later. I have no more to ask you today about how you found the envelope. However, there's one other matter that I'd like to clarify.'

'I will if I can.'

Patterson flipped a page over. 'Let's move forward to the night before the murder. You and the victim had dinner and drinks in the Glenavna Hotel. Quite a bit to drink, I see.'

'We were both well oiled.'

'When you arrived, where did you go?'

'We went into the main bar. I ordered two large gins and asked to see the menu.'

'This would have been about seven-thirty?'

'Yes.'

'Did you recognise anyone?'

'There were two or three groups drinking there. I didn't know any of them personally. They seemed to be a mixture of strangers and locals.'

'Nobody from the College?'

'Not that I noticed. We weren't paying much attention.'

'Miss Neil didn't talk to any of the drinkers?'

Matt thought back. 'She went to the Ladies before we moved to the restaurant. I remember her smiling at one of the groups.'

'Did she comment on anyone in the bar?'

'No. Sue tried to be friendly with everyone. She would have smiled from politeness if someone caught her eye.'

Patterson looked down at the file. 'Then you walked to the restaurant together and were shown to the table that you reserved.'

'I told them not to squash us up in a corner. I like to have room to breathe when I'm eating.'

'How many others were there?'

'I remember that two other tables were occupied by couples. When we left, the place was crammed.'

'You drank white wine and then two bottles of expensive red wine.'

'It was very good Beaujolais. Nothing out of the ordinary.'

'I don't know about these fancy tastes. I don't touch the stuff.'

'I gathered that. Anyway, we drank too much. I can't be too specific about details later in the evening. I remember that the restaurant was full before we moved back to the bar where we had two Hennessys.'

Patterson looked down. 'You didn't mention it in your statement.'

'Didn't mention what?'
'You had more drink in the bar.'
'I thought that I had. Yes, I ordered two brandies to finish us off.'
'Around midnight.'
'It's a hotel. They have a late licence.'
'I'm not interested in harassing the Glenavna. Was the bar full?'
'Packed with Saturday night drinkers.'
'Did you or Miss Neil have a conversation with anyone in the bar?'
'I didn't.'
'Miss Neil?'
'Who knows? When I was trying to attract the barman's attention, she went to the Ladies. She was away for some time.'
'So she could have met and spoken to someone else without your knowing?'
'It's possible. She didn't mention it.'
'You were both well advanced by this time?'
'Yes. We left after the brandies.'

Patterson closed his folder. 'Thank you, Mister Quinn. You may go. We'll be in touch.'

On his way back, Matt stopped to buy a packet of Anadin Extra. Two were washed down with lager in the gloomy lounge bar of the Stag's Head. A tense day had resulted in a soft landing. Had there been a relaxation in Patterson's attitude or was he preparing a trap? Matt could not fathom the first line of questioning. As for the second, perhaps the police were following up on Barney's suggestion concerning the previous murder committed in the grounds of the Glenavna.

He ordered a second lager. The temptation to ring the girl returned. No, it was too soon. He would have to let the hare sit until mid-week. Barney had to be told about the meeting on Sunday. Matt hoped that he had taken his advice to postpone the visit to the Royal Victoria Hospital. Barney had done him a big favour by sending Patterson off in a different direction. He hadn't done enough to help his old friend. Barney needed all the money he could get and was doing most of the legwork to clear Wilson. Apart from the Examination Board meeting on Friday, he was free and knew that he should be pulling his weight more.

Matt finished his lager and returned along the coastal path. The tide was in and there was a briny smell of mussels. The grey water lapped against the pebbly beach. Across the Lough in Bangor, yachts bobbed in the evening sunshine. *Dover Beach* filled his mind to no purpose.

The Halls of Residence were silent. He let himself into his apartment. There were no messages pasted to the door. He wondered when Sue's funeral would take place. The fridge contained a pork chop which he fried in garlic butter and ate with new potatoes boiled in their skins. His mother was right. He needed a woman.

As he sipped Beaujolais-Villages with a slice of Coleraine cheddar, the memory that had been niggling Matt since Bloomsday resurfaced. Something Ellie Sullivan had said yesterday had stirred it but he had not been able to make sense of it. What exactly had she said before he left her? Matt froze in mid-sip and almost dropped the cold glass.

'How can you be certain that this is the house where the murder was committed?'

'I didn't say that I was certain, although I'm pretty sure. I hope it hasn't put you off it.'

'It was over twenty years ago. Why should it bother me if it was the same place?'

'Surely you must see...' Matt hesitated. 'If it was, your father owned the house at the time. He must have done.'

'You're accusing him of killing Teresa.'

'He's an obvious suspect.'

'The stowaway might have been the killer. He was on the run from the Army. Surviving the boat tragedy provides him with an opportunity to disappear without trace. The authorities will never know if he's alive or dead.'

Matt broke in. 'What's this got to do with your home?'

'This place is within walking distance of the City Centre. He comes ashore and gets a ride into Belfast. Then he walks north of town looking for somewhere empty to break into.'

'How do you explain Teresa?'

'He finds this house, keeps his head down and settles in. He was in the Army and would be well trained for survival. Somehow he meets her and she moves in as well. Eventually they have a row. She threatens to turn him in and he whacks her.'

Matt saw the sense of what Ellie was saying. 'It's possible. He goes to Wilson and confesses as part of his cover-up operation. Yes, I admit the police would find it plausible.'

'You don't seem convinced. I don't want to remember my father as a murderer.'

'I didn't say he was. I'm sorry. I've caused you pain. I'll leave.'

She called his bluff. 'No, please. I hardly knew my father. My mother told me how he was when he'd been drinking too much. One time he slapped her so hard that he scored her cheek with his wedding ring. I guess it was the final straw for her. It's possible that he killed this woman.'

19

RAIN BATHED the rainbow, reminding Ellie of the time she had spent in the Catskill mountains on an Autumn break from the New York hospital. Summer in the city had been swelteringly hot and humid. At night, the roaches invaded the plastic bags carrying the detritus from the wards. When the air-conditioning broke down, the seconds ticked by on an eight hour shift. There was an oppressive hum of stale urine battened down by carbolic. As she returned on the bus from Belfast City Centre, a thunderstorm had broken the long spell of sunshine. Walking from the bus, Ellie saw in the distance the rainbow settling across the gantries. She let herself in with the new Yale key and thought about having a shower before she remembered. If she was going to remain here, that was going to be a necessity. A stodgy meal in the hospital canteen had stifled hunger. She changed and made tea.

On her return from lunch, Sister had come on duty and chided her about the loss of her identity card. 'How did you catch on so quickly?' Ellie asked.

'About a week ago, I was in the Reception area when the grump who works there told me that a man had been looking for you. He'd found your ID in the York Hotel.'

Ellie wondered whether the bait had attracted the right fish. 'I apologise for losing it. We were having a drink to send me off on my vacation. I must have grown careless. I'll make sure it doesn't happen again.'

'I think he was hoping to meet you. Your photograph must have tickled his fancy.'

'What makes you think so, Sister?'

'He said you could buy him a drink the next time you were in the Hotel.'

'What did he look like?'

'How do you expect me to know, Nurse Sullivan? I wasn't there. I believe he left his contact details at Reception. You can check before you leave. It can wait. We have work to do. Let's go.'

When she had finished for the day, the guy had already gone. His female colleague remembered Ellie's caller and rooted in a drawer for the information. Ellie waited patiently and then threw the slip of paper into her bag without betraying anything to the clerk. She left the building, stopped and retrieved it. The hook had clasped the right palate.

Ellie sipped her Green Label tea and matched the contact details with those that had been provided by Perry. After getting his letter, she had been careful. Then, one evening, after the good spell of weather had started, she had walked from the hospital to College Green. There were benches for visitors to sit beside the manicured lawns. On her second trip, she had struck gold. A police car pulled up beside a red Escort and a plump man in his mid-twenties climbed out. She had expected him to go into the address that she had been given. Instead, he stood on the pavement until the squad car had gone out of sight. Then, he turned in the opposite direction. Ellie rose and followed but, within a few minutes, DS Mulvey had reached his destination. She guessed that it would be foolish to wait.

She worked out her next step as she finished her tea. The timing would depend on the next move of Matt Quinn. She had not expected that he would contact her immediately but he would probably make his call before the weekend. Normally, she would have stalled to keep him keen but there was no time for games.

A murder had been committed in this house over twenty years ago. Supposing her father had done it and the stowaway's story was true. He goes to Wilson, then disappears. Nothing happens until Ellie returns to Ireland, meets Wilson and sparks a new cycle of action via Perry. She gets her legacy. The gaps tormented her.

After his visit to the Toners, the blues gripped Barney. He drove home and made a dinner of sausages and mash potatoes that did little to ameliorate his mood. A mug of black Maxwell House revived him as he studied Boyle's file. Charlie had made a brief note in 1969 concerning his inability to contact Wilson. Barney wondered what had initiated this particular enquiry. There was no follow-up and so he assumed that it had been Boomer making a final attempt before moving to Belfast. After his transfer, he would have had plenty of other matters to occupy his time.

In November 1973, Boyle had been contacted by Wilson who had had an unexpected home call from Ballymena police. They were following up an enquiry from Belfast concerning the murder of a girl behind a Social Club. On this occasion, the priest had had an iron alibi and could not possibly have been involved. He had then been left alone until 1976 when Charlie recorded their final meetings. The file notes correlated with the meeting that Billy Craig had told him about. The record of it would be in Boomer's folder in the storeroom. He needed another session with it. The page that Barney had ripped out would also have to be replaced although he hoped that Boomer had lost interest. He must have found out from Kerr that Wilson was dead, although it wouldn't stop him if evidence was produced to close the case.

Barney concentrated on Charlie's notes from earlier in the year. Wilson had arranged a meeting with the solicitor in March. When he arrived, it was clear that he was in bad shape. His doctor had put him on a course of Diazepam. Charlie had attempted to elicit the reasons for the black mood. Wilson hadn't been feeling well for some time and feared the worst. It was imperative that he made a will and he wanted his good name cleared for posterity. He had thought of a method of doing it.

It touched Barney that Wilson should have thought of him and Matt. He broke off to make more coffee. As he did so, his will hardened. Celia Toner had to be wrong. A woman's intuition was all very well but wouldn't stand up in a court of law...and yet she seemed so positive. Right or wrong, she had probably frightened the priest into his grave. If he didn't know already, he'd have found out who she was and guessed the reason for her confrontation.

The last meeting with Boyle had finalised the details of the will. Wilson had appeared in a more relaxed mood and Charlie had put this change down to an increased intake of medication. Afterwards, a bottle of Lamb's Navy rum had been produced as they talked about old times.

Barney finished his coffee and looked out across College Green. Last night's rain had nourished parched lawns. He thought about Matt's message advising him to postpone his visit to the girl. Matt must have found something out about Ellie Sullivan. Barney banged the side of his head with his right palm. Wilson had meant him to have the money. There was no way that he could have murdered someone.

On Wednesday, Matt rang the hospital at midday. 'Ward 6, please. I'd like to speak to Nurse Sullivan.' He rubbed his stomach as he waited for a response.

'Ellie Sullivan here. Can I help you?'

'It's Matt Quinn. I was ringing to see if you might fancy a drink over the weekend.'

'Great. Which night do you suggest?'

'Friday? I could pick you up at eight o'clock.'

'Fine. I'll see you then.'

Matt's nerves settled. As he turned away from the call box in the Halls of Residence, the phone rang. It was Barney. Matt explained that he wouldn't have time to meet on Thursday as he had to make final preparations for an Examination Board meeting on Friday.

'What about tonight?...York Hotel. Fine.'

When they met, Barney was in an edgy mood. 'Can you get the drinks in, Matt? I'm short of cash. I'll have to see if the manager will cash a cheque for me.'

Matt ordered two bottles of Red Heart for Barney and lager for himself. 'If you're strapped, Barney, I can bail you out.'

Barney sank the first bottle of Guinness in two swallows. 'I might take you up on that, Matt. You know how I'm fixed. Jean never eases off the pedal and I've got to keep the two places going. The sooner I get the money from Boyle, the better.'

'Anything else bothering you, Barney?'

'There was something I wanted to check before meeting again.' Barney elaborated about Boomer and the file. 'I had a tip-off that he would be away tomorrow morning and I was going to do it then. I should have waited. Instead, I took a chance late this afternoon.'

'What happened?'

'I replaced what I'd stolen and made a quick check on what I needed to know. I locked up but, as I crossed the yard towards the station, I ran straight into Boomer.'

'Did he ask you where you'd been?'

'Didn't need to. I was expecting him to question me. When he smiled and turned away, I felt even worse. I don't know what his game is.' Barney wiped froth from his mouth. 'I was dying for this. We'll forget about Boomer and we have a lot to talk about. You first. What have you got for me?'

Matt updated him on the meeting with Patterson. 'I think you've put him on a different scent so thanks for that, old friend.'

'Thank God I'm some use to a mate. Anyway, now that you've got it out of the way, you can relax for a few days. Go on, tell me your news.'

Matt told him about the meeting on Sunday afternoon. 'When she explained who she was, I was stunned and she knew it. However, she lost her cool once the Wilson name came up. We'll have to find out why.'

'How do you propose to do that?'

'She's agreed to go for a drink with me on Friday night.'

'You don't waste much time. Red mist again?'

'I wouldn't say that, Barney, but she certainly looks the part. I think I'd better come clean with her and tell her what we're after.'

'You didn't mention me?'

'No, so that's going to be awkward. She hasn't tried to reach you?'

'No...I didn't go over to see her after your phone call.'

'We'll have to tighten up, Barney, and keep in closer contact.'

'I know, Matt, I know. I'm under a lot of pressure.'

'Barney, you need the money more than me. We've got to get our act together. After Friday, I'll have plenty of time on my hands.'

Barney smiled. 'So you hope, Matt. What about another round? I feel better already.'

Matt sketched out a course of action. 'I'll tell her who you are and where we're coming from.'

'Slow down, Matt. You'll need to play it by ear. See if she gives a little herself and responds in kind. You're not stupid. You know what I mean.'

'Trust me, Barney. Tell me more about Boomer's file.'

'I've told you about the assault on Celia Teeny and the investigations that followed.'

'You've tracked her down?'

'We'll come to it. She recovered and obtained a teaching post in North Belfast...a Dominican College. One day, Wilson was visiting and she thought she recognised him as her attacker.'

'Did she report it?'

'She sent an anonymous letter to Boomer but he twigged on where it had come from. He contacted her, she was interviewed and admitted sending it. She gave him her reasons.'

'They didn't stand up?'

'I think Boomer believed her but, when she gave him her full story, the waters became muddy.'

'How come?'

Barney explained about the trip to America and the advertisement in the newspaper. 'You can see what happened, Matt. It supported the story that Sullivan was out there somewhere and didn't want to be found. She'd shot herself in the foot.'

'That's all to our benefit.'

'Not quite. As you guessed, I've found her. She married a guy called Joseph Toner. Very big in the wine trade.'

'I recognise the name. Very reputable dealer.'

'I rang up and they agreed to see me. A very attractive woman. He's a few years older.'

'Did you learn anything more from her?'

Barney swirled the remains of his Red Heart around the bottom of his glass and told Matt what she had said. 'It's depressing. She's convinced herself that it was him.'

'Did she follow it up as she had before?'

'She was reluctant to stir the pot and she realised that she had no proof. One day, the obituary notice appeared. She saw it and decided to drop the matter. She'd had her revenge. He was in bad health and the meeting probably was the final straw.'

'Do you believe her, Barney?'

'No, she has to be mistaken. Can't prove a thing, especially now that he's dead.'

'It doesn't make it any easier for us, Barney. Maybe we *are* fooling ourselves. There's something else I haven't mentioned. It's been eating at me. It was something that Ellie Sullivan said. We'll have one for the road and you can tell me what you think.'

20

FRIDAY AFTERNOON was warm but overcast. She washed her breakfast dishes in the white enamel sink and scrubbed the gas cooker. Afterwards, she had a bath and washed her hair. There had been no suggestion of dinner later. She cooked wholemeal pasta and ate it with a light tomato sauce. One glass of red wine accompanied the meal. With a half-hour to spare, she thought of the evening ahead.

He arrived sharp at eight o'clock. She saw from her front window that he had had a haircut and wore brown brogue shoes instead of trainers. She smoothed down her pressed Levi jeans and adjusted her white linen blouse before opening the door. The yellow Spitfire gleamed in the evening sunshine. Without asking her whether she minded, he removed the soft hood from the car. The leather seats felt cool.

'I thought that we might drive outside town to a traditional pub. When I say traditional, I mean it.'

'I'm in your hands.' The wind wrecked her hair as she enjoyed the ride out into open country. As the car roared down rural lanes between foaming hawthorn hedges, she was assaulted by the powerful smell of slurry. They came to a crossroads and Ellie saw to her right a thatched house with whitewashed walls. The car pulled over and stopped. She saw two crossed keys inscribed on a sign swinging above the entrance.

Matt got out of the car and put up the hood. 'The passenger door sticks. Let me give you a hand. I hope you like this place. It's one of the few genuine ones left.' He pushed open the front door and let her pass.

Two farmers nursed pints of brown ale in the public bar. She followed Matt into a back lounge. A barmaid wearing an apron came to ask them for their orders.

'Two bottles of Harp, please,' said Matt.

'I can't guarantee they'll be cold. I'll see what I can do.'

There was only one other couple drinking. Ellie heard the man request two more Bacardis and a bottle of Coca-Cola. Faded hunting prints hung on the yellow walls. A battered piano sat in a far corner of the room.

Matt grinned. 'Probably not what you're used to. The place will fill up soon and there's usually a music session on Friday night.'

She relaxed. 'It's great. Very atmospheric.' Ellie waited for him to begin. 'I didn't expect it to be so isolated. Where exactly are we?'

Matt sipped his lukewarm lager. 'The nearest town is called Portglenone. It's about twenty minutes drive from the pub.'

He hadn't wasted much time, she thought. This could prove to be a surprising evening. 'I spent some time in upper New York State. In the middle of nowhere, you sometimes found a spit-and-sawdust bar that wouldn't serve females.' She paused. 'OK, Matt. Let's not beat about the bush. What are you hiding?'

He looked around the smoke-stained room. 'It's been a long day. I had an Examination Board meeting at eight o'clock and we didn't finish until late afternoon. We heard yesterday that the External Examiner wanted to meet a cross-section of the students. It caused a panic.'

'How did they perform?'

'They all passed. I'm not avoiding your question. I was looking forward to seeing you again but I was worried.'

'Why?'

'When you told me your name, it rocked me. I should have given you the whole story.'

'I guessed you were holding something back. As a matter of fact, so was I but I'll tell you later. Let's hear what you've got to say.'

Matt retraced the story leading up to Teresa's death. 'You didn't ask me about the man who the stowaway met on the *Princess Victoria*. Later, you told me your father's name. We believe that they are the same person.'

'We?'

Matt ordered two more lagers. 'That's something else you didn't ask me on Sunday.' He explained to her about Barney and how they had met again in Boyle's office. Her eyes dropped.

'So that's your motivation. Don't worry. It doesn't bother me. I've been brought up in the States. I know how it is. Is that all you have to tell me?'

'There's more but there's something I need first. How did you know Wilson?'

'I didn't.' Ellie explained how she had come to meet the priest in the hospital and the follow-up. 'After you left on Sunday, I had to think everything out. If it was the same guy, it explained why he'd never contacted me again. When I saw him for the last time, he didn't look in good shape. What you've told me fills in some of the gaps.'

'When did you hear that your father had left you the property?'

'In April. I assumed that Wilson had mentioned my existence to someone and sparked off a chain reaction.' Ellie told him about the letter. 'I assume the name at the bottom was false.'

'What was it?'

'A Perry.' She watched him choke. 'Are you OK? Do you know someone by that name?' His response made her swallow hard.

Two violinists joined in a set of reels as the bar lounge filled up. Ellie began to speak but Matt advised her to remain silent until the music had stopped. The pause in conversation gave them both time to think. In the break, he began. 'I'm finding it hard to take in. Perry was also the name of the stowaway.'

'How can you be certain?'

Matt told her how he had obtained the name from Kerry. 'He thought that it was a pseudonym as well.'

Ellie sipped her lager. 'I suppose that it makes some kind of sense. My father helped this guy and maybe they became friends. By the way, my mother never told me that my father was a deserter.'

'She probably didn't know.'

'I can check it out.' Ellie hesitated. 'There's something else I must tell you. When I was in Greece, I met this man Gilbert. It doesn't matter how. Before I left, I told him part of my background. He got rattled.'

'Maybe he's the link.'

'He also knew Wilson well. I'm convinced of it.'

'Did he tell you how?'

'There wasn't time. My ferry was coming in. When he'd recovered his composure, he said that he would write to me.'

'He's expected back in August.'

'He's an odd guy.'

'Let's see what the letter says.'

'You want to read my mail?'

Matt apologised. 'I was getting carried away.'

'I was kidding. I'm as anxious now as you are to solve this whole thing.'

'One of them murdered Teresa. There's more that you need to be told. It will take time. Shall we move? These guys don't like conversation when they're playing.'

'Let's see Wilson's house. I guess that's what you had in mind in bringing me up here.'

'Let's go.'

As the violinists fiddled, Barney sat parched. His salary would go into his bank account at midnight but that wasn't much good to him now. He could have tried his luck again with Doug Stewart but decided against. Instead, he prepared Maxwell House coffee, adjusted his armchair and looked out over College Green as the light faded. He had had a frantic two days.

By lunchtime on Thursday, Barney had convinced himself that he had escaped Boomer's attention. As he was about to go to the canteen, the phone rang. 'Inspector Boomer would like you to come round right away,' said the girl with a voice like a jackhammer. 'Drop everything.'

Barney did as he was instructed. He rapped twice and entered. 'You wanted me, Sir?'

'Sit down, Sergeant Mulvey. I'd like to have a chat with you before you get yourself into big trouble.'

'Sir?' Barney sat ramrod straight and kept his nerve, on the outside at least.

'When I first found Craig and you out in the store together, I let it pass. I can't keep a continual eye on all my men and, when I'm out of the station, I have to trust them to carry on with their allotted duties.'

Barney detected a conciliatory note. 'You can be certain of it, Sir.'

Boomer's eyes twitched. 'I'm not out to carpet you, Mulvey. You have the making of a good career, especially the way things are going.'

'I take it you have a concern, Sir?' He tried to control the rumbling in his stomach.

'I'll get to the point, Mulvey. Little that goes on in this station escapes my attention. Don't forget it.'

'I don't, Sir.'

'When I found out that you were out there again on Monday morning, I bided my time. Then when I discovered yesterday that you were making a habit of it, I had to act.' Boomer raised his right palm in the air to halt Barney's protest. 'When you find yourself in a hole, stop digging. Before you say a word, I must tell you that I've spoken to Craig.'

Barney's shoulders sagged. 'I asked him to help me. It wasn't his fault.'

'I'm aware of that, Mulvey. Let's get down to brass tacks. What's your side of the story?'

Barney explained his motivation. 'I'll make up the time, Sir. You know that.'

'You should have come to me in the first place. It would have saved us all the wasted effort.'

'I'm sorry, Sir. I assumed...'

Boomer smiled. 'So, you think he was innocent?'

'I knew him well, Sir. He couldn't have done it.'

'You are a police officer, Mulvey. Emotion can't come into an investigation. On this occasion, I'm going to let your time wasting pass but don't do it again.' Boomer glanced at his watch. 'Would you like to join me for sandwiches? I'll get the girl to fetch some. Then I will tell you why you're wrong.'

Boomer sank his teeth into a ham sandwich and began. 'When the Belfast boys first interviewed Wilson, he was nervous but not to an unusual degree. However, his demeanour was enough to make them suspicious that he was hiding something. When a woman made a statement that she'd seen him going into the house, they raided the place.'

Barney swallowed. 'And found a blood stain.'

'They eventually matched it with the remains of the dress clinging to the dead woman's skeleton.'

'Did they identify her?'

'No, but samples have been retained in the Regional Forensic Laboratory. If progress continues to be made with DNA profiling, we might be able to do something with them.'

'What about fingerprints?'

'Good question, Mulvey, and it made them even more suspicious. There were none. The house had been scrubbed clean of those. Wilson could have gone in and wiped everything.'

'What did he say when they interviewed him again?'

'You've seen the file. I tracked down the interviewing officer when the second case came up. His memory was hazy. Reading between the lines, I suspect that Wilson simply said that the woman had to be mistaken. Then, when the house was proven to belong to Sullivan, it supported Wilson's original story. They had to drop the case and your friend scarpered to Portglenone.'

'He might have been terrified of Sullivan.'

'The officer involved was never satisfied. He felt that Wilson had got the better of him. On the other hand, he was a man of the cloth. He had to be pretty sure of his facts before charging him. It would never have stood up in court.'

'So the case was closed.'

'No. It's still open. There was no progress until the attack on Celia Teeny. You've read through my file. How much do you know?'

Barney gave him an outline without mentioning his recent visit. 'There's nothing solid, Sir. As far as I'm concerned, he's in the clear.'

Boomer paused. 'Don't forget, Mulvey. I conducted the interviews personally. I saw it in her eyes. She was positive.'

'The Ballymena police must have had her parents' home checked for fingerprints.'

'He was too cute for them as well. The place had been wiped again.'

Barney coughed. 'Sullivan could have done it. Wilson's story still holds. In many ways, even more so.'

'Yes, Mulvey, I agree that the advertisement business threw me. A good barrister would have seized on it. Our second case wasn't strong enough either.'

'Sir, what makes you think I'm wrong about his being innocent?'

Boomer wiped his mouth with a white handkerchief. 'Let's come to the third case in 1973...girl found dumped behind a Social Club.'

'He had a cast iron alibi.'

'Oh yes, he didn't do it. There was paramilitary involvement in that one.'

'Sir, what's the problem?'

'We received an anonymous letter accusing him of doing it.'

'It could have been Sullivan again.'

'The letter was typed. I had it placed in the file. You've probably seen it.'

'Yes, sir.'

Boomer produced a lopsided grin. He bent over and pulled open a drawer at the bottom of his desk. 'Have a look at this letter, Mulvey.'

Barney scanned it quickly. 'It's his original story typed out for the police in 1953.'

'Yes, Mulvey, and here is the anonymous letter that we've talked about. Compare the two. If you do it as well as I have done, you'll see they have been produced on the same typewriter.'

21

THE MOON shone on the back of Wilson's house. They sat on a bench beside a path that ran along the lush garden. 'Are you sure it's OK to do this?' Ellie shivered. 'You seem positive that nobody will hassle us.'

Matt smiled. 'We're not going to break in. I thought you might like to see it. Here, take my jacket.'

'Thanks. This place must be worth a lot of money. I'm not surprised you want to prove Wilson innocent.'

'I wouldn't do it if I thought he was guilty.'

'What else have you got to tell me?'

'He was linked with a second attack on a woman in 1966 and your father's name appears again. I will repeat what Barney has found out.'

Ellie gasped. 'If this story is true, I have a half-sister back home. What did you say her name was?'

'Lucia.'

'I have to meet Celia Toner.'

'It won't be easy. We'll have to talk it over with Barney.'

'You've taken my breath away.'

'You told me not to beat about the bush.'

'I'm not blaming you. I'm grateful.' Ellie looked up to see the moon split into two crescents by a purple haze. 'It's getting colder. This place is spooking me.'

'We'll go back to the car.' They walked to the white gates where the Spitfire was parked. He pulled the passenger door open. As Ellie climbed in she grasped his hand. He held it tightly for a few seconds.

She levered the seat back and closed her eyes. 'Any more surprises?'

Matt switched on full beam. 'We'll not meet much traffic on this route. I've told you most of what I know. I guess Barney and I have hit a stalemate.'

'If the murderer was my father, I have to know.'

'Let's switch to Perry.'

'If he's guilty, then he tried to fit up my father. It doesn't square with his letter to me.'

'Maybe your father is alive and he used the pseudonym as a smokescreen.'

Ellie was silent for a few minutes. 'I feel sure that he's dead. If your theory is true, it implies that Wilson contacted my father to inform him that he'd met me. Are you suggesting they made up and became pals again?'

'I guess you're right. It doesn't hold water.'

'Matt, I'm not sure how to begin...'

He heard the tremor in her voice. 'You need to think things out. It can wait.'

'No, I'd like to talk it out. You haven't asked me about my time in Greece.'

'You've told me about meeting Gilbert. Do you think he's involved in some way?'

'I don't know. We'll leave him until he writes to me. It's not what I meant.'

'I'm listening.'

'We've discussed Perry and I want to come back to him in a moment. Let's recap. My mother liked to tell me about how she'd met my father in Syros. She was fond of this period in her life. In their early time together, they were happy and I love to hold on to the memory. It was only later...when he returned to Ireland...that he reverted to type.'

'We're not all the same.'

'I didn't mean it like that. Perry knew about their time in Greece. He was aware of how they'd met. I was sure that he had been a close friend of my father. Men don't give those kind of details out to everyone.'

Matt grinned. 'Most Irishmen don't let them out to anyone, friend or not.'

'It makes it all the more convincing. I believe that Perry was acting in my interests.'

'Why so certain?'

'You can never be absolutely sure of anything, I suppose. It was Perry who asked me to go to Syros and to take photographs.'

'Motive?'

'I don't know. I did what he asked. On Wednesday, I left the film in to be processed. I'll have it back next week.'

'How are you going to get the photographs to him? You have no address for him.'

'The letters bore postmarks from Donegal. That's all I know. He wrote that he would get in touch with me when I returned.'

'He must have been in a good position to oversee your movements.'

'If he knew Wilson, it wouldn't have been difficult.'

'Wilson is dead.'

'You don't need to remind me of it. However, I just have a feeling that Perry will try to reach me soon. He'll find out that I'm back.'

Ellie felt her eyes droop. Matt drove through the night in silence. By the time they reached the outskirts of Belfast, she was asleep. He drove to her home, parked and sat back. She woke up with a start. 'It's been a long week. I'm looking forward to my day off tomorrow.' She yawned and turned around to him. 'Come on, I'll make us some coffee. I'm not finished with you yet.'

Barney spent the rest of the same Friday evening sitting in his armchair. The silence was only broken by students returning from the pubs which closed sharp at eleven o'clock. He turned over in his mind his conversations with Boomer.

'He sent us the letter himself, knowing that he hadn't done it. It demonstrated to me a weirdness in his mentality. Too clever by half, apart from anything else. Almost as if he was teasing us to make a stupid mistake.'

'You could have booked him for wasting police time.'

'I decided to wait for the next move. Doing nothing is sometimes the best option.'

'You couldn't prove that he had typed both letters.'

'Probably not. In any event, we didn't act. I forgot about him until I was at a social affair with Kerr earlier in the year. When I found out that he was dead, I filed the case away for posterity.'

'Until I put my foot in it.'

'You've had your warning, Mulvey. We'll leave it.'

Barney had one last shot. 'I've been thinking about your information on the two crimes. If you're going to close the case, I've got something else.'

Boomer looked at him sharply. 'Are you suggesting that I've missed something?'

'Of course not, Sir. You couldn't have known. My friend Quinn found it out by accident.' Barney outlined Matt's discussion with Kerry.

'I never believed this story of Wilson's, but we did make restricted calls to the Army. They denied all knowledge of a deserter. There *was* one person unaccounted for among the survivors. It was well known at the time. Wilson could have seized on it.'

'With respect, Sir. This guy Gilbert is a well-respected academic. He's identified the name and has evidence that a second man survived the tragedy.' Barney knew that he had got under Boomer's skin.

The Inspector rubbed his chin for several minutes. 'I agree that it might be worth looking at. You say that he's in Greece and won't be home until August. It can wait.'

Barney pressed home his advantage. 'If you would allow me…in my own time of course…to check something myself. I have substantial leave owing. I'd only need a couple of days off.'

'What have you got in mind?'

'A visit to Stranraer. I'd need help at the other end.'

'It could be arranged. I could square it, I suppose, with my equivalent over there. In your own time, you say? You must be keen to get your hands on this estate of Wilson's. We'll talk again tomorrow.'

Barney returned to his office. He sat down, clasped his hands behind his head and put his feet up on the desk. His shirt was drenched with sweat. It could have been worse, he thought. A seed of doubt had been planted in Boomer's mind. He had to concentrate on the stowaway and there was only one person alive who claimed to have met him. Apart from Sullivan.

He spent the remainder of the afternoon on his current cases. It was going to be important to keep on the right side of Boomer. In late afternoon, he met Billy Craig who said there had been no time to warn him. 'It's fine with me, Billy. As a matter of fact, it all went well.' He saw that his friend did not believe him. 'I'm having two extra days off next week to pursue a new line of enquiry. It's a pity you can't join me.'

Barney left the station at six o'clock and drove home. After frying bacon and eggs, the rest of the evening was spent in a fresh examination of Boyle's documents. He collated fresh notes and searched for clues in a fruitless attempt to shore up his theory. His good mood evaporated. At midnight, he went to bed but found sleep impossible. He arose at two o'clock and made tea. He watched the moon sink beneath a black cloud and then returned to a troubled sleep.

He rose early on Friday morning and arrived at the station before Boomer. The call did not come until early afternoon. 'Inspector Boomer will see you now,' said the girl. 'Thank God someone is going to keep him off my back for a while. I'm sitting here like a scalded cat.'

Barney pulled in his stomach as best he could before knocking on Boomer's door. Boomer must have changed his mind. It had been foolish to get one up on him.

'Sit down, Sergeant Mulvey. I'll get the girl to fetch us some tea and biscuits.'

'Thank you, Sir.'

'You caught me off guard yesterday. I don't like that but you gave me pause for thought. You'll have to work very hard to change my mind about Wilson's guilt. I've seen these guys get all the cover they need when they hit trouble with us. The usual trick is to move them right out of the country. He only got as far as Portglenone.' Boomer smiled. 'However, we must not let emotion clog up an enquiry. I'm granting your request.'

'I appreciate it, Sir. I'm grateful.'

'No need for thanks, Mulvey. You'll make a good officer yet. I've spoken to our brothers in Scotland. Here is your contact when you get to Stranraer.'

'Thank you, Sir.' He turned to leave. At the door, Boomer called him back.

'Just one more thing, Mulvey. It slipped my mind. It's been a hectic week and I haven't caught up since my day out on Monday.'

'Sir?'

'I spoke to the second woman this morning. You know who I mean.'

Barney felt his buttocks clench. If he could track her down, so could Boomer. 'Sir?'

'You can't hide anything from me, Mulvey. Remember it at your peril. We'll talk when you return.'

Barney went back to his office, tidied up his desk and signed out. Doubt gripped him. Boomer had spoken to Celia Toner and was even more convinced of Wilson's guilt. His sadistic streak would enjoy seeing Barney waste his leave on a fool's errand.

It was midnight. He decided to ring Charlie Boyle on Saturday at home. The solicitor had said that he would cover all expenses. Barney also needed to know when he was going to get his slice of cash from the legacy. It looked as if it was all he was going to receive unless he came up with something in Scotland. He suddenly felt exhausted and went to bed.

In the morning, he rose at nine o'clock, made tea and toasted his last piece of bread. He went out for shopping and paid by cheque. From a call box, he contacted Charlie. 'Sorry to get you out of bed, Mister Boyle. I've been moving on our case. I'm going to Stranraer on Monday morning to check on a vital development. I will require significant expenses. You said you would cover me.'

'It won't be a problem.'

'Any progress on my other money?'

'It'll be ready for you at the end of next week. While you're on the line, is there any progress with your friend? I couldn't get down to Belfast. And before I forget, there's something useful you could do for me in Scotland.'

Barney updated him and assured him that he would call next week. He rang off and searched in his pocket for Matt's number. A student replied that he would attach a note to Matt's door if he wasn't in his apartment. 'If you see Mister Quinn, tell him I'll be dropping by later today.' Barney scanned the telephone directory for the number of the ferry company.

'Twenty-eighth of June? First sailing...no problem. Turn up early and you'll get on board.'

Barney returned to College Green in a better mood. He boiled water in a saucepan and cracked in two large eggs. These were devoured with four slices of wheaten bread. He studied the *Irish News* for hot tips. Four horses were selected for a Yankee. The bookmaker could be persuaded to accept a cheque.

With bets placed, he drove to the Ulster College and parked the Escort. The deserted campus bathed in afternoon sunshine. Barney saw the message pinned to Matt's door and knocked three times with no response. He returned to the Ford and read his newspaper. The second visit also produced no reply. Giving up, he returned to spend an afternoon in front of the racing. Two of his horses romped home, enough for an evening's drinking in the York and additional cash for Monday before the banks in Scotland opened.

On Sunday morning, he tried again. There was no sign of life in the Ulster College. A bell tolled in the distance. Barney looked at his watch. Twelve o'clock. If he wasn't in the Halls, perhaps it meant that he had gone to stay with his mother again. He knew that her health wasn't good. The note had gone from the apartment door. Barney rapped and listened. He heard the sound of someone approaching. 'Matt, I called yesterday. We need to talk.'

'Come in, Barney. I didn't get your message until after you'd gone.'

As he followed Matt in, a woman's voice came from the bedroom. He began an apology but Matt held up his hand. 'It's OK, Barney. Take a deep breath before you meet your sister.'

MYRRH

22

THE LAST MONDAY of June began early for Ellie and Barney. Matt watched the Larne ferry sail towards Stranraer. The Lough was as flat as a semi-ellipse on a graph. Barney was scheduled to arrive by mid-morning. Ellie could look forward to a hectic week of hospital duties. Matt felt guilty about his contribution and the other threat teemed in his brain. He knew that Patterson's men had been questioning staff and residents but he was in limbo. His mood lifted as he thought of Ellie and his weekend. On their return from Crosskeys on Friday night, the conversation had developed cautiously.

'I only have Instant, I'm afraid.'

'That's fine.' Matt sat down and glanced around the freshly painted cream walls of the living room.

She returned with a silver pot and miniscule white cups. 'I bought them in Greece. I grew fond of their bitter coffee.'

'I'd like to go there sometime.'

'You should.' Ellie looked at her watch. 'It's late and we've got much to talk about.'

'Go ahead.'

'It's time you opened up about your friend.'

'Barney?'

'Come on, Matt. Give.'

'He was drinking in the York Hotel on the Sunday night before you flew to Greece.'

'He found my ID card. I know.'

'Perhaps *you* would like to tell me what you were up to.'

'I will...when you've finished.'

'Barney drove us up to see Boyle later in the week. He showed me your ID.'

'Didn't you recognise me when I first opened the front door of this house?'

'We were more disturbed by the name. I didn't concentrate on your photograph. In any case, it wouldn't have done you justice.'

'Thank you.'

'Barney guessed that you worked in one of the three hospitals...Royal, City or Mater. He struck lucky. They informed him that you were in Greece.'

'Syros?'

'They didn't know. In the meantime, I had spoken to Paul Kerry who told me that Gilbert was in Syros on business.'

'What did you make of it?'

'Barney then found out that Wilson had gone on a trip to Syros in Easter 69. Nobody knew why.'

'And?'

'The three visits had to be connected.'

Ellie frowned. 'How could they be? I knew nothing about the Wilson visit until now. As for Gilbert, I met him by accident.'

'You don't know that it hadn't been engineered.'

'You could be right. Let's hear what he has to say when he writes to me. Would you like more coffee?'

Matt nodded. 'OK, your turn.'

'You've been honest with me. I appreciate it.' She paused. 'I dropped the ID on purpose.'

'Why?'

'I've told you about Perry's second letter. I omitted a piece of information. It said that my father had had an affair after the Second World War with a married woman.'

'And?'

'Well, Perry...if you can believe him...stated that there had been a child. She passed the boy off as her husband's, but Perry knew better.'

'How?'

'I don't know. He advised me that, in the event of trouble at any time, I should contact Detective-Sergeant Barney Mulvey and seek help. His address was included.'

'What did you do?'

'I waited until finalising arrangements for my Greek vacation and deposited a letter in the safety box to inform Perry of the dates. I tracked my suspected brother down and got the hang of his movements. Towards the end, fear gripped me that I might meet with trouble in Greece. Dropping the ID was a crude way of establishing contact.'

'It worked. Our meeting with Barney might be explosive.'

'You'll keep me right.'

'I wouldn't be too sure about that. Do you mind if I ask you something else about the Perry letters?'

'Go ahead.'

'He asked you to take photographs.'

'I was given specific directions to go to a lonely place in the hills behind the port. When I arrived there, I found a Church adjacent to a small cemetery.'

'Any idea what Perry wanted?'

'I'll let you study the prints when they come back from the processors. I was instructed to photograph a grave at a particular spot that was isolated from the rest. At the head, there stood a simple cross bearing the initials T.S.'

'Any idea as to what they stood for?'

'I thought that S stood for Sullivan and that the dead person was my birth mother. Maybe I had been adopted. In the aftermath of the Second World War and with a Greek Civil War looming, it would not have been difficult to arrange.'

'Anything else?'

'I assumed that my real Mom had died in childbirth and my father had married again.'

'What changed your mind?'

'I can't say exactly. My mother used to comment that I took after my father in looks. Black Irish, she used to say. No, I was close to my mother before she found her current partner in Seattle. She would have told me. I'm positive.'

'You don't seem convinced.'

'It can't be true. It can't.'

Matt saw the tears bubble. 'Let's leave it until we see the photos. Maybe we can spot something new.'

'I'm tired.'

'I'd better go.' She showed him out. 'Shall I give you a ring early next week?'

She kissed him on the cheek. 'Call over tomorrow afternoon.'

On Saturday morning, he visited his mother. She enquired if he planned to stay again for the weekend. 'No, I dropped in to see if you needed anything. I'm going to the City Centre.'
'Do you want lunch?'
'A sandwich would be fine.'
She prepared John West salmon sandwiches and a pot of tea. 'I hope you're feeling better.'
'I'm fine.'
'How's your girlfriend?'
'Early days to be calling her by that name but, as a matter of fact, I was out with her last night and we're meeting again this afternoon.' He explained where they had gone for the evening.
'I can't fathom what people see in those old pubs.'
'Americans love them. She was impressed. Afterwards, we drove out to Father Wilson's house.'
'You're moving fast. Has Barney Mulvey done anything to clear his name?'
'He's doing his best.'
'It all sounds very difficult.'
Matt hesitated. 'Barney is a good detective. While we're on the subject, you told me about his mother last weekend. I didn't realise she had a reputation.'
'The poor woman's dead. I shouldn't have spoken about her in that way, especially now you and Barney are friends again. I hope you didn't repeat it to him.'
'Of course not. Someone else told me a similar story.'
'Who?'
Matt lied. 'I was in company one day and mentioned Barney's name. An older guy remembered his mother and made a sarcastic remark.'
'Barney's father was an abstemious man who liked a quiet life. She liked to go out on the town with a peroxide blonde from your Dad's part of the world. Dancing at the Plaza and the Floral Hall on

Cavehill. There was many a sailor who enjoyed their company. I'll say no more. Would you like more tea?'

'No, thanks. I'll have to get going. I'll see you next week.'

He arrived at Ellie's at two o'clock. Her tiredness had disappeared and she offered coffee. He hated to dispel her good mood but, if he didn't do it at this stage, she was bound to find out later and despise him. Somehow, he got the story out.

Her lack of reaction surprised him. 'You slept with this woman once. This guy Watt sounds like the killer.'

'I should have told you before.'

'We've only known each other for a week.'

'It feels longer.'

'Let's go outside. There's a garden at the back. It's not up to Wilson standard but we need some fresh air.' A white trellis table with two chairs sat at the bottom of the lawn beneath a decrepit apple tree.

'You might get some results from this in the Autumn.'

'Forget the tree, Matt. I hope this whole business is sorted out before September.'

'I hope Patterson comes up with a result.' He told her of Barney's other ideas about a suspect.

'Sounds like a long shot. There's nothing we can do about it this afternoon. I can't get over everything. My head's spinning.'

Matt placed his right hand across her left. 'You will have to contact your mother.'

'I can't do it just yet. I will when we find out more.'

The sun stroked the lawn and they sat back to catch its rays. He thought of driving across town to see Barney but dismissed the idea. At this stage, they could not arrive on his doorstep to discuss the good news. Matt had a graphic image of Barney's big jaw dropping in disbelief.

'Let's drive somewhere and have a drink. I know a pub near here with a beer garden overlooking the sea.'

He drove along the Antrim Road to The Shaftesbury Inn. After securing the black hood, they walked to the rear where groups of drinkers basked in the late afternoon sun. 'What would you like to drink, Ellie?'

'Gin and tonic with lots of ice.'

'Grab a seat and I'll go inside to order.'

Ellie veered away from a group of men whose table was strewn with pint glasses. She found a table beside an older couple. 'Do you know if this is free?' The woman nodded and smiled. Ellie noted the expensive sunglasses and long legs. Her companion looked ten years older and was drinking from a tall glass of whiskey.

Matt returned with lager and gin. 'I thought you might like this place.'

'It has a great view of the Lough.' From the side of her eye, she caught the woman staring at her.

Matt looked across the sea. 'It's difficult to imagine today how terrifying it must have been when the *Victoria* sank.'

'Even harder to think of my father swimming to the shore and surviving.'

'Did Perry's letter say when he died?'

'No, just that he was dead.' Ellie glanced across at the couple. She whispered to Matt. 'I think the woman is talking about us.'

'What makes you think so?'

'Intuition. Burning ears...call it what you like. I can't hear what they're saying.'

Matt finished his lager and looked at his watch. 'Would you like another drink?'

'I'll get it.' Ellie searched in her handbag for cash. 'You won't believe it. I've left my purse behind.' She emptied the contents onto the table.

'Forget it. I have a better idea. Why don't we drive back to the campus. We have time to pick up two steaks and some wine at the off-licence near the College. I'll cook dinner.'

'First the ID and now my purse.' She looked up at him. 'That's a great idea. Let's go.'

They nodded at the couple as they left. When Matt had parked at the front of the pub, he had noticed a silver Mercedes and guessed that it belonged to the whiskey drinker. He drove to Jordanstown. A master butcher cut two fillet steaks from the remains of a slab of beef. 'You got here just in time.' Matt thanked him and went into the adjacent off-licence. 'I'd like two bottles of your best Burgundy.'

A plump woman behind the till said that they had a batch on special offer. Matt inspected the shelves. He chose a bottle of Puligney-Montrachet and a bottle of Gevry-Chambertin. Ellie inspected his choices. 'I like a man who knows his wine. I'm looking forward to having dinner cooked for me. It's a change.'

He drove to the Halls and Matt ripped the message from the door. 'Barney has been trying to catch up with me. We keep missing each other.' He placed the white Burgundy in the fridge and opened the red. 'The beast will need to breath for an hour or two. I'll show you around the campus and then I'll start dinner.'

'Let me check my handbag again.' She rummaged about for a few minutes. 'I can't find my house key either.'

'Maybe you dropped it back at the Shaftesbury.'

'You might be right. What should I do?'

'I'll ring them from the Halls phone.'

Ellie stood behind him while he called to enquire. There was a delay, then a response from a barman who probably didn't need a phone. 'Yes, a key was handed in by one of our regulars. Pick it up anytime.'

'We'd like to thank him.'

'You've missed him. In any case, I heard Mister Toner say he was going on holiday.'

23

THE FERRY sailed into Loch Ryan on water as calm as the Sargasso Sea. It was just as well for he had eaten a breakfast of ham, eggs, sausages, black pudding and a tomato. Afterwards, inhaling the brine, Barney avoided the stare of a bald deckhand wearing Doctor Marten boots. As he disembarked, a seagull splattered its insides onto his tweed jacket and he rubbed it off in disgust. A passenger behind him said that he must be coming into money. Barney advised the Scot to sidestep a dog turd melting on the jetty. Three taxis sat behind a railing fifty yards away from the ship. He chose a squat Ford Cortina and gave an address to the driver.

Ten minutes later, the car pulled up in front of an establishment bearing the name COAST ROAD B&B. Barney checked in and was shown to his quarters. He placed his battered valise on a chair beside the single bed. The room contained a washbasin with two taps. There was also a wardrobe and a chest of drawers. A framed inscription above it read:

'In the midst of life we are in death. Therefore be ye also ready for in such an hour as ye think not the Son of Man cometh.'

Barney lay on the bed to plan his strategy. It had been an early start and soon he was fast asleep. On waking up an hour later, his mind was clear.

He left his key with the proprietor, Mrs Cameron, and asked for directions to the police station. It was a five-minute walk away. Barney asked for Detective-Sergeant Walter Martin who had been told to expect him.

'I'll be glad to help. There's not much excitement in this town. We have to keep an eye out for terrorist suspects travelling home by ferry. Apart from that, we try to keep the pubs in check at the weekend. Sometimes your boys give us trouble when there's a Rangers-Celtic match on in Glasgow.'

'I understand Boomer has briefed you.'

'To some extent. The disaster is not forgotten here. Many local folk died. I gather you want to track down Albert Steele.'

Barney hesitated. 'It's possible there was an army deserter on the ship. He survived the tragedy but later may have been involved in a murder.'

'Why all the excitement twenty years later?'

'One of the suspects has died and left behind documents with the aim of clearing his name.'

'Can you be more specific about why you want to speak to Steele?'

Barney related the story of the tossed coin. 'He and his friend John Wallace spoke to the suspect before he boarded. Wallace went down with the ship so all we've got is his mate. I'm hoping that he might remember something vital to assist us in our enquiry.'

'I'll put some feelers out. You can't come out of the blue and make a cold call.'

'I know. That's why I'd appreciate your help.'

'Where are you staying?'

'The Coast Road bed and breakfast.'

Martin grinned. 'You needn't look forward to a dram in that establishment.'

'So I gathered. Maybe we could meet later for a couple of nips.'

'I'll call with you later in the afternoon. Maybe around five?'

'Whatever suits.' Barney left the station and walked around the town. He found a tourist shop where he bought a book, *The Short Sea Route*, by Fraser G. MacHaffie. On his return to his lodgings, the landlady offered to make sandwiches. Barney patted his belly and said that he had eaten a huge breakfast. 'Do you mind if I work in my room for the rest of the afternoon?'

'Of course, Officer. It's nice to have a well-behaved gentleman with a proper haircut.'

Barney felt guilty. 'I'm working with local men on a case so it's good to get some peace and quiet.'

'You'll get it here, Mister Mulvey, and your room has been freshened up.'

Barney thanked her and ascended the stairs to his room. He sat on the bed, propped a pillow behind his head and opened his book. Soon he was engrossed in the story of the *Princess Victoria* and her predecessors. After two hours, he broke off to extract the folder from his valise. Leaning on the chest of drawers he made notes and compared extracts from his file with key passages from the book. In the late afternoon, a chilly feeling came over him. If anything happened to him before he returned, at least Matt could follow up the trail.

Thinking about his friend brought yesterday back to him. He could not believe that the woman was his sister. He sat on the edge of the bed and rubbed the sides of his forehead. As his mind raced, he heard a rap on the door and the Scottish burr. 'We have a Sergeant Martin downstairs. He'd like to have a word. Says you're expecting him.' Barney opened the door and asked her to send him up.

'I'll fill you in on what I've discovered. Then we'll have a dram.'

Barney invited him to sit on the chair while he lay back on the bed. Martin wore a grey flannel suit, white cotton shirt and a red tie with blue stripes. He looked the same age as himself. 'Anything of interest for me?'

'I didn't know how to approach Steele. It's a very sensitive subject we're dealing with. However, as I said to you before, folk have long memories. I asked around the station and got lucky. One of the older cops overheard me enquire. He'd been on duty on the day of the tragedy and had been involved in the subsequent investigation.'

Barney rose from the bed. 'It's warm in here.' He struggled for a few minutes with the sash window and gave up. 'We'll just have to put up with it.'

Martin pulled three folded pages from his inside pocket. 'I photocopied these for you. Sergeant Kane dug them out for me. They contain Steele's original statement and confirm what you told me. There was a stowaway and he was convinced that the guy was deserting from the British Army. Have a look. Do you mind if I smoke?'

'Go ahead. Give me ten minutes to study these papers. You're bigger and stronger than me. See if you can get the window opened.'

Martin put a cigarette to his lips, lit up and pushed from below the middle section of the window. 'It's jammed solid with paint. I have a penknife that should do the trick.' He scraped for a few minutes and pushed again. The window flew up with a bang. He leaned out while Barney read through the papers.

'It's eerie to see it written in black and white. The whole story rings true.'

Martin placed his cigarette on the bottom of the open window. 'Do you still want to speak to Steele?'

Barney sensed that he did not want to stir the matter up. 'If at all possible. I'll read through these again.' Barney kept calm. 'You say that I can keep these?'

'Be my guest. How about that dram?'

Barney woke early with a raging thirst. He reached to the side of the bed for a glass of water but it had been drained. His mouth felt like poultry litter and there was the familiar pounding in his skull. He opened one eye. Six o'clock. At least, he had had five hours sleep. The pub had closed sharp at eleven o'clock. They had lined their stomachs with cod and chips. He remembered devouring them but could not recollect going to bed. Breakfasts, he recalled, began at seven o'clock and finished at eight-thirty.

He got up, sprinkled his face with water and drank from the cold tap. A dry shave would have to wait. As he edged down the stairs, he heard plates jangling in the back kitchen. The front door was open. He tiptoed out and walked along the strand road. The sky was grey and the air chilly. After twenty minutes, he turned. As he did so, a fraction of the evening's conversation stirred.

'Barney, I'd like you to meet Sergeant Kane.'

'Call me Peter.'

Martin was deferential. 'I was telling you about him earlier. He'll have all the information you need, but we don't want any paperwork.'

'I understand. What will you have? It's my round.' Barney went to fetch pints of Heavy Ale. On his return, Martin and Kane broke off from their discussion. 'Walter's told you why I'm here, Peter, so I'd appreciate what you have...off the record.'

Kane drained half of the beer. 'Take your time, Mister Mulvey. Let me unwind for a bit.'

The three exchanged small talk about football and gambling before Kane opened up. 'It's better that you don't poke about too much in an official capacity.'

'You can trust me.'

Kane covered familiar territory. 'It's all in the statement. Afterwards, of course, all kinds of rumours and stories flew about the town. It was difficult to separate the wheat from the chaff.'

Martin interrupted. 'It's my turn.' He stumbled as he went to order more pints. Kane waited until he came back.

'Before I begin again, tell me what you're after.'

Barney went over his story. 'And so I think it's highly likely that either the stowaway or Sullivan was the killer.'

His colleagues looked at each other. Martin's eyes were glassy. 'Peter, come on.'

'I can give you some stuff that's not recorded anywhere...well, not as far as I'm aware.'

'Please.'

'Some of what you say makes sense. We were never able to determine the exact number of passengers on the ship. Also, there were all the usual stories about folk who were supposed to be on it but, for one reason or another, had been unable to sail at the last minute.'

'You always get it. I know.' Barney waved him on.

'As for this fellow Sullivan that you've talked about...I might have something of interest.' He paused. 'We interviewed most of the boat's staff. Some talked about a man who travelled at regular intervals on the crossing. A taciturn person who passed his time in the lounge bar. Although always maintaining a reasonable head, he appeared well-used to drink.'

'You don't have a name?'

'Well, this is what attracted the attention of staff. He travelled under different names. Nowadays, of course, such deceit would result in an investigation on someone from your part of the world.'

'So, he was Irish?'

'Most certainly. I can check tomorrow but the names were false.'

'How about descriptions of him?'

'They correspond with what you've told us about Sullivan. Now, it's my round.' He put up his hand. 'No, I insist. You're one of us.'

'Was he ever spotted again by anyone?'

'Not as far as I know. After the tragedy and the subsequent inquest, many folk went off travelling by ferry. He might have been one of them.'

Martin butted in. 'Could he have been one of the passengers who was booked on but didn't sail?'

Barney looked away from him. 'Peter, I understood from what you said earlier that someone had seen him aboard the ship on the day it sank.'

'I didn't say that, Barney. The passenger list contained one of the aliases that he used but we never obtained absolute confirmation that he sailed on that particular day. Walter may well be right. You seem very keen to prove that Sullivan made the trip.'

'If he didn't, the stowaway was creating a smokescreen and it would point the finger in his direction as the killer.'

Kane wiped froth from his mouth. 'Let's take a step back. I meant that Sullivan, or whatever his real name is, wasn't seen again by anyone who worked on the ferry crossings. However, that's not the end of the matter.'

Barney looked at his watch. 'It's nearly closing time. How about three of those malts we had earlier? I'll get them in.' As soon as he returned, Walter Martin rose to repeat the request.

When they were settled, Kane began again. 'We managed to establish that he...we'll call him Sullivan...usually travelled from Carlisle. At one point, we had an actual address for him there. It was checked out but didn't lead to anything.'

Barney's hopes rose. 'What type of address?'

'A rented flat. New tenants had just moved in. The landlord said that the previous couple had scarpered, owing him money.'

'Did he have a name?'

'He eventually coughed up. The name corresponded with one of our aliases but the trail had gone cold by then. This was months afterwards. It wasn't perceived as that important and the file was closed.' Kane jumped up and squeezed in an order for three malts.

* * *

Barney was shown to his seat in the breakfast room. Two commercial travellers sat at an adjacent table. He heard their Geordie voices discuss targets for an unspecified product. In front of him sat a flat object which he had heard about but never eaten. He saw Mrs Cameron approach from the kitchen.

She sniffed the air with disapproval. 'What would you like after your kipper, Mister Mulvey?'

Barney looked up from the handwritten menu. 'Kelloggs followed by tea and toast, please.'

'We do a proper Scottish breakfast. Bacon, eggs…'

Barney felt a spasm. 'I'll skip it, if you don't mind.'

She brought a pot of tea and left him to help himself. Afterwards, he felt better and made his plans. It was eight o'clock. He had a second day and night to do something useful. His return sailing had been booked for early evening. He returned to his room and rubbed the electric razor around his face. It was time to talk to Kane again.

'You look as if you could use coffee, Mister Mulvey. At least you've appeared. DS Martin hasn't arrived yet. Let's go into one of the interview rooms.'

'You were going to check the aliases for me. I'm grateful.'

'Think nothing of it. I enjoyed our drink together.'

'If you're ever in Ireland, I hope I can return the favour.'

'I'll take you up on that. Now, let's see what we've got for you.' Kane flipped through his set of documents. 'Ah, here we are.' He scribbled them on a piece of A5 paper and passed it over.

Barney scanned the names. 'I don't recognise any of these. They mean nothing to me.'

'I've omitted one of them as the relevant bill is attached to a separate file. You'll recall that a detective was sent to Carlisle in order to check an address with a landlord. The rental flat was no more than a bedsit. The man was an infrequent visitor, it seems. The other occupants of the block had recollections mostly of the woman.'

Barney waited. 'You said that an invoice existed?'

'Yes, I have it here as proof. The landlord also demanded formal identification. Here is the name of the couple who rented the bedsit.'

Barney felt his stomach gyrate. He stared at the slip of paper. 'Are you absolutely certain?'

Kane looked at him. 'Are you OK, Barney? Let me check again.' He extracted a pair of glasses. 'Yes. That's right. Mr and Mrs Wilson. The neighbours said her name was Teresa.'

24

AS BARNEY landed in Scotland, Matt arrived at his office. He unlocked it and found the room empty. Once the examination season was over, Derek Scott made weekly visits but Watt was unpredictable. Matt sat down and collected his thoughts.

As he did so, he heard a gentle tap on the door. It opened and a woman peeped through. 'Is it OK to come in and give the room a clean-up?' she enquired. 'I wasn't expecting anyone here. Apart from the big office at the end of the corridor, the others are empty.'

Matt smiled. 'No, it's fine. Come in. I haven't seen you before. What happened to the other lady?'

'She's not well. I'm covering her work. I usually do a different block. I'll not be too long.'

'I was going for coffee. Will you lock up when you're finished? I assume you have a key.'

'The girl in the office gave me a master key. I'll make sure the door is locked. If you have any rubbish, I have a bin bag.'

Matt threw out papers for disposal, thanked her and went up to the Mall. So, Deirdre had finally returned after her clash with Watt three weeks before. He remembered that it was Sue who had fed him the gossip. Now that Walton's PA was back, there were bound to be leaks.

He scanned the Common Room. In a corner, he saw Kerry in a huddle with his own Head of Department. Matt ordered coffee and found a seat. His mind returned to the day when he had discovered the photograph. The door had been locked, the office empty but with Watt's briefcase sitting beneath his desk. If Watt had nothing to do with it, he wondered how the envelope had got there.

'May I join you for a moment?'

Matt looked up at Paul Kerry. 'Of course.'

Kerry turned to his Head of Department. 'I'll sort the matter out shortly. I'm going to have a word with my mathematics friend as I mightn't see him again for a month.' He sat across from Matt.

'Are you off on holiday?'

Kerry smiled. 'I've managed to book a gite for the family in the South of France. We're driving to Rosslare this afternoon and making our connection early tomorrow.'

'Don't let me hold you back.'

Kerry hesitated. 'It was about our conversation from a few weeks ago. Josh Gilbert has telexed us through information about his movements. You might be interested.'

Matt's ears pricked up. 'I certainly would.'

'I'll give you a brief summary.'

'Thanks.'

'The last time that we spoke, you were keen to hear the name of the nurse whom Gilbert had met in Greece. He's met her twice since then. Appears very taken with her. Same girl?'

Matt hesitated. 'Yes, the names matched.'

'Is the girl in trouble?'

'No. My police friend said that someone was trying to contact her urgently. Something about a missing relative, I understand.'

Kerry looked at his watch. 'I must press on. Gilbert has asked our PA to access his *Princess Victoria* file. In particular, he wants her to check the W section. His interest has arisen from his last conversation with the nurse.'

'Her name is Ellie Sullivan. She's returned home. The police have spoken to her.'

'Did they find her relative?'

'I believe they did. Please, continue. I know that you're in a hurry.'

'It appears that the girl had a relative aboard the ship. He thought it may have been her father.'

'Victim or survivor?'

'Good question. I told you before that Gilbert believed that there had been one other person on board who was never accounted for...apart from the stowaway, of course.'

'Yes, you gave me his name.'

'Perry. Gilbert thinks he has a lead on the identity of the second person. Believe it or not, the answer may lie in Greece.'

'I don't suppose I could have a look at this file myself?'

176

'You'll have to obtain his permission. If you come with me now, I'll introduce you to our PA. She has a contact number for him.'

Matt jumped up. 'This is very kind of you.' They left and walked down the Mall towards the Marine Department. Kerry explained to the PA that Matt was interested in the *Victoria* disaster and would like to speak to Josh Gilbert.

She gave Matt a curious stare. 'I'll be talking to him shortly in order to clarify exactly what he's looking for. Shall I give him your number?'

'If you don't mind. Tell him that I might be of considerable assistance to him.'

Kerry interrupted. 'I'll leave you two to sort this out.'

'Have a good holiday.' Matt returned to his office. The door was locked. When he went in, there was a smell of fresh polish. The window sills had been dusted and the bins emptied. Half an hour later, the phone rang.

'Mister Quinn? We spoke earlier. I have Josh Gilbert on the line for you. I'm connecting you now.'

'How can I help you?'

'Thanks for contacting me.' Matt explained.

'I'm hooked. I have no personal interest in the matter although I'm thinking of writing a book…especially given the pace of recent developments. I would be happy to help you.'

'And I will be able to return the favour. Paul Kerry has been very helpful. When he mentioned the W factor to me, I hoped we could share information.'

'Of course. I've been trying to explain to our PA what I need but I may as well have been talking to the wall. Perhaps we could liaise while I'm out here. It might make matters easier.'

Matt decided to trust him. 'That would be great. We will have much to talk about.' He hesitated. 'I understand that you've met Ellie Sullivan whose father may have been aboard the *Victoria*. She is a friend of mine.'

'I see. She never mentioned you when she was out here.'

'We've only become friendly since her return. Our paths have all intersected because of Wilson. I was hoping to obtain permission to access your file.'

'By all means. I'll be interested in your views. Phone me when you've had an opportunity to read it. You'll know what I want. Connect me back to our PA and I'll clear it.'

Matt raced back to the Marine Department. The full file sat on the woman's desk and she handed it over. 'You must sign for it. Look after it, he said. He will be in touch.'

As Matt walked back to his office, he saw Watt open the door that led from the Mall to their office. Sure that he had not been spotted, he turned away to go to the Halls of Residence. He opened the file and skipped through to the section headed W.

When Ellie returned home in the early evening of the same day, she made tea and drafted a letter to her mother in Seattle. She had been putting it off for months and was unsure how to proceed. Her mother had married a man called Daniel Ferris to whom Ellie had taken an immediate dislike. She suspected that he was the type to read the letters of others without their permission. He worked in the property business and possessed all the mellifluence of the caste.

She began by apologising for not having written since taking up the post in Belfast. Although there was violence, the crime level was less than that of New York where it was not safe for a woman to travel alone on the subway at night. After a dull beginning, she explained, an unexpected development had occurred. A Catholic priest called Wilson had made himself known to her. He had served with her father during the Second World War.

Ellie finished her tea, sighed and continued. Jack Sullivan was dead. Ellie wrote that she should have phoned but it would hardly come as a devastating shock to her mother after all this time. The big news was that he had left Ellie their original home and she had moved in. The property was in bad repair but she was attempting to restore it.

The sum of cash which she had been left had been spent on a vacation in Greece. She had found the naval base where her parents had met. Ellie thought hard about how to phrase the next paragraph. The will had requested her to photograph a grave in Syros. The person buried there had a surname beginning with S and an initial T. Suspicions had passed through her own mind including the obvious one. Ellie sketched the passage out as best she could for she knew that there could only be one other answer.

On her return from Greece, she continued, a new man had entered her life. Her mother would be informed of any developments. The letter was finished with a delicate touch. Her new home had once been occupied by a ghost...a lady called Teresa. Had her mother ever known, from her stay in Belfast, a friend of her father's by that name?

She heard the throb of the Spitfire at seven o'clock. Ellie ran to the door. 'I wasn't expecting you so soon. I've been writing to my mother. Maybe she can help.' She felt his excitement. 'You have some news?'

Matt explained about Kerry and the follow-up with Gilbert. 'He was very helpful...not at all what you led me to believe.'

'You have the file with you?'

'I've been studying it this afternoon.'

'Have you eaten or perhaps you'd like something to drink? Wine?'

'Red if you have it.' She fetched two glasses and listened as he paced the floor. 'Gilbert became fascinated by the *Victoria* after reading an anniversary article in the Times in 1973. The structural faults in the ship were of particular interest. Then, after preliminary enquiries, he got hooked by the human side of the story. That's where his file begins.'

'Sit down, Matt. You're making me nervous.'

He apologised. 'Through his marine contacts, he persuaded some of the survivors to speak to him directly. He also gained access to material that had not been published. A Harbour Office friend was particularly useful to him. The story of the stowaway was remarkably consistent. I needn't go over it again. However, what you'll want to know is how he met Wilson.'

'Calm yourself, Matt. Have some wine.'

'He interviewed a man who had survived on a raft. I have his name here. Nobody else was aboard and one aspect of his story fuelled Gilbert's curiosity.' Matt hesitated.

'Go on.'

'Gilbert felt that the story had been subsequently misreported. I'll come back to it. At one stage, a woman had also clung to the same raft. A gigantic wave washed them off it. He managed to climb on again but she appeared to drown.'

'Appeared?'

Matt held up his hand. 'When they were on the raft, she told him that her name was Lily and that she had been going home with a friend from Carlisle to visit her mother in Donegal. Shortly afterwards, the wave swept her away but she was seen later clinging to a different raft.'

'What happened to her?'

'It was reported in newspapers that she was washed away to her death. A woman called Lily was subsequently identified.'

'Where is the twist?'

'Gilbert pressed the man as he seemed uncertain about one detail.'

Ellie sipped her wine. 'Hardly surprising in the circumstances.'

'The sinking haunted the guy. He wondered whether anything more could have been done. Let me come back to the detail. Gilbert felt that he wasn't absolutely sure that the woman on the raft was the same person whom he subsequently saw clinging to a different piece of wreckage.'

'What did he read into it?'

'Let me go back to...'

'Wilson?'

'Yes. The survivor became upset and spoke about his return to shore. Many of the survivors were at death's door. An ex-chaplain had arrived to offer Last Rites.'

'Wilson.'

'On hearing of the disaster, he had driven to Donaghadee to see if he could be of help to any of his flock.'

'I can't link all this up.'

'Gilbert made further enquiries. Wilson did not hang around for long and reports omitted any reference to him. It wasn't difficult for Gilbert to track down a Navy chaplain. He thought that an interview might yield a unique angle for a book.'

'So that's how he learnt about my father and Perry.'

'Gilbert went up to Portglenone and got the story about your father and believed it. The contact must have been mistaken. It was not a woman clinging to the piece of flotsam.'

'It would have been impossible to be certain given the force of the gales.'

'He persuaded the man to speak to him again…about a month after the first interview. There's something else. Wilson and Gilbert talked of Greece. Wilson told him about Syros. He encouraged his new friend to go there should a chance arise.'

Ellie closed her eyes. 'I see.'

'Gilbert changed his mind again after the second visit to his survivor contact. A month had elapsed. The man had had time to think.'

'What was new?'

'The name of Lily's friend in Carlisle.' Matt looked across at Ellie. 'You got it. The survivor had a hunch that it might have been *her* on the second piece of wreckage.'

25

BENEDICT ARTHUR CASEY had waited a long time to meet Barney Mulvey for the second time in sixteen years. 'I can't say that I remember much about you personally, but I can recall the visit of the troupe of altar boys to Captain Higgleston's submarine. Just before Christmas 1959, wasn't it?'

'You showed us around the boat and gave us lemonade while the two of them drank each other's health.'

'You look like a man who could use a dram. Would you like a nip of malt? I was about to have a drop of Sheep Dip. An unusual name for whisky, I know, but it hits the spot.'

'Don't mind if I do. I've been travelling all afternoon.'

Casey poured two large measures into plain tumblers. 'Stranraer to Edinburgh is a tedious train journey. Would you like water?' Barney nodded and the old sailor splashed some in from the kitchen tap.

Barney cradled his glass. 'How long have you left the Navy?'

'1965. The WINDSOR was my last posting. I'd been with it for about ten years. I collected my money and returned home. My wife and I opened the restaurant downstairs. Our two boys had left the nest by then. I never got a chance to know them. That's my biggest regret.' He paused to drink. 'Where are you staying tonight? We could put you up if you're stuck.'

'No, thanks. You've done enough by agreeing to talk to me. I've booked into a B&B off Chambers Street.'

'I know it. It's just around the corner from here.' A glint came into his eye. 'So, you tell me you became a Peeler. Where do you want to begin?'

Barney blew through his lips. 'Good question. When Charlie Boyle gave me your name at the weekend, I suppose.'

'How much has he told you?'

'He wasn't in the best of moods.' Barney hesitated. 'My business here isn't wholly official. Wilson left me and my friend, Matt Quinn, money.'

'Be frank with me, son. Then you'll get another reward.'

'Earlier in his life, Wilson was implicated in a murder enquiry. Despite being a man of the cloth, he came under suspicion. The cloud hung over him to the end of his life. It contributed to his death.'

'Cancer, was it?'

'Yes, in the final analysis. He'd suffered from stress for many years. My friend and I will inherit a piece of property if we clear his name. It will take time to explain everything.'

'I've got plenty of that. We'll have another malt and get something to eat.'

Barney explained the background and continued. 'It's possible that Perry killed Teresa. That's why I came over here to see what I could discover on this side.'

'Give me a chance to chew your story over. We do a classy steak and chips.' He rose and Barney followed him to the restaurant. Casey introduced his wife who noted their order and left. When the food arrived, both ate with a sharp appetite.

Barney wiped his mouth. 'Let me pay for the meal. I insist.'

Casey put up his hand. 'I wouldn't hear of it.' He glanced up at his wife. 'Mister Mulvey and I have a lot to talk about so I'll not be much use to you this evening.'

'Nothing new there, Arthur. I'll leave you to it.'

Casey rubbed his chin. 'I've digested your story and don't know what to make of it all.'

Barney sipped his tea and waited. 'Take your time.'

'You'll remember that the Captain and Wilson were close friends.'

'They'd served together throughout the Second World War.'

'Joe Higgleston used to blow his trumpet about their exploits together. They were brave men.'

'Nobody's denied it. Is he still alive?'

'No, God bless him. That's what I'm going to tell you. He died eight years ago. We remained in close touch after retirement and met up every month for a drink. He had a part-time post up in Holy Loch.'

'The nuclear submarine base?'

'Yes, that's it. He used to fill me in about all the latest developments although he may as well have been talking to the wall.'

Barney raised his right hand to his mouth. 'Another dram?'

'We'll go back upstairs.'

Casey restarted. 'Joe stopped talking about the War except towards the end when his health was failing. He'd always smoked and drank heavily. Exercise was anathema to him. The big C struck and they got him into a hospice in Glasgow. I visited regularly.'

'Do you mind if I take notes, Arthur?'

'As long as they're informal. I'm not signing statements.'

'I understand. They're for my own use.'

'One evening, Joe began to talk again about his wartime friends. I knew that something was nagging him, but I waited until he was ready.'

'Sullivan and Wilson?'

'Always. Joe was close to both but the pair often rubbed each other up the wrong way, especially with drink on board.'

'It fits in with what we know.'

'He said that he'd like to have met them again before he died. The last he'd seen of them was when Wilson visited at Christmas 59.'

'What about Sullivan?'

'He believed that he was dead and that's why he wanted to unburden himself to me. Joe wanted to die with his soul as clean as a whitewashed wall.'

'Any idea of when Sullivan died?'

'Be patient, son.'

Barney drank his Sheep Dip. 'It's been a rough week.'

'He gave me an address for Wilson and asked me to write to him with the bad news.'

'And you did?'

'He replied to say that he had made arrangements to visit the hospice in Glasgow. When I saw Joe again, he said that Wilson *had* come to see him. Whatever they talked about, it hadn't brought the relief he wanted. I could be wrong. By then, the cancer had got him on his last legs.'

'So he never told you much about the visit?'

'No, but before the end he gave me a sealed envelope with specific instructions attached in a separate letter.'

'Which were?'

'The letter contained the address of the solicitor. If Wilson died, Boyle had been asked to inform me, but only after the priest was well and truly buried.'

'What was in the envelope?'

Casey finished his glass of whisky and reached for the bottle of Sheep Dip. 'So, Mr Mulvey, you're a Peeler and haven't guessed yet. Let me fetch it for you.'

Matt threw his folder onto the coffee table and sat back. 'Yes, Ellie, Lily's friend was called Teresa.'

'Surely someone would have come to claim her.'

'I was thinking about it as I drove here. It's possible that Lily met an Irish friend in the factory where she worked in Carlisle. Perhaps a girl with no family. My father worked in a pub in England for a year before he got married. He used to tell us stories of the lonely lives many Irish emigrants led in England. Men from rural backgrounds worked on the roads and spent all their spare time drinking. Country girls scratched out threadbare existences in bedsits.'

'How does all this fit in with my father?'

'One possibility is that Perry and Teresa were lovers. She tells him that she has decided to escape from factory life and return home. He deserts from the Army and races up from London to follow her to the boat. They both survive and find their way back here. Then they quarrel and he kills her. Later, to cover his tracks, he gives Wilson his desertion tale but shifts the blame...to your father.'

'How did they know him?'

'Your father *was* on board and helps them. Perhaps this part of the story was true. He gives them this address but later drowns. Like Teresa, nobody is looking for him or interested whether he lives or dies.'

'It doesn't stack up, Matt. We've been over it before. Why would Perry write to me years later with power of attorney? No, there has to be another explanation. I think I have one. Let's get something to eat first. A Chinese takeaway has opened at the end of the Avenue. There's an off-licence nearby.'

'They got into the Spitfire and drove to the Double Dragon. An aroma of onions, boiled rice and curry sauce pervaded the warm evening air. They ordered and Ellie waited while Matt went to buy wine. He returned with two bottles of Beaujolais. 'Not bad. Two for three pounds.'

Ellie collected silver cartons containing noodles, stir-fried chicken and King Prawns. 'This is much different from how they'd cook it in the States. San Francisco has a large Chinatown quarter. I ate there often.'

He placed the food behind his seat and cruised back. Ellie studied the labels on the bottles of Beaujolais but said nothing. As they walked to her front door, curtains twitched on either side and were swiftly replaced. She found a white tablecloth and set out knives and forks. Matt poured the wine and they ate in silence. Finally, as he wiped curry sauce from his chin, she began.

'Don't you find it strange the way Wilson behaved on the day of the sinking?'

'He *was* a Navy Chaplain.'

'He didn't hang around for long to help nor did he return.'

'We don't know that he didn't.'

'Let's wipe the blackboard clean. Suppose that he and Teresa had been lovers. She'd become pregnant and he'd paid for her to live in England. He wouldn't want scandal.'

Matt looked at her in disbelief. 'I find that idea...'

'It's happened before. I've heard of it many times in the States. There's usually a cover-up.'

'OK. Let's hear what you've got to say.'

'She gets rid of the baby and finds work but life is tough. When Teresa hears that her friend is coming home, she gets homesick and contacts Wilson. We can guess how he would take the news.'

'Not with a big smile.'

'Exactly. Then he hears about the tragedy and survivors coming ashore at Donaghadee. There is turmoil but he finds her half-alive. On the pretence of giving her the Last Rites, he obtains privacy and sweetens her up. They drive back to Belfast. A fight develops. He's been drinking and kills her. Later he cooks up the Perry story to cover himself.'

'You're forgetting something.'

'What?'

'According to Barney, the police believed that she'd been murdered here before being dumped in the Lagan. Remember the bloodstain.'

'Yes but you also told me that a signed statement existed saying he'd been spotted here after Teresa's body had been found seven years later.'

'It wasn't confirmed. He denied it. Someone with a big imagination...led on by police who were keen to pin it on him. How could he have known about this place?'

'He knew my father owned this house but never used it. He's not the paragon you think he was. Teresa is brought back and told to lie low. He kills her and cooks up the story of the stowaway and my father. Wilson is the clever guy in all this.'

'What happens when your father returns to Belfast? Also, what about Perry and your so-called power of attorney?'

Ellie struggled. 'OK so there was a Perry and he was friendly with my father. She snapped her fingers. 'I've got it. My father returns to confront Wilson but the priest kills him too.'

'Slow down, baby.'

'Baby?'

'A blues tune was going through my head. When do you think he killed your father? How did he dispose of the body?'

'My father finds out what he's been up to, perhaps through Perry. Sometime in the 1960's, he pays a surprise visit.'

Matt interrupted. 'Barney said that Wilson was being blackmailed around 1967.'

'After the attack on Celia Teeny?'

'Yes. He might have paid up but kept it quiet.'

'My father *could* have blackmailed him, I suppose.'

'Who attacked Celia?'

'Wilson saw the advertisement. He stiffens himself up with a drink and goes to investigate. Doesn't want my father coming out of the woodwork and so he has to stop her. A battering is enough to warn her off. When trouble brews, he blames it on my father.'

Matt poured more Beaujolais. 'I agree it's possible. Barney won't want to hear any of this. He's determined to pin it on anyone but Wilson.'

'His judgement is clouded. I can see it now that I know about his debts but I can't have him framing the wrong man. How would you like it in your current position? I can help him with money. He should have had a cut of this property.'

'We'll suppose that you're correct. What do you think happened next?'

'My father saw or heard of the advertisement looking for news of him. He has contacts in the area and catches on. He may or may not have blackmailed Wilson. It doesn't matter. Wilson has plenty of motivation to kill him.'

'The body?'

'Maybe they met in Wilson's house. There's a stretch of ground at the rear and a river. Plenty of possibilities for burying a body.'

'It would be ironic if the body was lying back there somewhere. Barney inherits a property containing the corpse of his murdered father.'

'If my theory is correct, he won't be inheriting anything nor will you.'

'I'm not convinced.'

'Neither am I. There is, of course, the other scenario.'

Matt yawned. 'Let's relax for a while. My head is swimming and it's not the plonk.'

She smiled. 'I have to go to the bathroom. I've had a long day and need to freshen up.'

As Matt drank, he thought about what she had said. Maybe she was right. After half-an-hour, he went up. 'Ellie? Ellie? I was wondering where you'd got to.' He saw her fast asleep under the bedclothes and undressed. She stirred. Later, he was surprised by her waxed lips.

26

'ANYONE SEEN MULVEY?' Billy kept his head down as he waited for Boomer's assault. 'Craig, you should know where he is. I take it that he's come back from his trip across the water?'

'He's not expected back until Thursday morning. I'll tell him you were looking for him.'

'I thought he was only away for two days?'

'Wednesday was one of his days off-duty this week. I'll not see him until tomorrow.'

Boomer snarled. 'It wasn't cleared with me.'

'He assumed there was no problem.'

Boomer glanced at his watch and turned away. 'He'd better not let it happen again.'

Billy relaxed. Later, on his break, he checked the duty roster. Barney had *not* been expected on Wednesday. Billy breathed a sigh of relief. Boomer made him nervous. He felt guilty about letting Barney down before. The special directory gave him the number of Stranraer police station.

'I'm trying to contact Detective-Sergeant Mulvey who's over with you guys for a couple of days.'

Martin came on the line. 'Are you a friend of DS Mulvey?'

Billy explained. 'The boss is on the prowl at this end. I wanted to warn Barney not to be late for duty tomorrow morning.'

'I understand. Barney's a good guy. We enjoyed a few drams together on Monday night.'

'I'll bet. I wanted to advise him against repeating it this evening. Do you know if he got what he wanted?'

'He seemed surprised by some of what he discovered before he left for Edinburgh.'

'Edinburgh. He didn't mention that.'

'We assumed he was pursuing a new line of enquiry based on what we'd given him.'

'You're expecting him back?'

'He has a ferry booked for this evening. I don't know if there'll be time. If he calls in with us, I'll give him your warning.'

'Many thanks.' Billy put down the phone and crossed his fingers.

When Barney had not arrived by nine on Thursday, Billy became anxious but not alarmed. There was no sign of Boomer although he knew it was only a matter of time. By mid-morning, he assumed that Barney was sleeping off a bender. He made an excuse about checking with an informant before driving to College Green. The downstairs tenant opened the front door. As he was about to let off steam, Billy produced his badge. 'We need to contact DS Mulvey. It's urgent.'

'There's been no sign of him since Sunday night. I remember that he was out for most of the day.'

'You didn't hear him coming back last night?'

'No, I'm certain. Go up and check if you want.'

Billy raced upstairs, banged on the door but heard nothing. He thanked the man and drove back to the station. Afterwards, he knew that he should have obtained a key and gone into Barney's bedsit. When he was back at his desk, he asked if Boomer had made an appearance. There was time yet, he thought. He's missed the evening ferry and caught a morning one. He could just about get away with such an excuse.

By midday, Barney had not arrived and, after lunchtime, Boomer toured the main office on the rampage. A meeting of Senior Police Staff had been called and left him in a foul mood. Catching sight of Billy Craig, he pounced. 'You mean that he's not back. I'll have his guts. Find out where he is. If he turns up, he knows what to expect from me.'

Billy rang Stranraer. He was informed that DS Mulvey had not called back. They would ascertain whether he had boarded the evening ferry and get back to him. Billy turned around in his mind any other methods of reaching Barney. He knew Jean Mulvey's address but realised an approach would be pointless. From what Barney had said, only a big cheque would produce the slightest co-operation. Then he remembered the other contact number that Barney had provided. He rang. A student answered. She would leave a message with Mister Quinn.

The minutes ticked by throughout the hot afternoon. At five o'clock, Martin rang back. Billy broke out in a cold sweat and made a phone call. Then, he searched for the Halls number again. He instructed the student who answered to check Quinn's apartment. It was vital that he talked to him. The phone was left off the hook. Billy heard sounds in the background. Finally, he heard the voice of Barney's friend.

'Matt Quinn here. I just got your earlier message, Mister Craig. I've been out all day. What's it all about?'

'You may well ask. It's bad news, I'm afraid. I thought he might have been in touch with you after leaving for Scotland.'

'No, not since Sunday afternoon. What's happened?'

'He's in hospital with major concussion.'

Ellie studied the photographs as she travelled on the bus from Belfast to the Ulster College. She had requested magnitude larger than normal, thus delaying their processing. The quality of the Greek light was stupendous. Apart from those taken after dark, all displayed a rich blue background that intensified every scene. She flicked over the tourist snaps to concentrate on the important one. Yes, a J not a T.

She walked from the bus stop to the Halls of Residence and arrived before seven o'clock. Matt was ashen. At first, she thought that Patterson and his men had paid him a visit. He told her about Barney.

'Barney's colleagues in Stranraer went to the ferry offices this afternoon to check if he had boarded one of the Wednesday sailings or any of today's.'

'Which one did he travel on?'

'He boarded the early evening ferry as scheduled. They believe that he came off the Glasgow train but had spent the night in Edinburgh.'

'Did they know who he was going to meet there?'

'No.'

'What happened?'

'The boat was being cleaned after the passengers had disembarked. One of the toilet doors was locked which was unusual. A key was found. Barney was lying beside a urinal with his head battered in.'

'Did they realise his identity?'

'His pockets had been stripped. They rang for an ambulance and he was transferred to the Mater Hospital.'

'How did the cops at the other end find out?'

'Billy Craig grew alarmed when he didn't return this morning. He contacted Stranraer. A guy that Barney had worked with on Monday made enquiries at the terminal office. He heard about the assault and jumped to the right conclusion after hearing the description of the victim. The ferry staff gave him the name of the hospital. Billy rang it. Barney had come round briefly. I got the news about an hour ago.'

'You've done nothing since?'

'I was waiting for you.'

'Shouldn't we go to see him?'

'He is being transferred to the Royal Victoria. I explained who we were but they said there was nothing to be done tonight. They'll contact us if he surfaces again.'

'I can check it out in the morning. Matt, do you think it was random or connected with…?'

'It has to be the latter.'

'Matt, could you drive me home?'

'Can I get you a drink or something to eat?'

'No, I'm not feeling well. It's been a traumatic seven days. I need to go back and lie down.'

'Don't be frightened. Maybe I'm wrong.'

'I don't think so. Let's both get a good night's sleep. You don't have to stay with me. I'll be fine.'

After he had dropped her off, she changed, made tea and went to bed. She extracted the photographs from her bag and studied the important ones which she put aside. A night breeze rattled the sash windows. She heard rain bang against the glass as she fell asleep.

In the morning, she caught an early bus for the City Centre. The rain had stopped. She walked to the hospital in the cool sunshine. There were forty minutes to spare. Reception informed her that he was in intensive care. After changing into her uniform, she called to see him. On Sunday, she had searched his features for traces of herself. On this Friday morning, recognition was impossible. His face was covered in blue/black bruises already beginning to turn pale yellow. The lack of an oxygen mask raised her hopes. There was a honking noise from his snores. She heard a cough behind her.

Billy Craig introduced himself. 'We were here last night but were prevented from talking to him. They told us to come back this morning. What's the prognosis?'

Ellie smoothed out a crease in her uniform. 'I'm not his care nurse. I'm a friend of Matt Quinn. I'll go over his condition with the consultant when he arrives. Have you any idea who tried to kill him?'

Billy hesitated. 'We don't know if murder was the objective but whoever did it almost succeeded. We're following up a lead on the other side of the water.'

'I know why Barney was over there. Matt has told me all about it. We think it's connected.'

Billy stared at her. 'Don't I know you from somewhere? With your accent, I can't think where I've seen you before.'

'It's curious you should say that. I don't believe we've met.'

'It must have been the way the light shone on your face.' He looked down at Barney and back up at Ellie. 'Probably my mistake.'

'You said you had a lead?'

'I'm not certain of how good it is…especially after what you've said. Barney's been wrapped up in this legacy business. He hasn't been himself for some weeks. If it's connected, Quinn better be careful. I don't want to frighten you, but this can be a dangerous town if you cross the wrong people. Man or woman, it doesn't matter. If you have any clues, tell me right away. Barney is a good mate of mine. One of the best.'

'I'm glad to hear you say it. I'll warn Matt. Here is my direct ward number. Call me later when I've had a chance to talk to the doctor.' When he had left, she remained until it was time for the briefing from night staff.

At eleven o'clock, she received a call from intensive care to report that the policeman was in a stable condition. He would be kept under strict observation. A cop had arrived to block access. If there were any further developments, she would be contacted at once. Ellie rang for Matt.

'You think he's going to be OK?'

'Too early to say. His condition hasn't deteriorated although he's in bad shape. His face is in a mess.' She told him about her conversation with Craig. 'He's warned you, Matt. Watch out. I don't want to lose you both because of a lousy property. Call for me at seven.' Ellie had just replaced the phone when a second call came through from intensive care. Horror-stricken, she tried without success to get back to Matt. She worked until midday. Then, complaining of feeling unwell, she was told to go home.

Matt had postponed contacting Josh Gilbert but could leave it no longer. As he walked to his office, the attack on Barney focused his mind. The room was locked and he glanced at his watch. Greece was two hours ahead. He might catch him.

Gilbert was chewing on a slice of feta cheese as the phone rang. 'Good to hear from you. I was having lunch. Well, any conclusions?'

'I can see what you'd been thinking. Jack Sullivan had a girlfriend called Teresa. They both survive but he doesn't want it known. Later, they quarrel and he kills her.'

'The story doesn't make sense.'

'Perhaps he planned to stitch up Perry.'

'I think you know that can't be true either...especially in the light of what his daughter has told us.'

'We can't be sure that Perry wrote the letter to her about her father's will.'

'True, but then...who did write it?'

'I don't know.'

'I believe you do. It's the only explanation. Ring me back when you've had a think about it.'

Matt sat in silence. Gilbert had twigged on, helped by his enquiries in Greece. There was a tap on the door. 'Come in.'

The cleaner opened the door. 'Sorry, Sir, to disturb you again.'

'Is the other lady still unwell?'

'She's gone for good.'

'Sorry to hear it. Go ahead. I was just leaving. You'll lock up?'

'I don't have a key. The girl in the office hasn't been here.'

Matt returned to the Halls. He rang Ellie's ward number and was informed that she had gone home. After being transferred to Barney's ward, he heard the news. Alarmed, he raced to the Spitfire and drove to the Antrim Road.

A curtain twitched as he walked to the front door. There was an overpowering smell of gas. He knocked but received no reply. As he moved to the adjacent bay window, it exploded. Flames ripped through against his face as he was thrown into the air. Somewhere in the distance, bells tolled for a one o'clock Requiem Mass.

27

BOOMER reclined in his chair at the head of the Conference table. To his right sat Billy Craig while Patterson fidgeted on his left. It was eight o'clock on Saturday morning. He gave them permission to remove their jackets. 'All hell has broken loose about this one. Politicians from both sides and the American Embassy have been on with the Head of Service. The Press are expecting a statement by midday. He has told me to respond so let's get going. Craig, you first.'

Billy opened his file. 'You know most of it, Sir. I informed Quinn on Thursday evening of the news that I'd got from Scotland. He told Miss Sullivan. I spoke to her at the RVH yesterday morning and warned both of them to be careful. After hearing the bad news, she was sent home. Quinn rang the hospital and went to meet her.'

Patterson interrupted. 'He was seen leaving the Ulster College around twelve-thirty.'

Boomer sat up. 'It was news to me that Quinn was a suspect in your murder enquiry.'

Patterson continued. 'We'd more or less cleared him. He was unlucky to have slept with the victim on the evening before her death. We put him under pressure. Mulvey assured me that Quinn couldn't have done it. From what I saw of him, I believed him.'

'Guilty or innocent, the Press will make a meal of it. Craig, continue.'

'I visited the RVH again at lunchtime, heard what had happened and rushed around to Sullivan's ward.'

Boomer butted in. 'But she had already left.'

'I got her address. Something about the whole business stank. I had a strong feeling that she was related to Barney in some way.'

Boomer looked at his watch. 'We'll come back to it. Stick to the facts.'

'It was too late. The Antrim Road boys, fire brigades and journalists were everywhere. An ambulance had already taken Quinn and her away.'

'What do you believe happened?'

'A neighbour reported someone who had been behaving suspiciously earlier in the morning.'

'Have you got a description?'

'A bald man of around forty, wearing denims and black boots.'

Patterson broke in. 'Scar on his cranium?'

'Yes, why?'

Patterson looked at Boomer. 'Our chief suspect in the murder of Sue Neil fits the same description.'

Boomer gripped his fountain pen. 'Got a name?'

'Called himself Whitley. He has paramilitary connections in Jordanstown. We also have extensive evidence of his involvement in a vice ring operating around the same area.'

'Why isn't he locked up?'

'We didn't have enough to go on.'

'What do we know about him, besides what you've told us?'

'He worked as a part-time security guard on campus. His partner worked on site as a cleaner. We believe she kept an eye out for hornballs that they could suck in and blackmail. A colleague of Quinn's...an English guy called Watt...fell into her hands without much trouble.'

Boomer exploded. 'Where is Whitley?'

'I'm coming to it, Sir.' Patterson scanned his notes. 'We interviewed Whitley and Quinn on the same afternoon last week. At one point, we left them together in a Reception room. Whitley tried to play friendly but it was clear to us that Quinn didn't know him. We released both.'

Boomer looked up from his notepad. 'Together?'

'No. We let Quinn go later. Whitley followed him at a distance, then gave up as they neared the College campus. There was no connection.'

'Did you collect samples from them?'

'That was going to be our next move. We thought we'd begin with Whitley but he must have got a tip-off. When we went to interview him, Personnel informed us that he hadn't come back. They were waiting to give him his cards.'

'Did you try his home?'

'If you can call it that. His partner said that he'd left her. She said she was off sick. Her nerves were wrecked. I said we'd call back. If he turned up, we had to know at once.'

'What about other informants?'

'It took a week for us to get anything solid. A few days ago, one of them told us that Whitley often got work on the cross-channel ferries when things became hot. He also had plenty of connections in the West of Scotland.'

'I wish we'd known.'

Boomer waved Billy down. 'What good would it have done?'

'Surely, Sir, you can see what's happened?'

'I can guess.'

'Whitley links Quinn and Barney. When he sees Barney on the ferry he jumps to the wrong conclusion.'

Boomer held up his hand. 'I have to get everything typed up and checked before lunchtime. Mister Patterson, have you anything more for us that I can use this morning? If not, let Craig continue.'

'I want to come back to the explosion itself, Sir. The girl had moved in about two months ago and had begun to renovate the property.'

'Did she own it?'

'Must have done. The neighbours reported nobody else living there. Another nurse was the only caller apart from the recent visits of Quinn.'

Boomer made a note. 'A new boyfriend?'

'As far as I can make out. As I said before, the girl had been spending most of her free time updating the place. It hadn't been occupied for twenty years. You know the background. Do we need to go over it again?'

'No, proceed.'

Billy glanced down at his notes. 'She hadn't got around to replacing the gas cooker that we know was the source of the explosion.'

'I take it she wasn't trying to do herself in?'

'I don't think so. My theory is that Whitley attacked Barney on Wednesday evening and left him for dead. Then he jumped ship.' Billy turned to Patterson. 'Has anyone been back to check with his partner?'

Patterson squirmed. 'As a matter of fact, no. Get me a telephone and I'll organise it right away.'

Boomer waved towards his desk. 'Use mine. We'll take a short break.' He rose and beckoned to Billy. 'We'll go over some facts while he phones.' They heard Patterson give the necessary instructions.

When they came back, Patterson had finished his call. 'It's all fixed. I doubt if he'll come anywhere near in the daytime but my boys will rattle his partner. It wouldn't take much to make her crack if she has any new information.'

'Billy, continue with your theory.'

'After assaulting Barney, he goes through his pockets. He knows Barney is a friend of Quinn and they are both acquainted with Sullivan. On Friday morning, believing she will be working, he breaks in. When she returns unexpectedly, he hides in the kitchen and jumps her from behind. After a further search, he turns on the gas. As he does so, he gets a second surprise. Quinn comes up to the front door. Whitley escapes by the rear but not before throwing a lighted match into the house.'

Boomer sat back. 'It sounds plausible. I'll have the Antrim Road boys check with their paramilitary informants in the North and West of the city. If your theory is true, it's possible he's been staying with one of his cronies around those parts. If he found money in the house, there's no guessing what his next move will be.'

'Do you need anything more from me, Sir?' Patterson stood up. 'If not, I'll get back. We'll ring you at once if there's anything to report.'

'I have enough for a statement. We'll say we have a suspect with possible paramilitary involvement. It should keep them off our backs until Monday.'

Derek Scott watched the Press Conference on television. He had last seen Matt at the Examination Board meeting but there had not been time for more than a short conversation. When his wife heard what he had to say, she advised him to keep out of it. After all, it could have been him. He waited for an hour then rang the Head of Department.

'Yes, Derek, I did know that he was involved. I found out last night. It was my intention to talk to staff first thing on Monday.'

Derek detected a slur in Walton's speech. 'If you don't mind, Doctor Walton, I'd like to be briefed in private. Matt and I were friends. I would have problems if Watt was present at your meeting.'

'You can take it from me that he won't. However, I note what you've said. See me at nine o'clock.'

'You can't tell me anything new?'

'I have meetings with Personnel and police arranged for later this afternoon. I think it's better to leave matters until Monday.' He put down the phone.

Derek spent a tense weekend. He rang Kerry at his home number but there was no response. His mind was in turmoil. He decided to go for a walk but his wife warned him against it. She poured him a large glass of Bushmills. He waved away the tumbler of water. Somehow he got through the remainder of the weekend. He arrived at College shortly after eight o'clock on the first Monday of July. An hour later, he knocked on Walton's door. The outer office was deserted.

Walton looked at him with rheumy eyes. 'I apologise if I was abrupt with you on Saturday, Derek. The staff don't realise what a stressful time it has been for me.'

'I appreciate your seeing me alone. Have there been any developments?'

'I will tell you what they know. It must remain confidential. Your other colleague, Watt, is in hot water.'

'I guessed he had to be involved.'

'It's not *quite* what you may be thinking. Personnel had been receiving a number of complaints about him from female members of staff, including my own secretary, Deirdre. I should have acted sooner.'

'Sexual harassment?'

'I believe that's the term for it. He says that the urge is uncontrollable and that he is willing to undergo medical treatment. It's beyond my understanding. Perhaps it's time I got out and gave one of the younger men like yourself a chance.'

'I don't think it would be for me, Doctor Walton.'

'We'll leave the decision for another day. Let's get back to the tragedy. The cleaning lady heard about Watt's leanings and made herself available for cash. Her partner, a security guard called Whitley, ran a vice ring in the area. Watt might not have been aware of a paramilitary connection.'

Derek sighed. 'What do they think happened?'

'Matt Quinn had gone to Coleraine on Friday the fourth of June. Some business about a will, I believe. He returned late in the afternoon. You had gone home early as had most of the other academic staff.' Walton held up his right hand as Derek began to speak. 'I know, I know. It's been a hard year for you all. Earlier in the day, Watt had exposed himself to Deirdre.' Walton paused. 'Not for the first time, I understand. She told them that she was afraid to speak up. What might others believe? There were no witnesses.'

'That's why she's been off?'

'Yes. She came back last Monday but ran straight into Watt at lunchtime. On the Friday in question, she went home. The cleaning lady had a present for Watt. She believed the coast to be clear but had no key for your office. A sado-masochistic photograph ended up in the wrong hands. If Quinn hadn't returned, none of this business might have happened.'

'In fact, if he hadn't gone in the first place, everything could have been different.'

'We'll never know. Let me continue. Matters turned nasty. Whitley demanded money from Watt who refused to part with any more cash. On the fatal night, the police suspect that he saw Quinn coming from Neil's apartment earlier in the evening and jumped to the wrong conclusion. About a quarter to nine, Neil returned with a cape she'd borrowed from the nurse attached to Student Welfare. Meanwhile, Whitley has got the key and goes in shortly afterwards. You can imagine what happened next.'

'Have they caught him?'

'They say it's only a matter of time. I wouldn't be too confident. I'll try to piece together for you what happened last week. Would you like some coffee? With Deirdre gone, we'll have to make it ourselves.'

Derek sipped his Maxwell House as he listened to Walton. He knew that there was nothing he could have done. His wife would worry that he might be next. Whitley was out there somewhere. Belfast was a small town.

As Walton finished, the phone rang. He nodded at Derek who thought he recognised the voice at the other end of the line. As he rose to leave the office, Walton motioned to him that he should stay. Derek walked to the open window.

Walton rang off and continued. 'I don't think there's much more that I can tell you. The police have assured me that every resource will be devoted to hunting down this vicious killer. His partner has cracked but there's not much more to be obtained from her. Personnel should vet these characters more carefully. By the way, that was my fellow Head from the Marine Department. You know him, don't you?'

'Yes, I thought it was him.'

'One of his staff is in deeper water than Watt.'

'Not Kerry, I hope.'

'No, he's on holiday in France. It's a fellow that I don't know. Joshua Gilbert.'

'I've met him. I know that he is in Greece.'

'Not the best place at the present time to annoy the authorities. The Greek Colonels are a tough bunch to deal with.'

'What's happened to him?'

'He's been caught photographing a naval base on Syros. They've also accused him of attempting to steal relics from an Orthodox Church up in the mountains. They've interned him without a trial.'

28

THE SCARLET BERRIES of the mountain ashes trembled in the Autumn breeze as Barney struggled from the black-taxi outside the Chapel of the Resurrection. He adjusted his eye patch, inhaled and limped up to Belfast Castle, its lawns deserted and fountain dry. He found a seat overlooking the Lough and sat back alongside the Grecian urn. His right eye focused on the burnt horizon.

At first, the RVH prognosis had been that he might never see again. However, surgery by a consultant produced vision in one eye that had improved in late August. At the beginning of the week, he had returned to working on a part-time basis but found it difficult. However, Boomer had been sympathetic and ordered him to take it easy.

'There was no necessity to come back yet, Mulvey. Don't worry, there will always be a post for you in the service.'

'It's not the money that I was worried about, Sir. I need to occupy my time. I'd not be much good at any other job.'

'How are your family?'

'My wife and children, you mean? Nothing new there. I've settled back into my place in College Green. Thanks for arranging a telephone connection.'

'I want to have my men in close reach.' Boomer backtracked. 'Of course, it's for your safety. Whitley hasn't been caught and there is no shortage of thugs to help him. I feel bad about allowing you to go to Scotland on a fool's errand.'

Barney hesitated. 'You couldn't have predicted the result.'

Boomer glared. 'Do you want to talk?'

'It will do no harm.'

'I was convinced of Wilson's guilt.'

'I know.'

'It affronted me that we couldn't prove it. Let's look at the first case. A witness was certain that she saw him going into the house.'

'Not enough to prove that he murdered her.'

'No, but he behaved like a guilty man.'

'Innocent men have been jailed after being forced under pressure to admit to something they didn't do.'

'True. However, if Sullivan hadn't owned the place, who knows what our boys might have turned up? Let's move forward. I interviewed him myself in 1967 about the attack on Celia Toner. Fear dripped from his pores. The Sullivan story saved his bacon.'

'She advertises in a newspaper for information about Sullivan. Then she is attacked. His defence stands up.'

Boomer crossed his hands. 'We now have a victim who is certain about Wilson's guilt. You talked to her. Afterwards, she phones me. A pity she hadn't contacted me earlier.'

'I must say that she was convincing.'

'You didn't change your mind.'

'I admit that she got to me, especially when she told me about her visit to him.'

Boomer smiled. 'Then we have the business with the typewriter. A slippery act like that doesn't sit well with a man of the cloth.'

'I agree, Sir, but it could have been a defensive reaction from a man suffering from prolonged stress. He was taking medication for paranoia and depression.'

Boomer unclasped his hands and tapped his desk. 'As a result of his guilt, perhaps. As he got older, he couldn't handle it. There was increasing publicity about more powerful DNA tests that worked on small traces of blood.'

'Why weren't they performed?'

'They were submitted to the Regional Forensic Laboratory but sat in a massive queue. We'll never know the results. When you were in hospital, the site was fire-bombed by terrorists. All the samples have been destroyed. I'll never prove his guilt to you or anyone else.'

Barney smiled. 'I wouldn't go as far as that, Sir. You invited me to talk. I'd like you to listen to what I found out in Scotland.'

'I'd forgotten about that side of it. We focused on chasing Whitley over here.'

'DS Martin and Sergeant Kane were a big help.'

'They squared with you OK?'

'Very much so. A person by the name of Sullivan travelled regularly on the *Princess Victoria* before she sank. In fact, he was booked for the day of the disaster.'

'Did he sail?'

'The evidence suggests not. He used aliases, including the name of Wilson. It aroused suspicion but nobody was interested in finding out why.'

'So we are back to square one. Sullivan travelled on the ferry and sometimes used the name of Wilson. It supports the latter's story. You must have been pleased.'

Barney raised his hand. 'I admit that I was biased but wasn't going to fabricate evidence to make money. No, what I found out next changed my mind.'

Boomer relaxed. 'Give it to me.'

'When I came out of hospital, I made further enquiries through the Harbour Commissioner's Office. They weren't going to stand in my way given what had happened to me. I was given clerical assistance and my remaining good eye was up to scratch.'

'What did you find?'

'One night in June 1949, Wilson...accompanied by a woman called Teresa...travelled from Larne to Stranraer.'

'And afterwards?'

'They were on route to Carlisle.'

'You seem certain that it was him. Why?'

'We'll return to it later, Sir. Let's retain the name so as not to confuse the story.'

'Go on.'

'She had been pregnant. As a single woman, the baby had been taken away from her.'

'Are you going to tell me that the father was Wilson?'

'Yes. He made sure that the baby was looked after but he was in an impossible position. Also, Teresa was proving difficult to handle.'

'So he packs her off to England.'

'He probably told her that he would renounce his vows and join her.'

'I assume it didn't work out.'

'He made regular visits and was very good at creating smokescreens. Sometimes he was on official business and used his own name. At other times, he used the name Sullivan.'

Boomer sat back with his hands behind his head. 'I always knew he was a tricky customer. Continue.'

'I believe that he had no serious intention of giving up the priesthood.'

'So he kept fobbing her off.'

'Exactly. She gets work in a factory with enough to live on. She puts up with it for three or four years before realising he's conning her. She threatens to come home and spill the beans. He decides to go over to dissuade her on the return journey or at least keep a tight grip on her movements when she gets off the ferry.'

'The *Princess Victoria*?'

'Nobody could have predicted that one. Well, possibly, but we'll leave it for another time. He pulls out of the trip. She comes over with her friend from Donegal and survives the disaster. However, Wilson is ready to meet her and rushes to Donaghadee when he hears about the tragedy. He hides her in the house where she is later murdered by him.'

'You believe he did it?'

'All the evidence points that way. Then he gets rid of her in the Lagan. You can guess the rest.'

'The stories about the stowaway and Sullivan were a sham. I'm glad that you've proved me right after all these years. I *knew* that Wilson was guilty.'

'Not quite. There's more.' He told him about Casey's letter.

Barney raised the ashes, then limped behind the Castle to the path that Matt and he had wandered as boys. It meandered between green beeches and elms spread across the slope of Cavehill and brought him out beneath the black mountain face of Napoleon's Nose. He placed the urn on a rock and wiped the sweat from his face.

After a rest, he continued across the opposite slope of Cavehill until he reached the faded splendour of Floral Hall. White paint peeled from its walls and barricaded doors. He imagined the shades of a thousand dancers coupling in an everlasting September twilight, then sprinkled the dust into the lake in front of the ballroom and over the faded rhododendron bushes.

A tear bubbled faintly in his right eye. He wiped it into the cold clear air and descended the steep steps to the Antrim Road. His doctor had advocated regular exercise to lose weight and an end to smoking for the good of his future eyesight. Duty done, he caught a bus and got off at the Shaftesbury Inn. A glass of Powers was accompanied by a pint of Guinness as he awaited their arrival.

When they did not come, he recalled their telephone conversation from yesterday. 'Joe hasn't been too well since we came back from the USA. He's nursing an evil dose of the flu. You say that you have more information for me.'

'You know some of it but I thought you'd like to hear the remainder as you're the only surviving victim.'

'I'm touched that you've taken the time after all that's happened to you. It reached the American Press.'

Barney imagined her crossed legs. 'You were correct about your claims of assault.'

'What made you change your mind?'

'We could meet and I'll tell you. I'm free tomorrow.'

'Fine. We could have a drink somewhere.'

Barney glanced at his watch and his empty glass. 'Waiter, can I use your telephone?' When nobody replied, he rang for a cab. A diversion brought him past their home where he detected no sign of life. Then he directed the cab to the York Hotel.

'Barney, what will you have?'

He scanned the crowd of Friday evening drinkers before replying. 'Two bottles of Red Heart to wash my cares away, Billy. It's some time since we had a gargle together.'

When Doug Stewart set up their drinks, both swallowed with pleasure. Barney related the day's events and the information that he had not imparted to Celia Toner.

Billy interrupted. 'Boomer told me some of it. What made you turn?'

'On the Sunday before leaving for Scotland, my friends showed me a letter purporting to have come from Perry. I compared it with the one that Boomer had given me. They matched exactly.'

'What convinced you?'

'In Edinburgh, a sailor called Arthur Casey gave me a sworn statement from the dying hand of his ex-captain, Joe Higgleston. He had been a close friend of both Wilson and Sullivan for years.'

'The same Sullivan?'

'Yes. In order to explain, we'll go back to the letters.' Barney paused. 'I see Dick's not here tonight. Have you seen him lately?'

Billy stared into his glass. 'I should have told you before. They finally got him. I'll tell you about it some other time.'

Barney shrugged before continuing. 'It was not only that the letters were typed by the same person.' He sighed. 'Whoever wrote them was left-handed.'

'What was the significance?'

'My priestly benefactor pretended to be right-handed. It disturbed Matt Quinn but he didn't know what to make of it. He had his own problems, as you know.'

'How is he?'

'Scarred but well. I had a letter from him yesterday. He's living with my sister in her apartment in San Francisco. Her mother visited last week.'

'I saw the resemblance straightaway. You haven't fully explained it yet.'

'First things first, my friend. Without Casey's letter, I'd never have known how it happened.'

'Let me order more drinks.'

'Sullivan deserted after the war and made a good living in Australia but wanted home again. His wife in Belfast, Ellie's mother, had left him. She had suspected his adultery with Teresa although it was his violence that set the seal on matters. On one occasion, he gashed her cheek with the wedding ring on his left hand.'

'I'm beginning to get it.'

'Early in 1948, he gets a letter from Higgleston to say that his sub is docked in Syros. Sullivan has been planning a visit home but is wary about his status. He flies from Melbourne to Athens and makes a secret visit to the old team. A drinking party ensues. Matters turn ugly and Sullivan kills Wilson.'

'Premeditated?'

'Who knows? Even Higgleston wasn't sure when he'd had a few years to think about it.'

'What happened next?'

'A cover-up, after which Sullivan crossed the Rubicon by assuming Wilson's identity. Then he bided his time before writing to the Bishop for a transfer.'

'Surely someone would have caught on?'

'There was always a risk but one worth taking as it also gets him out of a potential murder charge. Wilson's only surviving relative was his mother who had Alzheimer's disease. Two close friends from seminary days had been sent to Africa on missionary work. A man changes a lot in ten years. Look at me.'

'In any case, he gets away with it.'

'Apart from some close calls. He was a right old stallion in his day.'

'And that explains your sister.'

'Yes. The bugger got both my mother and her friend pregnant. They ended up in the maternity hospital within days of each other. I survived but my brother died.'

'Your mother never gave you any clue?'

'You haven't got it yet, Billy. My mother was murdered by my father in February 1953. I sprinkled Teresa's ashes over the Cavehill this afternoon.'

It began to rain as Barney struggled home from the York. He fumbled for his keys, opened the front door and limped up the stairs. Faint noises indicated that the middle apartment had acquired a tenant. Barney let himself into his own rooms and checked the new answering machine. There was one message.

'Celia Toner here, Mister Mulvey. I apologise for missing our appointment. My husband has contracted pneumonia and was rushed to the Mater Hospital. I'll ring you next week, all being well.'

Barney changed and looked through the window. Rain speckled in the yellow light outside. Black pools of water glistened on the tarmac. He had acquired a taste for classical music while in hospital, especially Mozart and Bach. It was a night for the latter. He put the needle on the disc and heard the strains of the Concerto for Two Violins. After untwisting the cap from a quarter bottle of Powers, he pulled down the blinds.

His leather armchair with its intricate adjustments had been provided by the Service, courtesy of Boomer. He weighed up his ledger. Ellie had insured her house and had insisted on sharing the proceeds. Charlie Boyle was wrestling with the disposal of the other property. Barney wondered what they would do about Wilson's body lying beneath a crooked cross on a Greek hillside. As he tipped the bottle to his lips, the phone erupted.

He lifted it but the line had gone dead. Probably a wrong number at this time of night. The thought of his mother came to him. At least she had been buried at last, unlike poor Sue Neil whose body remained unclaimed. He drained the bottle. The violins reminded him of an Irish folk tune which Matt liked, *I will never see you again*. In turn, he was reminded of Kiltoy where Sullivan had met Barney's mother. As his eyes closed, the phone rang again. He waited but the burr continued. Reluctantly, he lifted it. His stomach turned when he heard the voice.

'Mulvey, your hour has come.'
'Who are you?'
'My name is Andy Perry. I knew Teresa Cross.'